TABOO EROTICA

THE LESBIAN SERIES

VICTORIA RUSH

COPYRIGHT

For the uninhibited...

TURN UP THE HEAT IN YOUR LIFE!

To receive more free books and other steamy stuff, sign up for my newsletter.

Victoria Rush Erotica

VOLUME ONE

THE HABIT

1

STACKED

I never particularly enjoyed going to the library. Beyond the hassle of dealing with crosstown traffic to get there, it always seemed such a chore to find what I was looking for. Whether I was searching through the card catalogue, the microfilm reels, or even asking the librarian, everything moved at a snail's pace. Having to search through the stacks, access the hard copy, then flip through all the pages to pinpoint my reference material—it all seemed so archaic.

Searching online was so much more efficient. From the comfort of my home office, I could tap in a few search words and within a couple of clicks, get exactly what I wanted. Unfortunately, today, I had no choice but to do it the old-school way. I needed to reference some old newspaper ads to get some ideas for a design project I was working on, and only the library went as far back as I needed.

At least I could count on a relatively quiet environment to do my research. Normally, there were few distractions to get in the way of completing the task at hand. People seemed to respect the rules of public decorum in a library more than other public places like the movie theater or a restaurant. Freed from trilling cell phones and loud side chatter, everybody went about their personal business quietly and politely.

But, today, as I walked toward the microfiche department, something unusual caught my attention. A nun in full regalia stood at the reference desk talking with the librarian. There was something about her manner of dress that seemed out of place among the casual jeans and shorts that other library patrons wore. Her black and white hooded frock stood in sharp contrast to the colorful and largely bare-skinned wardrobe of the other customers.

Like many other bystanders, I caught myself slowing down to stare at her. I saw a few people whispering and snickering amongst themselves as they pointed at her, and I began to feel sorry for the woman. Why should we judge her any differently, I thought, for quietly practicing her faith? There was something admirable about anyone in today's age who could so thoroughly dispense with the material and ego trappings of the modern world.

I was about to continue on my way minding my own business, when the nun turned around. She was much younger than I expected, perhaps in her early twenties, and absolutely stunning. The only part of her that I could see was the front of her face from her chin to her eyebrows. The rest of her head was covered in a white balaclava and hood that draped past her shoulders. She wasn't wearing any makeup, which only seemed to magnify her beauty.

Her pretty face was highlighted with plump rosebud lips, high cheekbones, and soft brown eyebrows. But the feature that stood out most prominently was her eyes. Her irises had an arresting—almost haunting—azure blue color, glimmering like glacial pools surrounded by the snow white hood encircling her head. She could have been a supermodel, and for all I knew, maybe she was. How someone that stunning could turn her back on all the temptations and opportunity that would have fallen into her lap, was a mystery to me.

Now I was even more intrigued by this stranger, and as much as I wanted to respect her privacy, I simply couldn't take my eyes off her. The librarian handed her a piece of paper and as the nun headed in the direction of the stacks, I followed a safe distance behind. Her billowing robe covered her body almost to the floor, but I could tell from the tight cinch of her belt around her waist that she had a slender figure under her heavy clothes.

As she walked toward the stacks, I tried to discern the shape and contour of her body, but her heavy vestments wouldn't betray what secrets lay beneath. But this only added to her allure. It was what I *couldn't* see that made her even sexier. I began to undress her with my eyes, imagining a model-perfect figure to match her face, and bit my lip trying to stifle my rising passion. As my panties began to moisten, I felt ashamed responding to this innocent creature in this way, but I couldn't stop.

Get a hold of yourself, girl, I admonished myself, under my breath.

When she retreated into the narrow space between two tall stacks, I stopped by a chair and placed my hand on the backrest for support. I could hear my breath escalating in excitement and had become weak in the knees. I'd never encountered another person— man or woman—who'd had such a powerful and visceral effect on me. I pulled out the chair and sat down, pretending to look through my purse so as not to be obvious that I'd been following her.

There were some loose textbooks in the middle of the table, and I grabbed one and opened it, pretending to read. I had no idea what the subject matter was because my focus was blurred trying to watch the nun's movement out of the corner of my eye. My pussy was burning in excitement, and I crossed my legs and rubbed my thighs together, trying to give my aching clit some direct stimulation. If there hadn't been so many people around, I would have torn off my clothes and cum within seconds fingering myself.

The nun stood in front of the stack tracing her finger over the spine of some books, trying to cross-reference the call numbers with the paper the librarian had given her. Her eyebrows pinched together in confusion, and for a moment I considered going over to offer some help. But I wasn't sure I could even talk, let alone make any sense, I was so smitten by her beauty. When she leaned forward to take a closer look at one of the books, I squinted to see if I could catch the protrusion of her bosom. But there was nothing to be revealed. It was almost as if she had multiple layers under her clothes to camouflage any hint of her female form.

Those Catholics sure know how to design a uniform to conceal a woman's shape. But I suppose that's the whole point. To minimize the possibility of any temptation—from within or without.

She was wearing a virtually impenetrable barrier to the outside world. My mind began to wander, wondering what kind of undergarments she might be wearing. Was she wearing a traditional corset or a push-up bra? Granny panties or boy-shorts? Nylons or bare legs? Or maybe nothing at all?

You could get away with just about anything under all that get-up, I thought.

I could feel the wetness beginning to spread in the crotch of my tight jeans, and I squeezed my legs together to pull the inseam harder against my throbbing clit. When the nun kneeled down close to the floor to pull a book from the bottom shelf, I couldn't stop myself.

I wish she were kneeling over my face. Oh, how I could give her a taste of earthly delights.

I began to wonder if she'd ever felt the loving touch of another man or woman. Or if she'd even touched *herself*, for that matter. I didn't know much about a nun's vows, but I knew they had something to do with remaining chaste and renouncing most worldly pleasures. It was hard to imagine having no sexual feelings, but if they kept their bodies covered in this manner, it would certainly minimize temptation. The nun never seemed to look beyond her direct field of interest or make eye contact with anyone other than the person with whom she was transacting. Perhaps she'd been trained this way, because there were plenty of scantily clad attractive young men and women scattered about the room to distract one's attention.

Suddenly, she stood up and placed a book under her arm. Then she walked to the rear section of the stacks and turned to walk down the rear aisle beyond my line of sight. After a few moments, I stood up from my desk and went into an adjacent column of stacks to see if I could trace her movement. I pretended to search for a book but instead looked through the space between the shelves to peer through the stacks. I saw her black robe moving to the far rear corner of the library, where she sat down on a large upholstered reading chair.

I grabbed the largest book I could find then headed in the direction of the nun. Not wanting to appear too obvious, I stopped at another upholstered chair about thirty feet away, turned slightly in her direction. I sat down and crossed my legs, then opened the large book on top of my knee. I laughed at my lame attempt at subterfuge, but at least it afforded a modicum of privacy while enabling me to continue spying on my new obsession.

As I peered over the spine of my book at the nun, I struggled to see what she was reading. I couldn't make out the title beyond the large cross appearing on the front cover.

Jesus—is she reading a version of the Bible? Now I'm definitely going to hell for having lascivious thoughts about a devoted woman while she's praying!

But there was no turning back. I was fascinated by this angelic beauty and couldn't take my eyes off her. As she read her book, I studied her face closely from the side. She had flawless alabaster skin, soft rosy cheeks, and a slender, perfectly-straight nose. Whenever she blinked, I could see her long, full eyelashes fluttering over her iridescent eyes. Her expression rarely changed, but every now and then I'd see the edges of her lips curl upwards in a gentle smile as if taken by a passage of her book.

How I'd love to feel those lips smiling around my love button, I thought, feeling my clit tingling in my tight jeans.

The more I looked at her, the more aroused I became, until it was impossible not to touch myself. Having the advantage of elevated padded armrests flanking me on both sides and a large reference book propped up on my legs, I was concealed in my own little cocoon. As long as I was quiet and careful, I could do just about anything I wanted on my chair and no one would be the wiser.

I looked around the room to ensure no one was watching, then I slowly uncrossed my legs and unzipped the front of my jeans and slid my fingers under my panties. But even with the front unzipped all the way, it was hard to reach far enough down into my tight jeans to reach my clit. My fingers pressed against the tight canvas, making it impossible to provide enough room to move around comfortably.

I braced my left arm on the armrest and lifted my hips up slightly, then shimmied my hips just enough to pull my jeans about one inch away from my opening. Now I finally had a little room to operate. My panties were thoroughly soaked, and as I began to circle my clit with the middle finger of my right hand, I had to clench my jaw to stifle my moans. When I redirected my attention back toward the nun, I caught her looking up at me before quickly peering back down at her book.

Shit! I thought. *Had she caught on to what I was doing? She probably runs into all manner of perverts exposing themselves to her whenever she leaves the safety of her convent.*

I froze with my hand down my pants, wondering what to do. The nun seemed to have refocused her attention on her book. My shifting position had probably distracted her temporarily. She couldn't possibly know what I was doing, walled off the way I was. I looked around the rest of the room to make sure I was clear, then slowly resumed fingering my sopping wet pussy.

As I touched myself, I watched the subtle changes in the nun's expression while she read. Her serious countenance made her appear even more model-like, as if she was posing for a camera.

Did she know I was watching her? Did she sense I was turned on by her? If she had, wouldn't she have excused herself?

Was she enjoying being watched?

As I watched her quietly reading, my mind raced thinking of all the dirty things I wanted to do to her if I could get her out of that habit.

What a funny term for a piece of clothing, I thought. I suppose it signifies her taking on a new form of habitual life. Whatever the garment's etymology, I was rapidly gaining a habit of my own for this sexy girl.

Forgive me, Lord. Forgive me the sins of my flesh.

As I began to feel the pleasure rising within me, my legs began to tremble, and I steadied my book on my thighs to disguise what was happening behind my armrests. As I neared my climax, my mouth unconsciously opened and just as I felt my orgasm take hold of me, the pretty nun looked up at me again. She must have known what I was doing from the tortured look of ecstasy on my face, and I looked away in embarrassment.

But I'd passed the point of no return and could no longer hold back the floodgates. As I jilled my clit furiously under my book, I felt the first wave of pleasure sweep over me. I fought to stifle my moans, gagging on the open air with my mouth wide open. I tried to remain as still as possible as the orgasm washed over me, but with each contraction, my chest heaved spastically in my chair.

The fact that I had to disguise the incredible pleasure radiating throughout my body only magnified its intensity. As I sat shaking uncontrollably in my chair, I thought the contractions would never end. I couldn't look at the nun for fear of betraying what was happening, so I peered straight ahead into the blurred text of my book.

When my contractions finally stopped, I slumped down in my chair and exhaled heavily. In my effort to disguise my orgasm, I hadn't realized that I'd been holding my breath the entire time. I panned the room to make sure no one else had witnessed my silent pleasure, then slowly zipped up the front of my jeans.

As I readied myself to silently slip out of the library, I noticed the nun shifting position in her chair for the first time. She crossed her legs and I saw a sliver of skin appearing under her frock above her shoes.

Was she giving me some kind of signal that she knew what I'd done and that she approved? Surely, she'd be discouraged from revealing any more skin in public beyond the small amount of her face?

After a few moments, I noticed a gentle bobbing of her upper foot over her leg.

Was she just indicating that she was happily engaged in her book? Or was this her way of revealing that she was really happy under her habit?

As I peered over the top of my book and watched her more

closely, I noticed that her hips were also squirming in her big armchair.

She's rubbing her thighs together as I was earlier, trying to stimulate her clit!

It was hard to be certain, because she continued staring expressionless straight ahead toward her book, but I noticed her eyelashes were fluttering more rapidly than normal. When her lips suddenly parted a few millimeters, there was no longer any doubt.

She was masturbating herself under her gown in plain view of the entire library! I looked around the room to see if anyone else was paying attention, then looked back at her face. Although she never directly returned my eye contact, the subtle changes of her facial expression and body movements told me everything I needed to know. As she rubbed her thighs together more firmly, her legs began moving more rapidly under her heavy tunic. The bobbing of her foot on her knee steadily picked up pace, and her face began twitching almost imperceptibly.

Suddenly, a deep flush fell over her cheeks and her back pulled away from her chair as the cloth of her habit rippled in shockwaves. She was cumming under her habit, and I was the only one to witness it! I jammed my hand into my panties and came hard again as I plunged my fingers into my soaking snatch. I'd never witnessed anything so sexy in my entire life. As I watched her sitting erect in her chair, spasming from her orgasm, my own pussy clamped down over my fingers in sympathy with her.

Although the pretty nun and I never spoke or made further eye contact that day, something told me this wouldn't be the last I was to see of her.

2

OBSESSION

For the rest of that day, I couldn't shake the pretty nun from my thoughts. It wasn't just her celestial beauty—there was something about her veiled appearance that got me worked up. Now that I knew she had sexual feelings, my mind raced with a million questions.

Was this the first time she'd acted on her impulses? Did she masturbate frequently in the privacy of her own room? Or had she simply gotten turned on watching me play with myself? Did she come to the library often for this express purpose? Was this her only safe outlet for expressing her sexuality? If so, why did she choose to live such a sheltered life, if she harbored such strong earthly desires?

But mostly, I just obsessed about what she *looked* like under all her formal vestments. As soon as I got home, I tore off my clothes and imagined our bodies bending together in every possible position. I imagined sucking her and licking her and fucking her, making her come in every possible way I could conjure. I fantasized about making her moan and scream in ecstasy, as I worshipped every square inch of her gorgeous body.

After I came for about the tenth time that day, I lay in my bed exhausted and naked, thinking about how I might see her again.

Searching for her at the local abbey was out of the question. They probably wouldn't even allow me to *talk* with her, and if so, it would only be through the front gate for a limited time. And my chances of running into her elsewhere in the Chicago area were practically nil. For all I knew, the library may have been the only sanctioned area outside the convent that she was allowed to visit.

My only chance for seeing her again was at the library. I knew that today's encounter might just have been a lucky happenstance, but I hoped that our silent tryst had awoken a primal urge within her that she'd want to revisit. My only hope was that she'd return to the library again soon and that this time we'd have a chance to connect on a more personal level. If so, I had no intention of letting her slip through my fingers again. At the very least, I hoped we could have a coffee together to give me a chance to get to know her a little better. I fell asleep that night imagining her lying beside me, our bodies intertwined, her skin still dewy from making love to me all day long.

<hr>

The following morning, I headed out early to be at the library for opening time. I didn't want to take any chance that I might miss my blue-eyed nun if she had the same idea as me. If I had to stay there all day every day for a month, I was ready to do whatever it took. I packed my laptop to work on client projects in case she didn't show up, but if she did, I planned to be ready. I wore a mid-thigh skirt and my favorite cream-colored silk blouse, with absolutely nothing on underneath. As I walked up the front steps of the library, feeling the cool morning breeze wafting up against my bare pussy, my nipples hardened, producing two protrusions in my blouse.

If she wants more of this, I thought, *I'll really give her a show today.*

When the library opened, I searched every floor and every corner of the facility, but the nun was nowhere to be found. I hadn't expected to see her right away, so I found an open table near the chair where she'd sat yesterday and flipped open my computer. But as much as I tried to concentrate on my work, I kept glancing over at the vacant chair, thinking about what had happened yesterday.

I glanced around the room to make sure no one could see my computer screen, then I typed in the search phrase *videos of nuns having sex*. I paused before hitting the Enter key, then added the word *lesbian*. I didn't want any men polluting my fantasy. A video titled *Confessions of a Sinful Nun* popped up. I clicked the pause button, then inserted my headphones into the audio jack so I'd be able to listen to the video privately. The video was different from most other pornos, with top-quality cinematography, multiple attractive characters, and a real forty-minute story arc.

This should distract me for a while, I thought.

The video began with the mother superior at a convent informing a young nun that two other nuns had missed communion, asking her to search the surrounding grounds for them. The pretty nun headed out along a trail in the woods, and after a few minutes heard the sound of two women giggling in a sheltered glade. She peered through the branches and saw the two nuns fondling each other under their habits. It didn't take long for them to remove most of their clothing, until they were wearing nothing but white stockings.

As one of the nuns lay on the ground, the other one straddled her face, grinding her bush into the nun's mouth. While she humped the girls face, she turned her body and began fingering the other nun's pussy. Before long, the nun on top began to shake, as her breasts quivered on her chest. "Oh yes!" she said, pulling the other girl's head tighter against her pussy. "Right there!" Just as she came on the other girl's face, the mother superior suddenly walked up behind the pretty nun and asked her if she'd seen anything. The other girls overheard the conversation and quickly scampered away, while the third nun covered for them.

If convent life is anything like this, I thought, *no wonder my blue-eyed nun felt the need to travel so far afield to escape the overprotective clutches of her abbey.*

The video was part of an extended series, and as I watched each clip, I fingered myself quietly under my desk. For over an hour, I took myself to the edge of climax, slowly backing down each time. I wanted to save myself for my *own* special nun if she came back. But when one of the scenes introduced a sister resembling the one I saw yesterday, I couldn't hold back any longer. I was just about to cum when a familiar black and white figure emerged from the stacks about twenty feet away.

It was the same blue-eyed nun from yesterday!

She walked directly past my desk looking straight ahead, carrying another book under her arm. She sat in the same chair as yesterday and opened the book on her lap, then peered up over the binding in my direction. Her eyes widened when she recognized me, then she quickly crossed her legs and directed her attention back to her book. I glanced at the chair I sat in yesterday and was disappointed to see that it was now occupied. But from my vantage point just a little further away, I actually had a more direct view of the nun. And from her seated position directly in front of me, she had a clear view of knees and skirt at crotch level.

This could actually work out better than I expected, I thought.

But as the nun kept her head buried in her book, feigning disinterest, I began to wonder if we'd crossed signals.

Had I frightened her away yesterday with my bold overture? If so, why hadn't she just gotten up and moved to a location where I wouldn't be such a distraction?

When her foot started bobbing again on her knee, her intention became clearer.

What a sly fox. She's signaling her interest in me through her body language.

I closed my computer lid to give her an unobstructed view of my upper body, then unbuttoned two buttons on my blouse to reveal my cleavage. As my breasts pressed firmly against the silk fabric, I could feel my nipples hardening once again. The nun looked up from her book and did a doubletake, before directing her attention back down toward her book.

"Yes," I whispered under my breath. "Did you like that? Give me a little more of your attention, and I'll *really* give you a show."

The nun had her head down, but I could see her long eyelashes fluttering in excitement against her brow. I knew she must have been torn between her vow of celibacy and her desire to engage me more directly.

She just needs a little more incentive, I thought.

I shifted position in my chair and spread my legs two feet apart. A few seconds later, she peered up, and I wobbled my knees under the table to redirect her focus. When her eyes dipped under my desk, they widened in shock when she saw my bare pussy exposed under my skirt. This time, she didn't look away.

As I spread my knees further apart, she stared straight into the junction of my thighs. I reached under the table with my right hand and hiked my skirt up a few more inches. She now had a clear, unobstructed view of my bare, glistening pussy. She froze for a moment, staring between my legs, then peered down again into her book, as a flush fell over her cheeks.

I smiled, knowing how conflicted she must have been between her pact with God and the tug of raging hormones racing through her system. There was something about the frustration she was experiencing that made this even more of a turn on. I looked around the room to make sure no one else was looking, then I placed my fingers over my clit and began to circle it slowly.

If she looks up again, I'll make it impossible for her to turn away this time.

I squeaked my chair, and within a few seconds, the nun's eyelashes lifted above her book again. When she saw my hand between my legs, her leg straightened over her knee and her book wobbled on her lap. As I placed my hand over my vulva and began to rub it over my slit, I could feel my juices spilling out of my pussy, coating my thighs and ass. The feeling emanating from between my legs was sublime, magnified all the more knowing my pretty nun was getting just as wet as me under her heavy habit.

As I began to feel my passion rising, my mouth opened unconsciously, and seeing the look of unadorned pleasure on my face, the nun's lips parted also. Recognizing that we'd made sustained eye contact for the first time, I felt an electric charge go through me, and I pressed my fingers tighter against my snatch. I could have come at any moment, but I wanted to savor this for as long as I could.

When her eyes dipped back under my table, I slipped my middle fingers into my opening and began to fuck myself as my two outer fingers slid up and down the inside of my thighs. I wanted to bring my other hand under the table to massage my clit directly, but it was too dangerous. It would have been far too suspicious for any onlookers to see a woman squirming in her library chair with two hands pumping under the table.

Instead, I pressed the palm of my hand against my mound and shimmied my hand up and down over my button while I pressed my two fingers as deep as I could into my hole. The nun was now bouncing her eyes up and down between my face, my bouncing tits, and my cavitating legs under the table. Her foot began bobbing more rapidly on her knee and I could see the front of her frock rising and falling as she breathed heavily.

For the first time, I could make out the bulge of her breasts under her gown, and although they were heavily concealed by all the layers of fabric, I could tell she had a plump set of tits. As I fantasized about sucking on them, I increased the pace of my finger-fucking and spread my legs wider, until they were almost a full one hundred and eighty degrees apart.

As my orgasm began rising within me, my mouth gaped open and I nodded, indicating that I was about to cum, and the nun did the same. Whether she was feeling the same sensations under her robe, or was simply mirroring my expression in sympathy with me, I wasn't sure. When my climax finally poured over me, I thrust my hand hard against my mound and clamped down over my fingers.

As the pretty nun watched the look of ecstasy wash over my face, I pressed back against my chair and sat shaking in a spastic seizure for a full thirty seconds. When my contractions finally abated, I sat up in my chair with my fingers still embedded in my pussy, savoring the heightened sensitivity inside my warm cavern.

When I finally regained my senses, I realized that I'd been so lost in my own pleasure that I'd temporarily lost focus on what the nun was doing. I wasn't sure if she'd managed to rub one out herself, or if she had just been concentrating on enjoying my show. But when she uncrossed her legs and spread her knees apart, her plan soon became apparent. A few moments later, her right hand disappeared from the edge of her book and I noticed some movement under her gown in the area between her legs as the textbook in her lap begin to shake.

Clever girl! It looked like she'd cut a hole in the side of her frock so she could have direct access to her private areas.

The movement under her gown began to take on a familiar and steady pattern as she began to squirm in her seat. Our eyes met once again, and her lips parted as her chest began to rise and fall more rapidly.

Fuck! I thought. *She's actually going to let me watch her come this time!*

I pushed my fingers harder into my pussy and began shimmying my palm against my clit again. But this time, I paced myself so I could cum with her. As her movements under her robe increased in intensity, I sped up my movements in kind. We were staring directly into each other's eyes now, and I could tell she was getting close.

When she nodded her head to me signaling that she was about to cum, I couldn't stop myself from moaning as my second climax took hold of me. The nun's thighs pulled together as she hunched forward in obvious climax, and I gushed all over my hand as the contractions inside my pussy sprayed my love juices all over my thighs and ass. I clenched my face trying to stifle my moans, but a few pitiful whimpers escaped. At this point, I didn't even care if anybody noticed what I was doing. I was on my own special wavelength with the pretty nun across the aisle, and for now at least, we were the only two people in the room.

After a few seconds, the nun's body relaxed and she lay back against her chair. The book resting on her lap popped up as she pulled her hand from between her legs, then she smiled at me softly and closed her eyes, laying her head on the backrest. I looked around the room to make sure no one else had witnessed our silent affair, then I pulled my sopping fingers out of my cunny and cleaned them with some wet wipes in my purse.

There was no way I was going to leave the library alone today without at least talking to the pretty nun. When she stood up from her chair ten minutes later and walked toward the stacks to return her library book, I quickly collected my belongings and followed her. A dribble of lubrication run down the inside of my thigh as my pussy pulsed in excitement, knowing I was about to have my first real contact with the blue-eyed beauty.

3

____

SISTERS

When I entered the row where I saw the nun go to return her book, she was bending forward squinting at the call numbers on the spines of the shelved books. I stepped forward and tilted my head down slightly, smiling at her.

"You know you don't actually have to reshelve library books when you're finished with them," I said.

She stood up, flushing in her cheeks when she recognized me.

"Oh—yes," she said, in a soft voice. "I just figured the librarians can use all the help they can get. There's so few of them looking after such a big place."

My heart raced as I listened to her talk. She was even more beautiful up close than I imagined. She had flawless unblemished skin, and her azure-blue eyes penetrated me like a laser, deep into my soul. Completing the angelic imagery, her melodious voice reminded me of the virtual assistant on my phone, lulling me with its lilt.

I glanced at some of the book titles on the shelf in front of her and the category banner at the side of the stack.

"You're a fan of historical fiction?" I said, trying to break the tension.

The nun glanced at the marker, then smiled as she turned her book cover around for me to see.

"Not usually. Normally I stick to scripture and other Christian themes. But the title of this one intrigued me."

"*Jesus and the Riddle of the Dead Sea Scrolls*," I said, reading the title of her book. "That certainly sounds like it qualifies."

"I think its miscategorized. It's really more of a critique of the Bible, suggesting that the Dead Sea Scrolls offer a somewhat different explanation for the events surrounding the time of Jesus."

"Sounds interesting," I nodded. "What was your impression of the book?"

"I...kind of lost interest after the first few pages," the nun hesitated, looking away. "I guess it didn't exactly fit in with my world view."

She looked at the laptop bag slung around my shoulder and peered back at me with her piercing eyes.

"How about you? What were you reading today?"

"Oh," I said, momentarily caught off guard. "I wasn't actually reading anything specific today. I just like to come here every now and then to find a quiet place to work on some...personal projects."

The nun turned to face me directly, holding her book over her breast like a schoolgirl.

"What kind of work do you do?"

"Freelance graphic design mostly. Book covers, ad copy, corporate logos, that sort of thing." I looked at the pretty nun's smock and frowned. "Pretty superficial stuff compared to your life's work, I would imagine."

"You mean *this*?" she chuckled, pinching her gown and pulling it away from her body a few inches. "I think most people imagine the life of a nun to be one of the most boring vocations possible for a young woman."

"I wouldn't exactly choose that word. I imagine you have plenty of spiritual and emotional stimulation in your chosen field."

The nun nodded gently and sighed.

"Yes, there's plenty of that. Perhaps not as much intellectual stimulation as in your field, though. That's part of the reason I like to come to the library. There are lots of other—*perspectives*—to be found here."

Now I was the one who could feel a blush spreading over my cheeks. I paused, wondering how I could steal a few more private moments with her.

"I'd love to learn more about your life. It's all so mysterious. Do you have time for a coffee? You could enlighten me on spiritual matters, and I could regale you with all the fascinating logos I've worked on."

The nun chuckled, then paused to contemplate my offer.

"I'm not sure you'll find the life of a cloistered nun terribly interesting. I'm sure you have a far more fascinating life. Coffee might be breaking the rules though. I'll be happy to share some fruit juice with you."

I smiled, beginning to realize how pure and unspoiled she was.

"Fruit juice it is. I know a quiet spot not too far from here."

I extended my right hand slowly.

"I'm Jade."

The nun extended her hand and clasped mine softly in hers. My heart thumped in my chest, sending a surge of hormones racing to my pussy.

"Sister Caroline," the nun said.

"Should I address you as Sister, Caroline, or Sister Caroline?" I asked, unsure of the proper protocol.

"Sister is fine."

"Pleasure to meet you, Sister. May I offer you a ride to the coffee shop?"

"Sure. It's got to be more comfortable than the two buses I took to get here."

The pretty nun and I continued making small talk on the way to the coffee shop, with neither one of us broaching the subject of what had happened between the two of us earlier at the library. When we got to the coffeehouse, I ordered two fruit juices and we found a quiet corner of the shop near the fireplace with two upholstered chairs.

"This is a cozy little spot," the nun said. She closed her eyes and took a deep breath through her nostrils. "And the smell is divine."

"I thought you didn't like coffee?"

"This aroma is bringing back the memories. After taking my vows, I gave up a *lot* of little pleasures I'd almost forgotten."

We paused for a long moment smiling at one another, then the nun took a sip of her juice.

"Do you mind my asking what kind of vows you've taken?" I asked. "I'm ashamed to admit that all I know about nuns is what I saw in the movie The Sound of Music."

"We could do worse than that in terms of public perception," the nun chuckled. "That was another one of my favorite things from my previous life, to steal a phrase. I always admired Julie Andrews. I think her depiction of a nun's life is partially what drew me to it."

My eyes crinkled, recognizing a common bond. I was rapidly developing more than just sexual feelings for Sister Caroline.

"You know you look a little bit like her," I said. "The same piercing blue eyes, soft pretty features..."

"You're far too kind, Jade. But to answer your question, we take three separate vows for poverty, chastity, and obedience."

"Obedience in terms of adhering to scripture?"

"Actually, the obedience part pertains to our promising to follow the rules of the abbey and the guidance of our abbess."

"Abbess?"

Sister Caroline chuckled.

"That's mother superior, to our Sounds of Music fans."

"And the poverty part? Is that why you can't drink coffee?"

"That wouldn't be breaking the rules, per se. But we're expected to follow a life of austerity once we enter the abbey. The menu at the abbey is kind of bland, but you get used to it pretty quickly."

I paused, unsure how to broach the delicate third subject.

"And the chastity part? Was that something that you had trouble adjusting to also?"

"At first, no. We actually go through a ceremony where we're literally betrothed to Jesus. Once the temptations are removed in the sheltered confines of the abbey, you soon learn to not think about the temptations of the flesh any longer."

"And when you *leave* the abbey?" I said, finally addressing the elephant in the room. "How do you manage the temptations then?"

"I was doing fine," she said. "Until I saw you."

I paused, looking into the nun's eyes with a pained look on my face.

"Sister..."

"I think perhaps you should call me Caroline. It feels a little strange under the circumstances you calling me sister."

"I agree," I said. "Caroline. I like that name. It's soft and pretty—like you."

"I was thinking the same about you, Jade. It's been hard for me to take my eyes off you. It wasn't just because..."

I leaned forward and placed my palm over Caroline's hand resting on her armchair.

"I'm sorry about being so forward," I said. "I couldn't resist. From the moment I first saw you, my body seems to have a mind of its own whenever I'm around you. And then when I saw you reacting to me the way you did—"

"Was it that obvious?" Caroline said.

"Not to anyone else in the library."

"I hope not. Otherwise, my abbey's switchboard will be flooded with calls from outraged Christians."

"You were very...*proper*," I chuckled. "I'm quite sure I was the only one who noticed that you were enjoying more than just your book in your chair."

"Not nearly as much as *you*," Caroline said, her cheeks flushing a deep shade of crimson. "It was a lot more—*obvious*—how much plea-sure you were experiencing on the other side of the room."

Hearing Caroline acknowledge our sexual connection for the first time suddenly sent a flood of juices pouring out of my pussy. I crossed my legs, feeling the moisture coating the inside of my thighs.

"You have that—*effect* on me," I said. " I think I could have just as easily—*enjoyed myself*—just watching you. I barely even needed to touch myself."

Caroline smiled at me warmly, as I noticed her bosom begin to rise and fall in silent excitement.

"I'm glad you did though. You're beautiful—everywhere. When I first caught you squirming in your chair yesterday, it was like a different power overtook my body."

I squeezed my thighs together, pinching my clit between my legs.

"While you revisited another one of those earthly pleasures you'd almost forgotten?"

"Yes," Caroline said. "And not just once. I've revisited those pleasures several times since yesterday. You're a difficult image to shake from one's memory, Jade."

As I crossed my legs trying to contain my rising passion, I felt the juices pouring out of my opening, dribbling down the crack of my ass.

"So what do we do now?" I asked. "Keep meeting for clandestine rendezvous at our local public library? Sooner or later, someone's going to catch on to us."

"I think you're right," Caroline nodded. "We're both taking unnecessary risks."

I looked around the coffee shop and noticed many people suddenly turning away. It was apparent that the pretty nun in her black habit had become the center of everyone's attention.

"Why don't we go somewhere where there aren't so many prying eyes? I can make us some more fresh juice at my place. That is—if you don't need to get back to the abbey right away..."

"What time is it?" Caroline asked. "I don't have a watch."

I pulled my phone out of my purse and tapped the screen to wake it up.

"Ten fifteen."

"It's still early," she said. "I might not be missed until the afternoon communion..."

For the entire duration of the twenty-minute drive back to my place, Caroline and I didn't say a word to each other, the sexual tension was so thick between us in the car. As she looked out her passenger window watching the passing scenery, I squeezed my thighs together, trying to keep my throbbing pussy from completely soaking the underside of my skirt.

When we got to my house, I opened the front door and invited her in. She looked around my living room and nodded approvingly.

"You have a lovely home," she said. "Tasteful and understated, just I expected."

"I wouldn't have thought you'd expect anything *understated* about me after today," I laughed. "Come to the kitchen and let me see if I can fix you up something more to your liking."

I led Caroline to my open kitchen and offered her a bar stool at the large central island.

"What do you feel like?" I asked. "Water, juice—or maybe something a little stronger? I don't suppose you're allowed to partake in certain other types of spirits?"

"We do occasionally partake in communal wine," Caroline chuckled, "so long as it's been properly consecrated first. Hopefully I won't be struck down for drinking something other than the blood of Christ, this one time."

"White wine it is then," I said, pulling a bottle of chardonnay from my fridge. "We don't need any more judging eyes upon us today."

I placed two wine glasses on the counter and filled the goblets halfway, then sat down beside Caroline.

"To rekindling forgotten memories," I said, holding my glass in the air.

Caroline tapped her goblet gently against mine, then took a small sip from the glass.

"There's been one other thing I've been meaning to ask you," I said, peering up at her white headdress. "Why is your hood white? Don't most nuns wear a black veil?"

"You're not the only one who's asked me that," she said. "Nuns normally go through a period of testing when they first enter the religious order, called a postulancy. For the first couple of years, we wear a white veil, signifying that we're still novitiates, or novices. Once we pass this initial test, if the nun and the abbess agree that the monastic life is what they desire, we take our final vows and receive the traditional all-black habit."

"So you're still—*testing* the waters, then?"

"I suppose so. I'm getting pretty close to the end of my postulancy period. My mother superior will be expecting me to take my final vows soon..."

"Do you feel ready?"

Caroline paused for a long moment with a pained look on her face.

"I thought I was. Until I met you. Then suddenly, my thoughts were no longer so pure..."

I set my glass down on the counter and stared into Caroline's eyes, imagining how conflicted she must have felt at this moment. We paused for many long seconds peering at one another, then she leaned her face toward me unconsciously. I quickly closed the distance and placed my lips against hers gently. As she closed her eyes, she pressed her mouth harder against mine.

I swiveled my stool until I was facing her directly, then I brought my right knee forward, parting her legs. As Caroline's mouth opened, I felt her cool breath on my face. I pushed my tongue gently into her, tasting the sweet vestige of wine on her lips. Within seconds, we were holding each other in a passionate embrace, pressing our bodies tightly together over the bar stools.

"Jade," Caroline panted, pulling away momentarily.

I looked into her eyes, trying to divine her intentions.

"Caroline," I said. "Do you feel ready?" I repeated.

She peered through glistening eyes at me and paused for only a moment.

"Yes."

Then she leaned forward and closed her lips around mine.

4

———

UNCLOAKED

Caroline and I kissed awkwardly on the bar stools for a few moments, then I pulled away and suggested we go upstairs where we could be more comfortable. As I led her by the hand through the hall, I felt an electric charge running through my body knowing I'd soon see her disrobed. But when we got to my bedroom, I paused looking at her habit, unsure where to start.

"I feel a bit uncomfortable touching your gown," I said. "Somehow, it just feels—*blasphemous*. I don't know how..."

Caroline smiled softly at me, then reached her hands up behind her veil.

"I can see how it might seem a bit daunting," she said. "Let me show you how I take off my armor."

She turned around and reached under the pleated fold behind her hood, then removed a hidden safety pin holding the two sides together, closing the pin and placing it in her pocket. Then she flipped up the back of her veil and unclasped another safety pin holding the inner flaps together. Then she turned around and lifted her hood off her head. Underneath, she wore a white cotton headdress covering her ears, neck, and the rest of her head.

I stared at her as she disassembled her wardrobe, mesmerized by the multiple layers of strange regalia. She looked so pure and inno-cent bound up in her tight white hoodie.

"Is there somewhere I can keep my veil?" she said, holding the white hood in front of her.

"Yes," I said, hanging it delicately over the back of my chair so as not to wrinkle it.

When I returned, she had her hands behind her head, slowly untying some more connections.

"Can I help?" I said, frustrated by the slow pace of her undressing. "Two people might make this go a little faster."

Caroline chuckled then turned around. At the back of her head, I saw two cotton ties holding her headdress together.

"You weren't kidding about the body armor," I chuckled. "They've really got you all tied up in this thing, don't they?"

"It's not as bad as it looks," Caroline said. "It's actually quite comfortable. You get used to it pretty quickly."

I untied the cotton bows at the back of her headdress, then gasped. Her hair was shorn down to short stubs, revealing an almost bald head.

"Are you *sure* you want me to take this off?" Caroline said with her back still turned to me.

"Yes," I said. "More than ever." I looked at the back of her hoodie and saw some more clasps. "What now?"

"Remove the safety pin holding the flap at the back of my neck."

I reached up and found the pin and gently slid it out under the band.

"Good God," I said. "How do you manage to get all these pins in and out every day without stabbing yourself? Or do you just sleep in this thing?"

"Heavens, no," Caroline said. "We're expected to keep our habits in pristine condition. That would produce far too many wrinkles. I actu-ally sleep in the nude most of the time."

My pussy pulsed at the thought of soon seeing her naked body.

"I'm dying to see you that way. How do we get the rest of this stuff off?"

"There's just one more pin to remove," she said. "At the bottom of my collar, you'll find another one holding the two flaps together."

I found the pin and removed it softly.

"Done."

Caroline turned around and smiled at me.

"Are you sure you're ready for this?" she asked.

"Yes," I said. "I want to see *all* of you."

Caroline reached behind her neck and removed her large oval collar and handed it to me. Then she reached behind her head and pulled her headdress forward off her head. When she showed her bare head for the first time, my eyes widened as big as saucers. Her baldness accentuated her soft features and beauty, reminding me of a young Sinead O'Connor.

"Caroline," I said. "You're stunning."

I leaned forward and kissed her on her lips and she pulled gently away.

"Don't forget about the wrinkling thing. I want to see you naked just as much as you do, but I've got to be presentable when I return to the abbey. Let's get the rest of these clothes off so we don't have to worry about it any longer."

She handed me the headdress and collar and I placed them flat on my work desk along with the pins. Now she stood before me wearing only her long black robe. The slow reveal was driving me crazy, and I could feel my pussy pulsing between my legs, anticipating what lay beneath.

Caroline threaded her fingers between the two sides of a long sash on the front of her gown, then pulled the strange garb over her head and handed it to me. Divest of the extra garment, I saw a long string of black prayer beads hanging down the side of her gown from her belt.

"This is called the scapular," she said.

"No wonder I couldn't make out your shape under your gown," I said. "How many layers do you have on this thing anyhow?"

"Just one more."

She reached around her back and unbuckled her belt, then handed it to me with the beads attached.

"Now the rosary..."

"Are you sure I won't get struck down by lightning touching this?" I joked.

"Let's hope not. But just to be safe, you might want to handle it by the belt only."

I held the belt out in front of me, being careful not to let the beads touch the ground, then laid it gently on my desk beside the other garments. When I returned, Caroline paused, looking at me unsteadily. I could tell she was a little nervous about revealing any more of her body.

"May I do this part?" I said, seeing the zipper running down the front of her tunic.

"Yes," she said, softly.

I slowly pulled the zipper down from under her chin and noticed that she wasn't wearing a bra.

"No undergarments?" I said, somewhat surprised.

"Not today," she said. "I wanted to feel...sexier. Normally, I wear an undershirt, bra, panties, and nylons. Something told me I might need to remove my habit a little faster today..."

I paused, realizing she was completely naked under this final layer. I stared into her eyes as I slowly pulled the zipper down. Listening to my heart pounding in my chest, I wasn't sure which one of us was more nervous. When the zipper reached the bottom of its travel, I pulled the upper halves of her tunic apart and peered down at her chest. When I saw her breasts, I gasped.

"Oh, God," I murmured.

Caroline's breasts were full and firm, standing in two perfect circles high on her chest. I reached in and cupped them with my hands and squeezed them gently, stepping forward and kissing her hard on her mouth. I could feel her chest rising and falling as she breathed heavily, blowing a soft breeze through her nostrils onto the sides of my cheeks. When I moved my thumb and forefinger over her nipples, I felt them harden, and she gasped in my mouth. As I rolled them gently between my fingers, she pressed her body firmly against mine.

We kissed for a few more seconds, then I moved my hands around the sides of her back, down toward her buttocks. As I ran my hands over her cheeks, they quivered in my hands and I pulled her toward me more tightly. When our mounds touched, we both let out a moan, and I felt Caroline's muscles contract in my hands as she pressed her mound against me.

"Jade," she panted. "This is all I've been able to think about. I want to make love to you."

She stepped back a couple of feet, then pulled her arms out of her sleeves and dropped her gown to the floor. When I saw her fully naked body for the first time, it took my breath away. She had a slender but shapely hourglass figure, with barely an ounce of fat anywhere on her body. Her whole body was white as fresh snow, except for a light brown triangle of pubic hair between her legs. I reached down and picked up her habit and folded it over the back of my chair, then returned to behold my pretty angel.

I stepped forward and ran my hands down the sides of her body, feeling the curvature of her hips, then I cupped her face in my hands and kissed her softly. Her body was shaking next to me, and as I touched her back, I felt goosebumps on her skin.

"Are you chilly?" I said.

"Maybe a little," she said. "I'm not used to being out of my habit for this long. Maybe I'm a little nervous too..."

"It's okay," I said. "We can take this slow. Let's get you under the covers where you'll be more comfortable."

I pulled the covers down from the edge of my headboard and gently sat Caroline on the side of my bed. Then I kneeled down on the floor between her legs and untied her black shoes and placed them beside my nightstand. With my face so close to her kitty, I could smell her sex wafting up from between her legs, and I wanted to pull myself into her so badly.

But I lay her down on the bed and pulled the sheets and comforter over her, then stood up. As she lay on my bed looking up at me innocently, I began to unbutton my blouse. Her eyes widened when she saw my full breasts pull away from my shirt, and I quickly pulled my arms out of my sleeves and threw my blouse on the floor.

"I'm not quite as worried about wrinkling as you are."

"Neither am I right now," she said. "Just get out of those clothes and get in here."

I quickly undid my skirt and dropped it to the floor. Even though Caroline had seen my naked vulva from across the library floor earlier, she was surprised to see my bare mound. Her eyes widened as she took in my body, squirming seductively under the covers.

"Now *you're* the one who looks pure and clean," she said, staring at the bare space between my legs.

I pulled off my shoes, then climbed in under the covers next to her.

"I'm sure I'm nowhere near as pure as you," I said, snuggling close to her. "But speaking of clean, I am feeling a little crusty from all the bodily discharges I produced watching you earlier today. Do you mind if I have a quick shower?"

Caroline wrapped her arms and legs around me and squiggled closer to me under the covers.

"Now?" she said. "You'd leave me to my own devices after teasing me so thoroughly?"

"Well if you don't think you can wait the five minutes it'll take me to clean up, you could always join me in the shower."

I turned around and opened my nightstand drawer.

"Or you could keep yourself amused with these other devices while I'm gone."

Caroline's eyes widened as she took in my collection of sex toys.

"Are those what I think they are?" she said.

"You've never used one?"

"Nothing quite so...elaborate. I've experimented using bottles and sundry pieces of fruit before, but these look a lot more —*sophisticated*."

I looked into Caroline's eyes and smiled a wide grin.

"You're in for a real treat then," I said. "But first, I want to have my *own* way with you before you get too attached to mechanical devices. Come, let's have a quick shower together to get cleaned up. It'll warm you up, too."

I threw the covers back then we scampered into my ensuite washroom, giggling like two little girls. I adjusted the water temperature in my shower until it was nice and warm, then I pulled Caroline under the spray. As the droplets bounced off her bald head and streamed down her face, I pulled her toward me and kissed her hard on her mouth. We rubbed our breasts together under the slippery water, clasping each other's buttocks, grinding our mounds against one another.

Caroline moaned gently, and I began to lower myself slowly down her body. As the water poured over me, I kissed her under her neck, tasting her sweet flesh. When I reached her chest, I paused to give each of her breasts plenty of attention, sucking and flicking her hardened nipples with my tongue, cupping and squeezing her tits between my two hands. The further I moved down her body, the more she moaned and whimpered, her stomach quivering in excitement from my touch.

It was obvious to me that she'd never been touched in this way by another person, and I savored every square inch of her magnificent, unspoiled body. When I got to her bush, I sucked the water droplets off her thatch like dew on the morning grass. Then I knelt down on the tiled floor, gently spread her legs, and kissed her pearl. Caroline gasped, grabbing the back of my head, and pulled me closer toward her.

"I thought you said we were going to get *clean* in here," she panted.

"That's exactly what I'm doing," I said. "I didn't say *how* we were going to get clean. Do you want me to stop?"

"God, no!" she said, pulling my head harder against her crotch.

When I slipped my tongue around her button and began to lather her with my serpent, Caroline threw her head back and moaned loudly.

"Yes, Jade," she whimpered. "Lick me. Lick me clean with your tongue."

Caroline's sexy comments surprised me, emboldening me to go further. I cupped her ass with my left hand and began trilling my fingers against her opening. Caroline bent her knees and tilted her hips, encouraging me to go further.

"Yes—take me," she said. "I want to feel you inside me."

I slipped my middle and forefinger into her cavern, and she pushed her hips down until my hand was buried inside her up to my knuckles. As she began humping her hips against my hand, I sucked her lengthening nub into my mouth.

"Oh God, yes," Caroline panted. "Suck me, Jade. It feels so good."

As her humping action increased in intensity, she pulled my head harder against her pussy. I could tell she was getting close, so I curled my fingers against her G-spot and flicked my tongue more rapidly over her rubbery clit. When I slipped my pinky finger further down her perineum and placed it over her anus, she gasped.

"Yes!" Caroline panted. "Jade, I'm going to—"

Suddenly, she emitted a guttural scream and pushed her muff hard into my face, as I felt her vagina and rosebud pulsing against my fingers. As she came into my mouth, I held her firmly in my hands, savoring her sweet nectar as the water streamed over my face.

"Jade—Jade—Jade!" Caroline panted with each pulse of her pussy. "I'm cumming! Oh—I'm cumming into your sweet mouth!"

It was odd to hear someone screaming in the throes of ecstasy without using any curse words, which just added to my excitement. As I felt the water streaming down over my ass and mound, my pussy quivered along with Caroline's. When she finally stopped shaking atop of me, I stood up and kissed her passionately, as the water streamed down over our faces.

Caroline wanted to return the favor, but I just wanted to get her back into bed as quickly as possible. I let her run the bar of soap over my body and between my legs, but I made sure to not get too worked up. There was so much more I wanted to do with her when we had the full and free roam of each other's bodies. When we were both thoroughly clean, we stepped out of the shower and toweled each other dry, then we scampered back into my bedroom and dove under the covers.

We kissed and intertwined our legs awkwardly for a few minutes, then I pulled myself away.

"Are you thoroughly warmed up now?" I said, looking into her eyes.

"Yes. You've practically brought me to a boil."

"Good," I said, throwing back the covers. "Because this is going to need a little more space."

Caroline pinched her eyebrows together and began to raise herself up.

"What did you have in mind? It's my turn to—"

I placed my hand on Caroline's chest and gently pushed her back onto the bed.

"It's okay," I said. "This is for *both* of us."

I lifted her knees off the bed then gently pressed her legs forward and apart until her thighs were resting on top of her chest. Then I moved my body forward and pressed my mound against hers.

"Uhnn!" Caroline grunted in surprise when our clits touched.

"Yes, Jade!" she said. "Make love to me."

She lifted her head and peered between her legs. Both of our buttons were hard and erect, protruding like little pencil erasers toward one another. I lowered myself slowly and swayed my hips over hers, watching out nubs bending and flexing in a playful little sword fight.

"Oh God," Caroline panted. "That feels so good! Stroke me, Jade. Rub me...*fuck* me!"

I widened my eyes and gasped at Caroline in mock astonishment.

"You dirty little girl," I said. "I sure hope no one else is listening right now. Otherwise you could be in a lot of trouble."

"So do I," Caroline said. "But right now it hardly matters. Take me. There's only one place I want to go right now."

I lay my body on top of Caroline's and began to grind my pussy into hers as we kissed passionately. For the first time, I felt her tongue press into my mouth, and we sucked and nibbled on each other as our hips gyrated together. I wanted to make this feeling last, but I was already so worked up from making Caroline cum earlier, I could feel my orgasm rising quickly within me.

I grunted into Caroline's mouth as my juices poured out of my cunt, coating her bush and thighs with my lubrication. I could feel myself getting close, and I pulled my face up so I could look at Caroline's face. As my mouth and eyes widened signaling my impending orgasm, Caroline suddenly began panting louder.

"Yes, Jade," she said. "*Cum* for me. I want to watch you cum all over me."

I lifted my body up in one last strain and thrust my pussy hard against hers.

"Caroline!" I screamed. "I'm cumming! I'm cumming in your sweet pussy!"

Caroline's pupils suddenly dilated and she called out my name.

"Fuck, yes!" she screamed with me. "I feel you! I'm cumming with you, Jade! Oh God—it feels so good!"

Suddenly, I felt a hard spray jetting up against my vulva as Caroline squirted her love juices into my opening. Feeling her cum against my pussy was too much. I swung my body around her and clamped our boxes together in a scissor position. I wanted to feel our pussies connected as we were cumming together.

"Uhnn—Caroline," I grunted. "Come in my pussy, baby! Fill me up with your sweet nectar!"

I pulled her leg up toward my chest, grinding our cunts together, feeling my contractions gripping my entire body. We jerked and heaved our bodies together for a full minute, watching the look of tortured ecstasy wash over our faces. When we were completely spent, I collapsed on the bed beside Caroline, panting and sweating. We lay beside one another for a long time, holding and caressing each other, then Caroline finally turned toward me.

"What time is it?" she asked.

My eyes widened and I shook my head.

"Oh no," I said. "You can't..."

"I have to," she said. "The abbess will begin to worry if I'm not back soon."

I looked at Caroline through glistening eyes.

"But I don't want to let you go. I wanted to feel you fall asleep in my arms."

I turned my head toward my nightstand, thinking of how I could entice her to stay a little longer.

"And besides, you haven't even tried any of my toys. I had a few special ones in mind for you. When can you come back?"

"I don't know if I can," Caroline said. "These library excursions were meant to be temporary. I'm supposed to stay within the abbey. That's the whole point of my vows—to abstain from worldly temptations."

"But I thought you hadn't decided yet? Hasn't this changed your thinking at all about continuing on your life of abstinence?"

"It has, but I'm not ready to give it all up just yet. I need a little more time to think—"

"Can I visit you at the abbey at least? I just need to see you. I can't just let you walk out of my life forever."

Caroline looked at me with a pained expression and shook her head.

"It's too dangerous. People will notice there's something different between us—"

I reflected back to the videos of the naked nuns I watched earlier in the day.

"Is there somewhere I could meet you then, where no one would notice? Can you ever leave the grounds temporarily?"

"Not really."

Caroline paused for a long moment.

"But—"

"Tell me," I said. "I'll do anything, as long as I can see you again."

"There might be one way," she said. "But it's very dangerous..."

"What? Tell me!"

"I might be able to sneak you into the abbey for a short time. There's a secret passageway that we're not supposed to know about. A few other novices and I occasionally use it to slip outside to go for a walk. But we'd have to do it at night, and we'd need to have a signal."

I paused for a moment, thinking how I could notify her when I was near.

"How about if I hoot like an owl? There's plenty of those around here. Will you be able to hear it from inside the abbey?"

"I'll keep my window open," Caroline nodded. "But not tonight. The abbess will be watching too closely. Let's do it tomorrow night, just after dusk. Hoot three times in succession, so I know it's you. But be sure to do it convincingly, so it sounds like a real owl. I'll meet you at the south gate at the edge of the forest."

"I'll watch YouTube videos and practice all day," I said. "Will I be able to stay the night? I want to feel you in my arms when I fall asleep."

"Possibly. But you'll have to stay holed up in my room until the following night. Then you'll have to leave. It will be too dangerous for you to stay more than one day."

"I promise," I said, feeling my heart beating again in excitement. " Even one more day with you will feel like a lifetime. I just hope you'll reconsider your vows so we can see each other again. I don't want to lose you."

Caroline turned her body to face me and kissed me softly.

"You're so sweet, Jade. If anything could pull me away from the ascetic life, it's you."

Then she paused as she smiled into my eyes.

"And bring some of your toys. That might help."

MOTHER SUPERIOR

The next twenty-four hours seemed like an eternity, as I waited to see Caroline again. All I could think about was her radiant face and her pale, supple skin pressed against my body. I'd gone online and practiced my owl imitation as promised, standing in front of my mirror contorting my face and vocal chords, until I thought I'd gotten the pitch just right. As long as nobody saw me huddled in the surrounding woodland, I was confident I'd be able to pull it off.

An hour before dusk, I collected my belongings and drove north toward the remote address Caroline had given me. When I got to the monastery, there was a long drive leading up a hill, protected by a wrought-iron gate. I parked my car on a side street and tried to find a pedestrian access point, but the entire estate was surrounded by a tall iron fence topped with pointed finials, with locked gates all around.

Caroline had warned me about the barricade, so I removed a heavily padded blanket from my tote bag and flung it atop the spikes. I threw my purse over the fence then awkwardly pulled myself up the front of the fence and swung my legs over the top. I could feel the finials poking through the blanket into my stomach and chest, and swung my legs over the other side and fell onto the manicured lawn on the other side.

"These guys don't fool around," I murmured, feeling like a cat burglar invading a hallowed ground.

I made my way up the hill, trying to stay under the cover of the many mature trees scattered over the estate. When I got to the top of the hill, I saw a tall, steepled church flanked by two four-story block buildings. Caroline told me she was in the west residence, so I moved to that side of the compound and waited about thirty feet behind the rear entrance under a large elm tree. There was no sign of any activity on the grounds, which just added to the spookiness of the scene.

What the hell have I gotten myself into? I thought, looking around the quiet estate. *If anybody sees me, I'll stick out like a sore thumb.*

I'd worn special clothing to not be too conspicuous, and with my long dark pants, black sneakers, and black turtleneck, it just added to the cat burglar mystique. As the light dimmed over the estate, bats began darting over the dark sky and I heard rustling in the branches overhead.

This place is creepy, I thought, wondering if this was an omen of bad things to come.

But as dusk fell, I began to hear the familiar hooting of owls in the surrounding woodland, and as I listened to their calls I prepared to alert Caroline. At precisely nine-fifteen, I let out my signal.

"Hoo—hoo—hoo," I called out in my best falsetto.

Within seconds, a nearby owl returned my call.

"Hoo—hoo—hoo," I repeated.

Almost immediately, the owl hooted back.

If I can trick a real owl, I thought, *hopefully I can blend in with the rest of the local fauna.*

I waited five minutes, watching the back door to Caroline's building, but there was no sign of movement.

Had her abbess suspected something different about Caroline when she returned to the abbey and was keeping a closer eye on her? What if she can't get away?

I repeated my owl signal two more times, then I saw the back door swing open a few inches and Caroline stuck her head out, motioning for me to come in. I looked around to make sure the way was clear, then I scampered toward the door and jumped inside. Caroline and I kissed for a moment, then she pulled away with wide eyes.

"Jeesh—" she said, "do you think you could have made more of a racket out there? You've probably woken up the entire western wing!"

"It wasn't just me," I protested. "Apparently, there was another amorous owl out there competing for my affections. We had quite a little conversation going on for a while there."

Caroline giggled, then pulled a folded habit from under her cape and handed it to me.

"What do you want me to do with this?" I asked.

"We're going to need to disguise you, in case we run into anyone. It's only three floors and a short walk to my dorm, but I don't want to take any chances."

"Oh my God!" I said. "As if we haven't already broken enough rules. Now you want me to pretend I'm a *nun*?! God will surely strike me down before I get to your room."

"I'm sure he'll understand, under the circumstances," Caroline said. She removed the long tunic component from the pile. "Put this on first. Do you remember how it goes?"

"I've replayed your undressing ceremony in my head only about a hundred times since you left," I chuckled.

I stepped into the toga, then pulled the sleeves over my arms and zipped up the front.

"Good," Caroline said. "Now for the scapular."

She handed me the long flap draped over the front and back of the habit, and I pulled it over my head.

"Now the guimpe..." she said, handing me the large white collar.

She placed it around my neck and fastened it with the safety pin behind my back.

"Almost done," she said, handing me the white headdress. "Do you remember how to put on the wimple?"

"Of course," I said, placing my face through the hole in the front, then pulling it up under my chin and over my head.

"We won't worry about tying it at the back," Caroline said. "We haven't got far to go. It should hold until you get to my room. Now for the veil."

She lifted a black hood from my hands and placed it over my headdress, fastening it with two velcro tabs on top of my head.

"Why do I get a black one?" I asked.

"You're going to be a fully professed nun for tonight," she said. "You'll attract less attention this way."

"No prayer beads?" I joked.

"Let's not push it," she said. "You're already living on borrowed time as it is."

Caroline paused, as she looked at me approvingly.

"You know, you look quite suitable in a habit. Are you sure you don't want to consider joining our monastery full time? At least we'd have a chance to be together more—"

"I don't think I could manage the chastity part of your vows very well," I kidded.

"What now?" I said, looking up the stairs.

"Follow close behind me," Caroline said. "If we encounter any other sisters along the way, just keep your head down. Hopefully, nobody will recognize that you're an outsider."

"And if I am?"

"Well improvise."

"Is that where the lightning comes in?"

"Quite possibly."

I shook my head as I followed Caroline up the three flights of stairs, then she opened the door leading to her floor's hall and peered through the crack.

"All clear," she said. "Remember—stay close behind me."

I paused, reaching out to grab her arm.

"Shouldn't the more senior nun lead the way? Won't it look unusual for me to be following you?"

"Don't let that uniform go to your head, my lady. Just follow my instructions and we should be fine."

Caroline swung the door open and stepped out into the hall, then began walking down the corridor with her hands embedded under the sides of her gown. I mimicked her movement, holding my purse tightly against my abdomen, walking three feet directly behind. When we were about halfway down the hall, another nun suddenly turned the corner about a hundred feet ahead of us and began walking in our direction.

My heart raced in fear thinking I'd be detected, and I scurried up closer behind Caroline.

"What do we do now?" I whispered. "Surely she'll recognize that I'm not part of the congregation!"

"Just be calm and keep your head down," Caroline said.

I lowered my head, feeling my loose headdress falling down over my eyebrows, and I lifted my hand to push it back. After we'd closed the distance to about fifty feet, the nun stopped and turned to one of the residence doors and nodded gently toward us. Caroline returned the gesture, then the nun entered the room and closed the door behind her. Twenty feet ahead, Caroline stopped outside another door on the opposite side of the hall and quickly pulled it open motioning me inside. I scampered into her room, and after Caroline checked both ends of the hall to be sure no one else was watching, she slipped in and closed the door behind her.

We giggled quietly, then I pressed her body against the door and kissed her passionately on her lips.

"That was a close one," I said. "Do you think the other nun suspected anything?"

"I don't think so, but just to be extra careful we're going to have to be super-quiet as long as you're in my room. The horarium has ended for the day, so we've got the rest of the night to ourselves."

I leaned in toward Caroline and slipped my knee between her legs, pressing my thigh against her crotch as I kissed her. After a few seconds, she stepped away, pinching her eyebrows.

"Wrinkles!" she said.

"You've *got* to be kidding me," I said. "Don't you have an iron? They must provide *some* appliances to make your life easier—"

"We do. But it will just be easier if we get out of these clothes. Besides, I've been dying to see you naked again ever since yesterday."

"You don't have to ask me twice," I said, eager to get out of my religious garb as soon as possible.

We helped each other remove our garments, then Caroline hung and placed everything carefully in her wardrobe closet. When we were both naked, we pressed our bodies together, mashing our breasts and mounds against one another, kissing passionately. I moaned unconsciously from the delirious feeling of holding her close to me again, and Caroline pulled her face away, lifting her finger to her lips.

"Sh!" she said. "Not a peep. This place is like crickets at night. You can hear everything."

"That's easy for *you* to say," I whispered. "I don't know how I'm going to possibly contain myself around you."

"Well then, I guess you'll just have to do *me* first," Caroline smiled. "I've had more practice keeping quiet around here."

She looked at my large purse resting on the floor and widened her eyes.

"Did you bring some of your toys for me to play with?"

"I did," I said, smiling at Caroline mischievously.

I picked up my purse and placed it on her narrow bed, then pulled out a large purple dildo with a V-shaped extension near the base.

"This is one of my favorites. It's called a rabbit vibrator."

I pointed it up and turned the dial at the base of the dildo. The purple shaft began to vibrate and the tip of the dildo began to wobble in circles, as a ring of beads midway along the shaft began to rotate.

"Those don't look like prayer beads," Caroline said.

"No, but I think you might find them divine in an entirely different sense of the word."

Caroline looked at the animated device, widening her eyes.

"Do I put it *inside* me?"

"It works best that way. The oscillating head twists and turns, providing a heavenly form of stimulation against your G-spot."

"G-spot?"

"That the place inside you where I tickled you with my fingers yesterday."

"Oh yes—I remember that very well. That was the first time you took me over the edge."

Caroline placed her fingers over the strange rubbery protrusions on the side of the dildo. "What do *these* do?"

"Those are the rabbit ears. They provide direct stimulation to your clitoris while the shaft is pumping and churning inside you. The combined effect is really quite something."

"I can see how you were worried I'm might become too attached to these devices." She reached into my bag and pulled out a leather harness with a long red phallus attached to the front. "What about this one?"

"That's what's called a strap-on dildo. It's something I can use to—um—*make love* to you like a man."

"Do women *do* that to each other?" Caroline said, pinching her eyebrows together.

"Some do. It can actually be quite fun, when you're in the right mood."

Caroline glanced in my purse seeing a variety of other sex toys and shook her head.

"Where do we begin? You've brought so many—"

I pushed Caroline gently down on the bed and lay on top of her.

"First, I want to touch and feel you with my *own* body parts," I said. "I've been dreaming about tasting your sweet body for the past twenty-four hours."

I rubbed my tits against Caroline's and ground my pussy into hers, thrusting my tongue into her pliant mouth. As her breathing escalated, I began kissing my way down the front of her body toward her pussy. I played with her breasts for a few minutes, pinching and sucking her nipples, then I drew my tongue over her quivering tummy until I reached her pubic patch. I flapped my face over her soft bush, breathing her fresh scent deep into my nostrils.

The lower I went on her mound, the wetter her patch became until my face rested between her slickly coated thighs. When I placed my tongue over her clit and licked it like a lollypop, Caroline gasped. I looked up between her legs and she tilted her head down toward me.

"*Now* who's being the noisy one?" I said.

As we peered into one another's eyes, I took her jewel into my mouth and began dancing my tongue over her hard shaft. Caroline bit her lip and scrunched her eyes, trying to keep quiet. It was such a turn-on seeing her face contort in private pleasure as I nibbled on her fiery love button. Her mouth opened wider with her rising passion, and I placed my fingers at her opening, preparing to thrust them inside her. But she reached out and placed her hands over mine, stopping me.

"Wait," she panted. "I want to feel you...*fuck* me...if you're going to be inside me. Can we try your strap-on sex toy?"

I lifted my head and smiled at Caroline like a Cheshire Cat.

"I thought you'd never ask," I said.

I quickly got up off the bed and wrapped the leather harness around my hips then rocked my hips in the air, flapping the big phallus sticking out from my mound.

"Is that what a *real* man's penis looks like?" Caroline asked, wide-eyed.

"More or less," I said. "This might be a little larger than most, and it has a few extra features distinguishing it from a regular cock."

I tapped a button on the side of my belt and the penis suddenly began bouncing and oscillating from side to side. Caroline's eyes grew even larger, and she tilted her hips up toward me.

"Yes, Jade," she purred. "Fuck me with your big man cock. I want to feel you inside me."

My pussy pulsed and I felt a dribble of lubrication run down the inside of thighs. I ran my hand over the slick patch then rubbed it over the top of my phallus, simulating a masturbation effect.

"Mmm," Caroline said. "I think it will feel even better *inside* me. Stop playing with your cock and put it inside me."

Caroline's dirty talk was getting me even more turned on, and I kneeled on the bed between her legs and placed the tip of my artificial cock over her opening. I rubbed it up and down her slit for a few seconds then I pressed the head against her clit. She rocked her hips forward to provide more friction against her love button and moaned softly. I looked into her soft blue eyes then grabbed her hips on both sides and slowly inserted the cock into her cunny.

"Oh, God yes!" Caroline panted. "Fuck me with your big cock, Jade!"

I thrust my pole deep inside Caroline's pussy and began pulling her hips toward me as I fucked her harder. Her tits bounced up and down on her chest with each thrust of my hips, and she began swinging her head from side to side in pleasure.

"It feels so good, Jade!" she said, seemingly no longer concerned about how much noise she was making. "Fuck me harder. Make me cum all over your big cock!"

I could feel the base of the phallus rubbing against my own clit as I thrust in and out of Caroline, and before long I began to feel the familiar pangs of an orgasm rising within me. I reached to the side of my belt and pressed the vibrator button, suddenly feeling the device throbbing between my legs. I pushed my hips hard against Caroline's vulva, grinding the oscillating phallus against her clit.

"Oh God, Jade!" she panted. "You're going to make me cum! Here it comes—I'm cumming Jade!"

I looked down between her legs and saw her spraying all over my artificial dick as I pumped in and out of her. Feeling her love juices dripping down under my belt into my own pussy soon put me over the edge too.

"Caroline!" I panted, trying my best to keep my voice to a whisper. "Cum on me, sweetie. I feel you. Momma's coming with you!"

I thrust my big dildo into Caroline's spasming pussy for a full thirty seconds, then I fell on top of her, kissing her passionately while I continued to pump my cock into her, savoring the slippery wetness between both of our legs. After a few minutes, I pulled out and lay beside her, kissing her face and neck softly.

"That was incredible," Caroline panted, looking into my eyes. "Those toys really *are* addictive, aren't they?"

"They can be. That's why I like to use them in moderation. There's still nothing quite like the natural feeling of skin on skin."

"Mmmm, I agree," Caroline purred. "Speaking of which, I think it's *your* turn for some good old-fashioned skin-on-skin lovemaking. What can I do for you now?"

"Well, now that you mention it, there *was* something I had in mind.."

I removed my harness and placed the strap-on dildo on the corner of the bed, then swung my legs over Caroline's midsection and shimmied my hips up toward her head. When I got to her shoulders, I lifted my legs and placed my knees on opposite sides of her head. I paused for a moment, watching Caroline stare at my dripping wet pussy, then I slowly began to lower myself toward her face.

Just before I touched her lips, we heard a loud rapping noise on Caroline's door.

"Sister Caroline," an older woman's voice said from the other side of the door. "Is everything all right in there? I heard some unusual noises. May I come in?"

"Um—one minute, Mother Margaret," Caroline called back, her eyes wide as saucers.

She raised herself up off the bed and whispered for me to hide in the closet. Then she went to the wardrobe and opened the doors, putting on a terrycloth robe. I quickly picked up my purse and slipped inside, retreating to the far corner behind the hanging frocks. Caroline closed the door quietly behind me, and I peered between the narrow slats with frightened eyes. Caroline lifted her bedcovers and threw the rabbit vibrator and strap-on dildo under the sheets, then straightened her robe before heading to the door. I couldn't see her and the other nun from my vantage point, but I overheard the conversation clearly.

"Good evening, Mother," Caroline said. "Everything is fine. I was just preparing my bed to go down for the night."

There was a long pause, and I looked around Caroline's room to make sure all of my belongings were out of sight. Fortunately, she'd had the presence of mind to hang my clothes in the closet, so for all intents and purposes, it looked like she was alone.

"May I come in for a moment?" Mother Margaret said. "I'd like to inspect your room to ensure everything is in order."

"Of course. But I don't think you'll find anything out of place. You know how neat and fastidious I am."

"I do," Margaret said. "This won't take long."

I heard some footsteps moving toward the closet, then a nun wearing an all-black habit passed by my door. I crouched lower under the hanging robes and held my breath so as not to be heard. The mother superior looked around Caroline's room and noticed a bump in her covers and bent over to smooth them with her hand. Her eyes widened when she felt a hard object under the covers, and she swung the covers down, revealing the rabbit vibrator.

"What's this?" she asked.

"It's a—" Caroline paused, trying to think of how she could explain the strange object, "...*massager*. It helps loosen up my tight muscles when I get cramps."

"*Really*?" Margaret said, in a condescending tone. "You know most electric devices are banned from use in this abbey. But I might make an exception in this case, depending on your need. Show me how you use it."

Caroline looked at the mother superior in shock as her mouth tipped open.

"It's okay, my child. I merely want to see how it relieves your —*pain*."

Caroline picked up the vibrator by its purple shaft and twisted the control knob on the bottom. The vibrator began whirring and twisting in her hand, and she placed it against the back of her neck, turning her head from side to side, simulating the relaxation of her shoulder muscles.

"That's quite an interesting device," Margaret said. "May I see it for a moment?'

Caroline hesitated, then turned the vibrator off and handed it to her superior.

Margaret held it up in her hands for a moment and twisted it around in her hands.

"Why is it shaped like a *penis*, I wonder?" she said. She ran her hands over the tip of the phallus. "It appears to be anatomically correct—except for these strange flaps on the side. Where *else* have you been placing this massager to relieve your pain?"

It was obvious to me that Mother Margaret knew full well how the sex toy was designed to be used and that she was enjoying watching Caroline squirm as she tried to explain why she had it in her possession.

"Just my shoulders and back, mostly," Caroline said.

"*Mostly*?" Margaret said. "Show me. Take off your robe and lie down on your bed and show me how you use this thing to stimulate your muscles elsewhere on your body."

Caroline froze as she looked at the mother superior with a terrified look in her eyes.

"Go on, child. I'm *ordering* you. By your vows, you must follow all of my instructions. Let me help you off with your robe."

Mother Margaret stepped behind Caroline's back and pulled her robe off her body, then threw it on the base of the bed.

"Please continue, Caroline," she said. "Lie down on your bed and place that massager where it is designed to go."

Caroline lay down tentatively on the bed and began to rub the dildo over the sides of her body.

"*Lower*, my child. I think it's meant to go lower."

Caroline traced the vibrator down the side of her body until it rested on the side of her hips, then she pushed it into the sides of her buttocks, pretending to massage her hip muscles.

"Now, bring it—*inside*," Margaret instructed. "Between your legs. Place the purple penis between your legs."

Caroline paused for a moment, and the mother superior nodded for her to continue. She pulled the vibrator over her thigh and placed it awkwardly between her legs, rubbing it up and down softly over her slit.

"Yes, my child. Doesn't that feel better than using it to massage your neck or shoulders? Now, I want you to turn it on."

Caroline lifted the dildo above her hips and turned the dial part way. The vibrator began humming softly.

"*All* the way," Mother Margaret said.

Caroline twisted the dial clockwise until it wouldn't go any further. Suddenly, the penis became fully animated, twisting and oscillating noisily in her hand.

"Now place it between your legs, and let's see how pleasurable this massager can really be."

Caroline placed the tip of the humming vibrator at her opening and gasped.

"Does that feel better, Caroline?" Margaret said. "Is this massager relieving your stress in your nether regions?"

"Yes," Caroline panted.

"I think it's designed to massage your *insides* too," Margaret said. "I want to see you insert it into your private area. You've had far too much stress built up these past few months. Let's see if this special massager might relieve you of some of your burden."

Caroline paused for a moment, then inserted the tip of the vibrator into her slit. I could see the oscillating head turning and dancing over her opening, tickling her clit. As her long eyelashes fluttered in obvious pleasure, I couldn't help reaching down between my own legs to play with my own clit. There was something incredibly sexy about watching her masturbate herself while being watched by such an austere authority figure.

"*Deeper*, my child," Margaret said. "Press it deeper inside you. Feel the phallus filling you up, massaging your deepest regions. Relax and enjoy the stimulation of your special massager."

As Caroline inserted the dildo deeper into her pussy, I could see the rabbit ears flapping along the side. When she pressed the ears directly against her clit with the oscillating dildo embedded all the way inside her, she grunted loudly.

"Yes, Caroline," Margaret said. "Doesn't that feel better? Is that relaxing all of your muscles now?"

"Yes, Mother," Caroline panted, beginning to hump her hips, thrusting the vibrator in and out of her. "It feels...very good."

"Continue, my child," Margaret beseeched her. "Continue massaging your inner regions to see if you can relieve *all* of your stress."

"Yes Mother," Caroline panted, beginning to lift her hips off the bed as she hammered the dildo in and out of her.

It was the sexiest thing I may have ever witnessed, and I bit my lip trying to stifle my moans as my juices poured over my hand trilling between my legs.

"Oh Mother," Caroline said. "I can feel it—beginning to—ease my pain. It feels very good."

"Yes, my child. Push it harder up inside you. Make sure it reaches all of your sore muscles."

Caroline lifted her hips high over the bed and pulled the vibrator as far into her as she could, holding the vibrating ears tight against her mound. I could see the wings flapping wildly against her clit as she opened her mouth at the height of ecstasy. Suddenly, she grunted loudly and began shaking her hips uncontrollably.

"Uhnnn!" she grunted. "Oh God, I feel it, Mother!"

"Yes, my child," Margaret said. "Feel his blessing sweeping over you. You are truly filled with the spirit of Jesus."

Watching Caroline cumming so hard in front of the mother superior unfurled my taps, and I gushed all over my hand as my pussy clamped down over my fingers. It took a superhuman effort to not utter a sound, as I jerked silently in the darkness of the closet.

Caroline held her hips up in the air as she spasmed in a long and sustained orgasm for many seconds. When the wave finally passed, she flopped back on the bed, panting heavily.

"There now," Margaret said. "Doesn't that feel much better?

Perhaps we can find a good use for this automated stress-reliever after all."

Margaret kneeled on the bed and took the dildo out of Caroline's pussy and inserted it into her mouth, sucking her juices seductively from the shaft.

"I've been feeling some built-up stress of my *own* lately..."

As she knelt on the base of Caroline's bed and began to lift the front of her habit, she suddenly paused and ran her fingers over the covers. Feeling something else under the covers, she pulled them back all the way, revealing the strap-on dildo.

"What have we here?" she said, looking at Caroline mischievously. "Have you been using these special massagers with some of our other sisters? I think perhaps it's time I reminded you who's *really* in charge around here."

As she began to remove her habit, Caroline glanced toward the closet doors. I wasn't sure if she could see me peering back at her, but I sure as hell could see her and the mother superior vividly. And I was about to get the show of a lifetime from my dark little peephole...

VOLUME TWO

THE EXCHANGE STUDENT

1

—————

I almost missed the ad while rushing out of the grocery store after a long day of work. Tucked away in a corner of the bulletin board near the exit door was a small poster with the headline *Earn Extra Income Hosting a Foreign Exchange Student*. I paused for a moment, then pulled my cart closer to the board to read the message:

Earn money while helping a foreign student expand their cultural horizons. There's no better way to learn a new language and appreciate other cultures than to live with someone from another part of the world. By hosting a young person from a different country, you promote friendship, understanding, and cooperation in your home and community. Welcome a foreign exchange student into your home today and open the door to an exciting new world of experiences. Contact exchangehost.com for more info.

After reading the ad, I suddenly became aware of how hard my heart was pounding in my chest. I'd lived alone after separating from my husband more than two years ago, and my big house had become far too quiet and lonely. Having never had children of my own, the idea of hosting a young person from another country seemed a perfect fit. I'd have someone to liven up my daily routine while helping the student develop a sense of independence in an exciting new environment.

When I got home, I went to the agency's website and read everything I could about the program. The more I learned, the more excited I became. I wasn't interested in the small monthly stipend I'd earn hosting the student so much as the sense of adventure taking in a boarder from a different country. It would be an opportunity to share cultural experiences, improve my foreign language skills, and make new friendships.

The following morning, I called first thing to book an appointment for an interview. When I got to their office, the receptionist escorted me into the director's suite where a smartly dressed woman in her fifties invited me to make myself comfortable while she took a seat in the opposite armchair.

"Welcome, Ms. Robertson," she said. "My name is Elise Laurent, the director of Exchange Host student exchange services. What brings you to our office today?"

"I'm interested in hosting a foreign exchange student," I said.

"I see you're here by yourself. Do you live alone?"

"Yes," I said, crossing my legs defensively. "Do you accept applications from single women?"

"Of course," she said. "It all depends on the individual's circumstances and motivation. Our primary concern is finding a safe and supportive environment for our clients. May I ask what attracts you to our program?"

"I saw an ad for your services at the supermarket. I've never had any children, and I like the idea of helping a young person supplement their education in a different country. With so much conflict and misunderstanding between countries and cultures, this seems an ideal way to foster better communication and friendship."

"You seem primarily focused on the benefits to the *student*," the director nodded. "What advantages do you see for you, personally?"

"It's not about the money, if that's what you mean. I'd do it for free, if that were an option. I live alone and work from home, so I have limited opportunity for social interaction. To be honest, I think it would be fun to have someone else to share my house with. Especially a young person who I could foster and take under my wing. I could take her shopping, go out to restaurants, visit national parks–it could be fun for both of us."

"So you're looking to host a female student only?"

"Not necessarily. I'd consider either gender, but I think it would be more fun hosting a girl."

The director nodded, scribbling some notes on a notepad.

"You say money isn't a consideration. May I ask what you do for a living?"

"I'm a freelance graphic artist. I help develop ads, logos, websites, and media campaigns for corporate clients."

"Do you own your home?"

"I guess technically the bank owns it until the mortgage is paid off," I chuckled. "But yes, I'm the sole title owner."

"Umm," the director hummed, scribbling some more notes. "Do you have an extra room and bath available for another occupant?"

"Yes," I said. "Frankly, that's another reason I'm considering this. My house is far too large for one person. I'll feel better making better use of the extra space and helping the environment by wasting less."

"Um-hmm," the Ms. Laurent nodded. "And you feel you'll have enough free time away from your work and other responsibilities to give your charge proper attention and care? It's not like taking in a boarder–these students will need oversight and companionship. They'll be a long way from home in a whole new environment. It's more akin to a foster parent situation."

"Absolutely," I said. "Being self-employed means I can make my own hours and work around my guest's schedule. I'm looking forward to taking her under my wing and making a new friend. Like I said, I'm not doing it for the money."

"Okay," the woman said, putting down her notepad. "We'll need you to fill in an application and provide three references. Then I'll need your approval to run a criminal record check and credit check. If everything pans out, we'll begin contacting you with possible candidates to find a good fit. The whole process can take two or three months and with a new school year approaching, you'll need to get started soon."

"Sounds good," I said, rising from my chair and extending my hand. "Thank you for your time and assistance, Ms. Laurent. I'll look forward to hearing back from you at your earliest opportunity. Let me know if you need any more information in the meantime."

"It's been my pleasure," she said. "Thank you for your interest in our program. I think you'll find this experience enriching and rewarding on both sides. My assistant will help you with the paperwork. We'll be in touch soon."

After filling in the application, I drove home with a sense of excitement wondering who the agency would find to connect me with. I had no idea what age, sex, or nationality the student would be and that was part of the attraction. It would be a whole new experience for both of us. But after a few weeks of not hearing from the agency, I began to wonder if they were having second thoughts about my candidacy. I'd checked with my references who told me they'd already been contacted, and I knew there wouldn't be any issues with my background or credit check, so with only a few weeks left before the start of the new school year, I placed a call to the director.

"Exchange Host," the receptionist said, answering the phone.

"May I speak with Ms. Laurent?" I said.

"May I ask who's calling?"

"My name is Jade Robertson. I had an interview with Ms. Laurent a couple of months ago and haven't heard back. I was just hoping for an update."

"One moment please," the receptionist said.

"Hello, Ms. Robertson," the director said when she picked up her extension.

"I'm sorry to bother you," I said. "But I haven't heard back from you and I know we're getting close to the start of another academic year. I was wondering if you had any problems with my application or if you'd vetted any potential candidates."

"No," the director said. "Your application came through with flying colors. Unfortunately, it was processed a bit late and all of the hosting spots for the new school year have been filled."

"That's disappointing to hear," I said. "So I guess I'll have to wait another year for consideration?"

"Not necessarily," she said. "We have a number of students who seek to transfer mid-year. There may be another opportunity as we approach the end of the first semester. We'll contact you if anything becomes available."

"Okay, thank you, Ms. Laurent."

I hung up, feeling dejected about prematurely getting my hopes up. The closer we'd gotten to the start of the school year, the more excited I'd become about having a new housemate. Now I'd have to wait a whole other year to have the opportunity to host a student.

For a while, I considered putting an ad in the local university newspaper offering a room for board, but I knew it wouldn't be the same. There was something about taking in a young international student that added an extra allure for me. I'd have the chance to nurture someone who really depended on me while we explored each other's language and culture. In the end, I decided to hold off, hoping to try again next year.

But much to my surprise, I received a message from Ms. Laurent a couple of months later indicating that she had a new candidate lined up for the spring semester. I picked up the phone and called her immediately.

"Hello, Ms. Laurent," I said excitedly when she picked up the phone. "It's Jade Robertson. I got your message regarding a possible candidate for the spring semester, and I'm still interested."

"That's wonderful news," she said. "We're ready to finalize the placement if you're sure you're ready to proceed."

"Absolutely," I said, still catching my breath.

"Would you like to view the student's profile before making a final commitment? We can send it to you via email if you prefer."

I paused for a moment, hearing my heart pounding in my chest. As eager as I was for more details, I couldn't wait for the most important information.

"That would be helpful, thank you," I said. "Can you tell me if it's a boy or a girl, and from which country they'll be transferring?"

"It's a girl who'll be completing the final semester for her senior year. She's transferring in from France."

France, I thought, feeling my heart skip a beat. I'd always wanted to travel there and learn to speak the language, but had never found the time. This would be my chance to learn more about their culture by experiencing it in a whole *different* way.

"That sounds exciting," I said. "When will she be arriving, and are there any final preparation requirements?"

"She's due to arrive January twenty-third, the weekend between first and second semester. The only other preparation requirement is a final in-home interview to ensure you have sufficient accommodation and resources to care for your guest. We can arrange a convenient time to visit next week if that will work for you."

"That's perfect. How about Wednesday at one p.m.? Thank you for keeping me in the queue for consideration with this placement."

"My pleasure, Ms. Robertson. I'll look forward to seeing you next Wednesday. Bye for now."

Later that day, I received the student profile via email. When I opened it, the first thing I saw was a single headshot photo. It was a bit grainy, but she looked pretty and fresh-faced, with wavy blonde hair and bright blue-green eyes. Her name was Luna, and she lived in Saint Denis, a suburb of Paris. She listed her hobbies as yoga, skiing, and dressmaking. Her father was an engineer and her mother was a nurse. She had two siblings, an older sister and a younger brother. Her career interests were international relations and fashion design.

Perfect, I thought. *We can exercise together, go skiing on weekends, and we both have an interest in women's fashion.* It sounded like a match made in heaven.

After successfully passing the home inspection and knowing I'd have a girl as my guest, I went about decorating her room like I was expecting a newborn baby. I went out and bought a new work desk and bookshelf at Ikea and new towels and linens from Bed, Bath, and Beyond. The closer I got to her arrival date, the more excited I became about having my new houseguest. For the next four or five months, I knew my life would never be the same.

2

———

As Luna's arrival date approached, I busied myself tidying up her room, decorating it with girly stuff. I painted the walls pale blue, bought lots of pretty throw pillows, and hung a beautiful photo of the Eiffel Tower to remind her of home. I even picked up a basket of beauty products from the French store L'Occitane, including lavender-scented bubble bath, shea-butter soap, and cherry blossom shampoo and conditioner. I wanted to do everything I could to make her adjustment as smooth as possible.

When her arrival date finally came, I drove with Ms. Laurent from the placement agency to O'Hare airport. While we waited outside the International Arrivals lounge, I tapped my foot nervously, checking my watch every two minutes wondering what was holding her up.

"Shouldn't she be here by now?" I said to Ms. Laurent. "Her flight arrived more than an hour ago."

"This is normal for international arrivals," she said, holding a sign with Luna's name on it as passengers began steaming out of the terminal. "She still has to clear through immigration, pick up her checked bags at the baggage carousel, and find her way through this maze of an airport."

"Does she have your phone number in case she gets lost?"

"Yes, but I'm sure it won't come to that," she said, placing her hand on my forearm, trying to calm me down. "Don't worry, there's only one exit from her arrival terminal, and she was told that we'd be waiting with a sign."

I scanned the swarm of passengers exiting the baggage claim area, trying to recognize her face from the picture in her profile. After another fifteen minutes or so, I saw a young girl throw up her hand and move toward us. When she reached our position, she stood her roller bags on the floor and reached out her hand to Ms. Laurent.

"Madame Laurent?" she said with a lilting French accent.

"Bonjour, Luna," Ms. Laurent said with an equally strong accent. "Comment était votre vol?"

"C'était bien," the girl said, shaking her head in dismay. "Mais c'est un très grand aéroport!"

"Je suis désolé," Ms. Laurent replied. "Je suis content que tu ne t'es pas perdu."

Then the director turned to face me, extending her hand in my direction.

"May I introduce you to your American host, Ms. Jade Robertson?"

"Pleased to meet you, Ms. Robertson," the girl said in perfect English.

"Please, call me Jade," I said, shaking her hand softly as she bent her knees in a gentle curtsy.

I was immediately taken by how beautiful she was up close and in person. She had wavy blond hair with a tinge of red, falling softly over her emerald-green eyes and creamy skin. With her high cheekbones, gently upturned nose and plump, rosebud lips, she looked like a young fashion model straight out of Vogue magazine. Wearing a sheepskin-lined leather bomber jacket overtop skinny jeans and Converse sneakers, I could see how she'd already defined her own unique sense of style.

"Do you need to use the restroom or get something to eat?" Ms. Laurent asked the girl.

"I had a snack on the plane, thank you," she said. "And I found the *toilette* in the baggage claim area."

Even the way she pronounced everyday pedestrian words like toilet in her native tongue was charming. I was already swooning over her, and I'd only met her for a few minutes.

"Can we help you with your bags?" Ms. Laurent said.

"Yes, thank you," the girl said. "I'm really getting a workout juggling these three bags."

Ms. Laurent reached out for the large check bag and I grabbed the smaller carry-on roller while Luna hiked her large tote bag over her shoulder.

"Let's get you situated, then," Ms. Laurent said, pulling the large roller bag in the direction of the ground transportation exit door. "Our car isn't parked too far away."

We packed Luna's bags in the trunk of my car, and I invited her to sit in the front passenger seat while Ms. Laurent sat in the back. As we exited the parking garage and pulled onto the 294 ring road heading south, Luna peered out the side window at the passing cityscape of downtown Chicago.

"You live in a very tall city," she said, gazing at the skyscrapers with wide eyes.

"Yes, I suppose it is," I nodded. "But Paris is a large city too. Doesn't it have a lot of skyscrapers also?"

"Very few, and they're all outside the main city. The city planners banned tall buildings to preserve its unique European flavor. Except for the Eiffel Tower, of course."

"Paris sounds so beautiful," I nodded. "I really must go there soon."

"Perhaps I can return the favor and host you when you visit?" Luna said, peering over at me through long eyelashes.

"That would be lovely," I said, almost missing my exit heading west toward the Naperville suburbs.

"So you live outside the city also?" Luna asked.

"Yes, but I'm only about twenty miles or so from downtown."

"I'm not familiar with miles..."

"That's equivalent to about thirty kilometers," Ms. Laurent chimed in from the back seat.

"Sorry," I said, reaching over to clasp Luna's hand gently. "I'll have to get in the habit of speaking European."

"Not at all," she said. "I'm a guest in your country. It's better that I begin learning about your American culture right away."

When we pulled into my driveway, I removed Luna's bags from the trunk and she peered up at my two-story house.

"What a beautiful home you have, Ms. Roberts–I mean, Jade," she said. "Everything in America is so *big!*"

"Thank you," I smiled. "But this really is just a typical middle-class home here in Chicago. Hopefully, you'll find plenty of room to stretch out. Come, let me show you around."

I escorted Luna and Ms. Laurent through the front door into the foyer, then hung their coats in the closet. Luna was wearing a tight cashmere sweater that matched the color of her eyes, and it took every ounce of my willpower to keep my gaze focused above her prominent, pointy breasts sitting high on her chest. We walked down the hall toward the kitchen, and I placed her bags at the foot of the stairs to the second floor. When she noticed the covered pool in my backyard, she rushed toward the window excitedly.

"You have a *pool* also?" she said. "Ms. Laurent never mentioned that!"

"Unfortunately, it's not much use during the long winter months," I said. "Hopefully we can get it up and running before you head back home." Then I pointed to the hot tub resting in the corner by the exit door. "But I *do* have a Jacuzzi that's quite relaxing on a cold winter day."

"I feel like I'm staying at a luxury hotel," Luna said.

"I wouldn't go that far," I smiled. "But I'm glad you find the accommodations suitable so far."

Ms. Laurent placed her briefcase atop the kitchen island and flipped it open.

"Shall we go over the final arrangements?" she said. "I think it's time you two settled in and begin getting to know one another."

"Certainly," I said. "Why don't you make yourselves comfortable in the living room? Can I get either of you a cup of coffee or tea?"

"Tea will be fine, thank you," Ms. Laurent said.

"Milk and sugar?"

"A little bit of both, thank you."

"Luna?"

"I'll have mine plain, thank you."

Plain it is, I thought, beginning to make a mental note of her preferences. But everything about this girl screamed she was anything but plain.

After I prepared the tea, I brought the cups into the living room and sat down on the sofa next to Luna.

"I've already gone over the protocol with both of you at some length," Ms. Laurent said. "So I won't bore you with too many more details. I just wanted to reiterate to Luna that as your official stateside sponsor, if you have any questions or concerns at any time, feel free to reach out to me at the number I've provided. That applies equally to you, Ms. Robertson. If you have any questions about legal matters or if any issues arise, please don't hesitate to give me a call."

"I've gone over the care package many times," I said, smiling at Luna as she beamed at me with a slight flush in her cheeks. "Everything looks pretty straightforward. I'm sure Luna and I will get along famously."

Ms. Laurent had us sign the final releases, then she glanced at her phone as it buzzed softly on the coffee table.

"It looks like my taxi is here," she said. "I'll look forward to hearing how you're enjoying your new surroundings, Luna. We'll talk again soon."

After I escorted Ms. Laurent to the front door and watched her pull out of the driveway, I helped Luna carry her bags upstairs to the guest bedroom.

"This is your room," I said, placing her bags by the bed. "I've tried to decorate it with a light feminine touch and some accents from your home country."

Luna peered around the room and smiled when she saw the framed print of the Eiffel Tower.

"It's lovely," she said. "You needn't have gone to so much trouble."

"It's the least I could do for someone visiting America for the first time. Let me show you your bath."

I led her into the washroom across the hall from her room, opening the empty storage lockers.

"Although it isn't attached to your room directly, you'll have the exclusive use of this bathroom. I've cleared out all the cabinets and bought you some toiletries to get you started."

Luna picked up the scented soap in the basket and held it softly under her nose.

"You've gone to so much trouble for me already, Jade," she said, peering up at me through her thick locks of hair. "It's *already* beginning to feel like home."

"I'm glad," I smiled. "Why don't you unpack, then if you'd like, we can go to the supermarket together and get some food for dinner. Or would you prefer to go out to a restaurant?"

"There's no need to treat me any different than any other houseguest," she said. "How does that American expression go? I don't want to eat you out of house and home."

As I watched her bend over to peer inside the shower curtains, I couldn't help staring at her tight, heart-shaped ass.

God forgive me, I said to myself. *Remember, you're her guardian while she's away from home. Get your mind out of the gutter.*

There was something about this precocious French beauty that told me she was going to be much more than just an ordinary houseguest.

3

After Luna finished unpacking, we went to the supermarket together and picked up some food for dinner. I wanted to spoil her on her first day in the U.S., so I baked a prime rib roast with mashed potatoes and gravy, corn on the cob, and apple pie. We chatted about her interests and life experiences, and when I learned that she'd recently turned eighteen, I couldn't help seeing her in a whole new light. She seemed more mature than other girls her age, talking about how the move to a new country to finish out her last year of high school was driven by her desire for independence and to explore new opportunities.

The following day, we went shopping for school supplies, and I got her a new SIM card for her mobile phone so she could make local calls. It was a colder January than usual in Chicago, and when we got home, I invited her to join me in the hot tub. She hadn't packed a swimsuit, and knowing it was too early to invite her to go nude, I offered her my one-piece suit. We were roughly the same dress size, but her waist was definitely narrower and her breasts were firmer and pointier than mine. Before we lowered ourselves into the bubbling water, I admired her tight figure, feeling my pussy throb as the hot liquid enveloped my hips.

"Wow," Luna said, feeling the Jacuzzi jets swirling over her body under the churning water. "You weren't kidding about how relaxing this is. This feels heavenly."

"It's especially nice on a cold winter day," I nodded. "There's something about feeling the hot bubbling water with the cold surrounding air that makes it even more refreshing."

"That, and all these water jets caressing my body," she smiled. "It's like getting a massage from a hundred masseuses."

"You've never enjoyed a hot tub before?" I said, peering at the top of her breasts protruding above the surface of the water as the churning liquid swirled over her erect nipples.

"Not like *this*," she purred, resting her head against her seat rest. "I've had a Jacuzzi bath before, but never outside and never with another person."

I was tempted to tell her about the secret location in the tub where she could receive special stimulation on a different part of her body, but I figured I'd let her discover that for herself another day. It was still early in our relationship, and I didn't want to overstep my role as her host.

"So what do you think of America after your first two days?" I said, changing the subject.

"You mean besides how cold it is in the winter?" she chuckled.

"Sorry about that," I said. "Perhaps you should have looked to relocate to a warmer state like Florida or California."

"Something tells me I'm going to warm up to this place pretty quickly," she said, glancing down at my breasts bobbing atop the swirling water. "Besides, I kind of like the cold weather. My family takes frequent ski trips to the Swiss alps. I don't imagine there's much skiing in Florida or California."

"Florida, no. But you'd be surprised how many ski resorts there are in California. The Sierras get a fair amount of snow in the higher elevations."

"Are there any ski hills near Chicago?"

"There's a few resorts in northern Wisconsin about four hours from here. It's a far cry from the Swiss Alps, but they have passable trails for an intermediate skier."

"I never even thought about bringing my gear with me," Luna said, shaking her head.

"Do you prefer to ski or snowboard?"

"I'm proficient at both, but I'm a slightly better skier."

"Not to worry," I said. "We can rent some equipment at the slopes. Once you get settled in at your new school, we'll make a weekend excursion soon."

"I'd enjoy that very much," Luna nodded, adjusting her position under the swirling water.

"Are you nervous about moving to a new school tomorrow?" I asked.

"Not too much," she said. "I've managed to maintain fairly good grades, and the curriculum between the two school systems is pretty well aligned, so hopefully it won't be too much of any adjustment."

I noticed Luna spreading her arms out to her sides, searching for the new locations of the underwater jets. As she squirmed in her seat, I could tell she was curious to see what they might feel like on other parts of her body, but she was too shy to make such a bold move in my company.

"What about socially?" I asked, eager to see if she had a boyfriend. "Do you make new friends easily?"

"It usually takes me a while to form those kind of bonds," she frowned. "Transferring in the middle of the school year doesn't help."

"Well, I'm sure with your pretty looks and charming French accent that it won't take long for you to find new friends." Then I looked at her with an arched eyebrow and a slight curl of my lip. "Is there a special someone back home that you'll miss *especially* much?"

"Not really," Luna smiled, understanding my meaning immediately. "I've been so focused on my studies trying to make sure I get into a good university. I don't have any time for boyfriends."

My pussy twitched when I heard she was unattached. Suddenly, *I* was the one shifting uneasily under the churning water, desperate to feel the jets pulsing against my pussy as I peered at the pretty French girl.

Later that evening while Luna checked in with her family back home, I went to my bedroom and propped up my pillows, picking up a book from my nightstand. About a half hour later, I heard her run a bath, and I wondered why she needed to bathe again so soon after our long hot tub. Listening to the sound of her body rubbing against the metal tub while she lowered herself into the water, my mind soon drifted away from the book, imagining what she looked like naked.

I wondered if it was true what they said about French girls not shaving their private areas, and I couldn't stop picturing her pretty tits floating atop the clear water. As much as I enjoyed watching her undulate in the frothy water of the hot tub, I would have killed to be in the bathtub with her right now. After a few minutes, I heard a scraping sound like she was shaving her legs, and I smiled.

So much for European girls going au naturel, I thought. *Apparently, they're just as obsessed as American girls about maintaining their smooth skin.*

I found myself holding my breath as I strained to listen to the sound of the razor scraping her skin and the water sloshing over her naked body as she shifted her position periodically in the tub. After a while, the scraping sound stopped and for a while I couldn't hear anything in the washroom. Then I slowly began to hear the sound of ripples lapping against the side of the tub, and I wondered what she was doing. Straining to listen, I heard her begin to mew as the sound of rippling water began to escalate in pitch and frequency.

Is she...? I thought, suddenly sitting up in my bed.

As her breathing and soft moaning began to grow more noticeable, there was no longer any doubt. She was masturbating in the bathtub!

Now I knew why she wanted to take a bath so soon after our hot tub together. She'd apparently gotten just as aroused as me feeling the swirling water jets caressing her body, and she wanted to re-experience the feeling in the privacy of her own room. I wondered if part of it might *also* have to do with a similarly strong attraction she was feeling for me.

I tiptoed across my carpet and opened my door as wide as it would go, then ripped off my clothes, sitting spread-eagled on my bedspread. As I listened to her soft sighs and moans, I placed my fingers against my clit, surprised at how wet I'd gotten in the last few minutes. While the pleasurable sensations began to spread throughout my body, I closed my eyes imagining what she looked like as she touched herself in the bathtub.

Did she like to squeeze her tits like me when she played with her clit? Did she like to place two fingers inside her pussy and stimulate her G-spot while rubbing her palm against her vulva? Did she have one leg propped up on the side of the bathtub while she jilled herself spread-eagled in the sudsy water? I could almost see the flush spreading over her chest and cheeks as her pleasure escalated in intensity. It didn't take long for the image I was cultivating in my mind to get me so worked up that I experienced a sudden orgasm, squealing softly as I bit my lip.

Suddenly the sloshing sound in the bathroom stopped for a moment as Luna paused to hear what I was doing. While I lay on the bed motionless with my fingers still embedded in my pussy, I felt my heart pounding in my chest as I struggled to slow my breath so Luna wouldn't know what I'd been secretly doing while she touched herself. Then a few moments later, the rhythmic sloshing sound resumed and I heard her moaning and sighing as her body squeaked against the slippery metal surface of the tub.

This time, I remained perfectly still while I curled my fingers softly inside my pussy, listening to Luna's breathing and groans growing more pronounced. Suddenly, I heard a loud splash as she jerked her body forcefully in the tub, and I knew that she'd reached orgasm. Consumed with desire, I began pounding my fingers in and out of my pussy while I tribbed my burning clit with the fingers of my other hand.

This time, my orgasm washed over me like a freight train, and I arched my hips high off the bed, gaping my mouth wide open in the throes of a powerful climax. Trying to stifle my moans, I held my body in an arched position for almost thirty seconds as wave after wave of intense contractions rolled over my body. When I finally collapsed onto my bed, the springs squeaked loudly, and the house became eerily silent.

I wondered if Luna sensed that I'd been pleasuring myself while I listened to her, just as she'd done with me. Either way, something told me there'd be a lot more than just *studying* going on in my household over the next four or five months.

4

For the next few weeks, things quieted down as Luna settled in to her new school and concentrated on her studies. We went shopping on weekends, watched movies together on the sofa on weeknights, and enjoyed frequent hot tub dips. But as much as I sensed the burgeoning sexual tension between the two of us, neither of us felt brave enough to make the first move for fear of breaking our unwritten host-student pact.

With the mid-winter school break approaching, I asked Luna if she wanted to head north for a few days of skiing. When she quickly agreed, I booked three nights at a cozy hotel near Granite Peak at Rib Mountain State Park. Luna was an excellent skier, and I had a hard time keeping up with her down the mogul-covered expert trails. In the evenings, we went out for dinner at local restaurants and by the time we returned to the hotel, we were both so exhausted, we fell asleep before ten p.m. But I saw enough of her in her skimpy underwear to have vivid dreams fantasizing about pouncing on top of her on the adjacent bed in our single hotel room. By the time we headed back home, I felt our relationship had reached a new level of comfort and closeness.

"Did you enjoy our little getaway?" I said, peering over at Luna as she stared out her window on the drive home.

"Yes, thank you so much, Jade," she said, turning to face me with a big smile. "You're the best host I could have ever hoped for. Sometimes I feel like I've hardly left home. Between the ski trips, restaurants, shopping, and everything else, you've made me feel like part of your family."

"Everything but the *hot tubs*, right?" I grinned.

"I have to admit, that's a lovely perk," she nodded. "Although with the weather beginning to warm up, we might not have so much need for it soon."

"In another month or so we can look into opening up the pool. It's heated too, so maybe you'll find it just as relaxing and refreshing on cool evenings and weekends."

"I'll have to look into getting my own swim suit soon," she smiled. "I'm going to wear yours out pretty soon with all the use it gets in the hot tub."

"Now that you *mention* that," I said, peering over at her. "I've been thinking. You've told me about your dressmaking hobby and your interest in exploring fashion design as a potential career. I'd like to buy you a sewing machine so you'll have something else to do with your free time."

"I could never expect you to buy me such an expensive gift," Luna said, shaking her head. "You've already spent far too much paying for the hotel and the restaurants on this ski trip."

"Hey, I enjoyed those just as much as *you* did. Besides, I've been wanting to get a sewing machine for myself for some time now. They're not that expensive, and I'll get almost as much use out of it after you've gone as you will."

"Only if you *promise* to use it after I leave," Luna said, peering at me earnestly. Then her expression changed as her eyes opened wide and her forehead wrinkled in delight. "Maybe we can have some fun designing and making patterns *together*!"

"I'd really enjoy that, Luna. We still have a few days left in the winter holiday. Would you like to go to the fabric store tomorrow and look around for ideas?"

"That would be awesome!" Luna said, bouncing up and down excitedly on her car seat. "Oh my God–you're the *best*, Jade!"

T he following day, we set out to the local fabric store to begin searching for material. We both agreed that we'd like to surprise each other with our initial designs, so we paid for our samples separately then we went home and began sketching some ideas. After supplying each other with our measurements, we set out crafting our garments. With Luna's measurements of 35-23-34, I wanted to make something sexy and flattering for her figure. While *she* worked in the evenings and on weekends on her design, I worked during the day while she was at school.

When the day finally came to reveal our designs to each other, we met in the living room like two kids at Christmas. We did rock-paper-scissors to see who would go first, and Luna won the first round.

"Okay," she said excitedly to me. "I've got your item wrapped up in this garment bag, so I want you to turn around before I reveal it."

"Now you've got *me* all excited," I said, turning around to face the windows looking out into the backyard. "Tell me when it's okay to turn around."

I heard Luna unzip her garment bag, followed by a slight rustling sound, then she giggled softly.

"Okay, I'm ready," she said.

I turned around and peered at a cream-colored linen mid-length dress with cropped sleeves and a small slit on each side of the lower hem.

"Wow," I said, widening my eyes. "It looks *gorgeous*! Can I try it on?"

"Absolutely," Luna smiled with a huge grin.

"Do you mind if I undress here?"

"It's just us girls," she nodded with a smile. "No one else is looking."

I kicked off my loafers then pulled my pants down and unzipped my blouse, laying them over the back edge of the sofa. Then I unzipped the back closure and stepped into the dress wearing only a bra and panties. The dress fit snuggly over my hips and ass, and the V-neck top hugged my bosom perfectly, creating a slim, tapered look.

"Can you zip me up in the back?" I said, turning around.

For the first time, I felt Luna's hands caress my bare skin as she closed the panels and zipped them together. I turned around to face her, feeling my nipples getting hard and my panties moistening.

"It fits perfectly," I gushed, swiping my hands down the side of the dress, stepping forward to see how much room I had to maneuver. "And the little side slits leave just enough room to move around comfortably. You absolutely *nailed* this one, Luna. How did you know linen was one of my favorite fabrics?"

Luna looked at me sheepishly and shrugged.

"I confess that I peeked in your closet when you weren't looking to get some ideas. I hope you like it."

"I love it!" I said. "It's classic, sexy, and timeless. Though I might not be able to wear it until summer. Because of that silly no-white-before-Memorial-Day rule."

"At least I'll see it on you before I leave," Luna smiled. "I was hoping you might also wear it when you come to visit me in France this summer."

"I'd love that Luna," I smiled, leaning in to kiss her on the cheek.

"Why don't you go for a walk down the hall to see how comfortably it moves with you?"

"Okay," I said, strutting down the hall using my best supermodel catwalk imitation, swinging my hips from side to side in an exaggerated manner as I stepped one foot in front of the other.

"Wow," Luna said. "It almost looks better from *behind* than from the front, if you don't mind my saying. Is there enough room for you to walk comfortably?"

"Absolutely," I said, swinging around and affecting a pouty model face as I strode back down the hall toward her. "There's just enough play in the skirt with the side slits to allow me to walk with a normal gait. This is the absolute perfect dress! Thank you, Luna, for making me such a pretty garment. You really do have a knack for this."

"The pleasure was all mine," Luna beamed. "But with a figure like yours, I suspect even a *potato sack* would look good on you."

"Hardly," I said. "But it's my turn now. Turn around while I get your surprise ready."

"Okay," Luna squeaked, barely able to contain herself as she turned to face the windows overlooking the backyard.

I pulled her two-piece garment out of a department store bag and held them up, one on top of the other.

"Okay," I said, excited to reveal my design. "You can turn around now."

When Luna flipped around and saw what I'd made, her eyes flew open and she jumped up and down excitedly.

"Oh my God–they're *beautiful!*" she exclaimed, moving in closer to examine the lacy camisole and matching silk shorts.

"I hope you don't think I was being too forward designing a sexy loungewear set for you," I said. "But I thought these would look beautiful on you and now that you're almost finished high school, I thought you might like something to make you feel all grown up."

"Are you *kidding* me?" she said. "I've always dreamed of owning something like this, but my parents would never let me wear them."

She stepped forward and pinched the fabric between her fingers, rubbing it softly.

"Is this...?"

"Yes," I smiled. "It's real silk. None of that fake polyester Victoria's Secret stuff for my pretty European model. I wanted to make a first-class outfit for a first-class girl."

"Can I try them on?" she said.

"Of course. That is, if you feel comfortable taking your clothes off–"

Luna practically ripped off her jeans and t-shirt then unclasped her bra and pulled down her panties, throwing them in a pile next to mine on the sofa. Seeing her for the first time naked, I couldn't help but glance down at her exquisite figure. Her breasts sat high and proud on her chest, pointing straight out like a Madonna corset, with large brown areolas and pink nubs. Her mound was shaved perfectly bald, and my mind suddenly wandered back to the memory of listening to her shaving in the bathtub while my pussy fluttered under my linen dress.

She pulled on the silky shorts first, then she lifted her arms as I watched the camisole slide down over her shoulders and her protruding tits. I was worried about getting the fit right over her uniquely shaped breasts, but when the straps fell over her shoulders, the fabric draped sexily over her mounds with just the right amount of cling and loose folds. And the lacy top hem swept down just enough to tastefully show off her tight cleavage without making it look trampy.

"How do I look?" Luna said, smiling at me sexily.

"*Mouth-watering*," I said, feeling my panties growing damper by the moment. "You could give any one of those Victoria Secret models a run for their money. How's the fit?"

"It clings to my body with just the right amount of drape. And the silk feels absolutely heavenly against my bare skin. Do you mind if I see what it looks like in your upstairs dressing mirror?"

"Of course," I said, taking her hand and leading her toward the stairs. "I was thinking the same thing."

When we got to my bedroom, Luna stepped in front of the full-length mirror and gasped. The soft baby-blue with cream-colored lace accents made her look sexy and innocent at the same time. While she peered at the front profile of her lingerie set, I ran my eyes over her tight ass perfectly framed by the clingy silk fabric.

"It fits me perfectly!" she gushed, twisting her body from side to side while she peered at herself in front of the mirror. "How does it look from behind?"

"Just as sexy as from the *front*," I smiled. "See for yourself."

Luna turned her body around then twisted her head to look at her reflection in the mirror.

"How did you get it to fit me so perfectly?" she said, pushing her butt out in a vampy pose. "It fits every curve of my body like a glove!"

"I've had a fair amount of time to study your body in my wet swimsuit in the hot tub these past few weeks. Your figure is indelibly imprinted on my brain."

"Thank you, Jade," Luna said, rushing up toward me and flinging her arms around my neck while she pressed her tits and hips against me.

As I hugged her softly, I desperately wanted to place my hand under her chin and kiss her, pulling her onto the bed only a few inches away. But somehow I managed to keep it together and release her after a few moments, while we continued admiring our fashion designs in the mirror.

If this was the best way to get her body pressing up against mine, I thought, I was already thinking of the *next* clothing design I had in mind for her.

5

———

Over the next few weeks, Luna and I continued to make increasingly sexy outfits for one another. My next design was a cut-out one-piece swimsuit with a large oval opening on both sides of her midsection that accentuated her curvy figure. For her part, she designed a matching lace bra and panty ensemble that took my lingerie set one step further. Feeling excited about carrying our mutual clothing design venture to the next level, I left a message for her on the fridge one afternoon while I went to the fabric store to shop for more material.

Luna,

    Running some errands this afternoon. Should be home around 5:00 p.m. Feel like pizza tonight?

    Jade

I received a text back from her when she got home from school saying pizza sounded great, but by then I'd finished most of my shopping so I headed back a bit earlier than planned. When I pulled into the driveway, I didn't open the garage door like usual because I wanted to sneak my new fabric design in without her seeing it.

Opening the door softly, I tiptoed down the hall and up the stairs, hoping to hide the material in my closet.

But as I approached my bedroom, I heard a soft buzzing sound and I paused at the partially closed door, peering through the crack. Luna was lying buck naked on my bed with a vibrator humming loudly between her legs. I recognized it immediately as my Rabbit vibrator and she was holding the end of it with two hands while she pressed the flapping ears tightly against her pussy.

Instantly aroused in a fit of passion, I placed the fabric bag down on the floor and unzipped my pants, thrusting my fingers under my soaking panties. As I watched Luna ramming the dildo in and out of her bare cunny, I trilled my clit rapidly, feeling my knees beginning to weaken. She looked even *more* beautiful with a soft flush filling her face and her pointy tits jiggling on her chest as she rolled her hips and flexed her arms, fucking herself with the buzzing vibrator.

As she began to arch her back and widen her mouth in mounting ecstasy, it took every ounce of my willpower not to barge through the door and take her into my arms. The more she tensed her body and arched her back, the closer my own orgasm steamrolled toward me. When she suddenly grunted and began jerking her body forward and back in the midst of a powerful orgasm, I felt my juices spraying all over my hand and jeans resting halfway down my thighs.

I was tempted to sneak away before she caught me lurking outside the door, but there was something about seeing the girl I'd fantasized about for the past two months naked on my bed that kept me hesitating in the hall. After she recovered from her orgasm, she pulled the still-buzzing Rabbit vibrator out of her pussy. Seeing her juices glistening on the whirring contraption made my pussy throb as two more steams of lubrication trickled down the inside of my thighs. When she reached over and pulled open my nightstand drawer to search for another toy, I smiled.

That's it, baby, I purred. *Go ahead and try out my entire collection. Give your momma a nice show.*

When she lifted the oversize Magic Wand vibrator out of the drawer, my heart fluttered.

You better be careful with that one, sweetie. It packs a hellova punch.

This was one of the few vibrators I owned that had a power cord, and Luna lifted herself off the bed, searching for the nearest outlet. While I watched her bend over, revealing the glistening slit between her legs as she plugged the device into the wall, I kicked off my jeans and panties, eager to free up my pussy for less restricted access. Something told me this show might go on for a while, and I planned on enjoying it to the fullest. But when she climbed back on the bed instead of lying back down face up, she surprised me by getting on all fours with her bare ass pointed directly in my direction.

Fuck me, I thought to myself. *You're making this damn near impossible for me, girl.* Now it was going to be even more difficult to restrain myself from barging through the door and pouncing on top of her.

As I watched her spread her knees apart then rest her chest on the bed as she angled her hips up in the air, I stood mesmerized outside the door. I could see her entire gleaming vulva from her bald pubis down over her splayed lips, all the way to her tight brown pucker. Even her swollen clit was visible from my position, poised like a ripe cherry at the junction of her folds under the bottom of her mound.

Oh, how I longed to be lying between her legs, taking her plump fruit into my mouth.

But when she flicked on the big vibrator and positioned the pulsating ball over her erect gland, I lost all sense of space and time. As her hips began to undulate against the vibrating head, I thrust three fingers inside my pussy and began fucking myself hard. I could see her tits hanging between the A-frame of her splayed legs, and when she grabbed one breast with her other hand and began squeezing it while she moaned in pleasure, I unbuttoned my own blouse and thrust my bra up under my neck, pinching my nipples.

I hadn't witnessed such an erotic sight in a very long time, and I bit my lip trying to remain silent while I watched the sexy nymph pleasuring herself. As I watched her juices pouring out of her snatch and rolling down the insides of her thighs, I could hear her cries and whimpers growing in urgency. But when she reached around behind her ass with her free hand and thrust two fingers into her pussy while she rocked back and forth on the bed, I almost lost it. I had to stop fingering myself for fear of falling off the cliff and making a commotion.

Besides, I wanted to save myself for the big finish. I wanted to dream that I was right there *with* her, grinding my sopping pussy against her while we came together.

As Luna began pumping her fingers harder into her hole, she turned her head sideways on the bed, and I saw the look of ecstasy on her face. As she opened her mouth wider approaching another orgasm, I suddenly felt my cunt clamping down on my fingers as I jetted my juices all over my palm. Seconds later, Luna emitted a loud squeal as she pulled her fingers out of her cunny and I saw her rosebud contracting in powerful convulsions while she pressed the vibrating ball of the magic wand hard against the base of her mound.

Oh my God, I panted outside my door, trying to control my breathing so as not to be heard.

Thinking that would be the end of it, I was surprised a few minutes later when Luna peered inside the drawer one more time then pulled out my favorite sex toy, the Osé vibrator. Designed to mimic the movement of a person's natural anatomy, the uniquely shaped device had a long bulbous finger-shaped projection that curled forward in rhythmic pulses to stimulate the front side of a woman's G-spot. The other part of the device had a small opening in the base with a flexible tongue designed to imitate the action of a person's mouth. When it was fully inserted into the vagina, the two parts together delivered an unforgettable experience unlike anything else, designed to give its recipient a blended, full-body orgasm.

Luna peered at the device with pinched eyebrows for a moment, turning it over in her hands trying to figure out how the various parts worked. Eventually, she found the power button on the base of the unit, and when she held it down I saw a small green LED light illuminate.

That's my girl, I smiled. *It takes a little getting used to, but if you just play with the buttons enough, you'll figure it out.*

Flipping the device upside-down, she noticed the control buttons under the base. She pressed one of the buttons, then her eyes lit up as the finger-shaped appendage began flexing toward her in a come-hither motion. When she pressed the little plus symbol next to the button, the finger began moving more rapidly. Shaking her head in shock, she ramped down the speed of the finger then tapped the other button. Suddenly, the aperture at the base of the unit began to pucker open and shut, mimicking the motion of a moving mouth. Luna leaned her head closer to the device, mesmerized by the strange object.

Pretty incredible, right? I muttered, teleporting my thoughts to her through the thin crack in the door. *You have no idea how heavenly it feels until you actually put it inside you.*

She turned all the power functions off, then sat up against my headboard with her knees hiked up toward her chest. Then she slowly inserted the long finger into her slit until the base was pressed firmly against her vulva. When she tapped the finger-control button on the base of the unit and felt it moving inside her, she groaned softly.

"Yes, Jade," she purred. "Finger my pussy while I look at your beautiful body."

I stepped away from the door, wondering if she'd seen my shadow moving in the hall. But when I peered back at her, her eyes were closed as she continued talking to herself. When she tapped the clitoral-control button, she slid her hips down while spreading her knees further apart.

"Oh God, Jade," she moaned. "That feels incredible. Lick my clit with your soft tongue. I want to feel your face against my pussy when I come."

Holy shit, I thought, plunging my fingers back into my dripping hole. *She's fantasizing about the device being my own fingers and mouth touching her instead of the artificial toy!*

Knowing she wanted me as much as I'd fantasized about having her, ratcheted up my pleasure tenfold as my juices began flowing out of my pussy in rivers. I was tempted to swing open the door and tell her I was waiting right here for her, but I didn't want to invade her privacy and embarrass her using my toys. I'd have to wait for another time to make my first move. But right now, I was going to *enjoy* this fantasy show to the fullest.

As she began to undulate her hips against the throbbing device, Luna tapped the plus button on the base of the unit, increasing the speed and intensity of the two simultaneous functions. Holding the base of the unit tightly against her snatch, she grabbed one of her tits with her other hand and moaned loudly.

"Fuck yes," she grunted. "Suck my clit while you finger my cunt, Jade. You feel so good, I'm going to come soon all over your face..."

Yes please, I hissed, watching her fuck herself with the animatronic device. My juices were now dripping all over my hand and my pants lying on the floor below my legs, and I wondered how I was going to put them back on and sneak past her without her knowing what I'd been doing.

"Jade!" she suddenly squealed. "I'm going to come. I'm going to come so hard all over your pretty face. Make me–*unghhh!*"

When I saw Luna climaxing again with the sexy toy embedded in her pussy, I watched her face contorted in sweet agony, wishing it was my face planted between her knees instead of the artificial vibrator. As her body quivered and writhed on the bed in the midst of another powerful climax, I clenched my jaw trying to control my breathing, pursing my lips to make sure she couldn't hear my own suppressed squeaks. It was most powerful orgasm I'd experienced in months, and it took almost a full minute for my contractions to stop pulsing inside me.

When I finally stopped shaking outside the door, Luna suddenly turned her wrist to look at her watch, then she got up off the bed and dashed into the washroom to clean off the vibrators. I looked at my phone, and realizing it was approaching five o'clock, I pulled up my pants and crept back downstairs. Then I quietly opened the front door and waited outside on the doorstep for a few minutes to allow Luna to put herself back together.

After three or four minutes, I opened the door with a flourish and called Luna's name to announce myself.

"Hello beautiful," I shouted. "I'm home. Are you hungry?"

I smiled listening to her scampering upstairs as she ran from my bedroom into her own. It looked like the two of us were going to continue our little cat-and-mouse game for a little longer. Holding the fabric store shopping bag in front of my crotch as I ascended the stairs to conceal the giant wet stain on the front of my jeans, I scurried into my room and changed into fresh clothes. After I stowed the shopping bag in my closet and washed the smell of my juices off my hands, I went downstairs and saw Luna sitting on the sofa watching TV like nothing had happened.

"How was your day today?" I asked, pressing my lips together to conceal my knowing smile.

"Pretty uneventful," Luna replied. "You?"

"I picked up some more material at the fabric store. I can't wait for you to see what I've got planned for my next surprise."

"I like surprises," Luna said, peering back at me from the sofa.

"Me too," I smiled. "Are you hungry?"

"Voracious," she said. "I could eat a horse."

That's not the only thing I could eat right now, I thought, gazing back at her like a Cheshire Cat.

6

———

For the next week or so, the sexual tension in the house continued to ramp up as Luna took more frequent baths, making little effort to conceal her increasingly noisy self-pleasuring activity. One day, not long after school ended, I came home from a shopping trip and saw her lying in the hot tub with a more flushed face than usual. As I began putting the groceries away in the cupboards, I glanced at her in the reflection of the microwave glass panel and noticed that she was positioned in the special spot where she could receive direct underwater stimulation to her private areas.

I turned around and motioned to her that I was coming out to join her, and she waved for me to come in. But this time, I didn't even bother going through the pretense of changing into a bathing suit as I stripped off my clothes and scampered out the back door, lowering my naked body into the swirling water.

"I hope you don't mind if I enjoy the hot tub in the *nude* this time," I said. "I think we've seen each naked enough times by now that there shouldn't be any more surprises."

"Of course not," she smiled. "I was thinking the same thing.

Though I have to admit I've been enjoying wearing this sexy new swimsuit you made for me."

"Are you finding the openings in the fabric provide enough stimulation from the underwater jets?"

"Yes," she said, subtly adjusting her position on the seat. "Although sometimes I wish there were a few *other* strategically placed holes for me to fully appreciate this experience."

"I know what you mean," I smiled. "I see you've found the special spot in the tub where you can receive an even *more* invigorating massage."

"It's pretty hard to miss," Luna nodded, spreading her legs wider apart under the churning water. "Is there a similar spot on the other side of the tub where you can enjoy it too?"

"As a matter of fact, there *is*," I grinned, positioning my pussy directly in front of the underwater jet shooting up from the base of the tub. "*Mmm*–that feels better."

"You seem to have quite a few toys in the household for stimulating your body," she smiled.

"How do you mean?" I asked coyly. "Like *what* other toys?"

"Um..." Luna hesitated as a deep flush rolled over her face.

"It's okay," I said. "I know that you found my secret stash of sex toys. I saw you using them one day when I came home a bit early."

"You don't mind?"

"Are you kidding me?" I said. "I enjoyed watching you almost as you did *using* them."

"Well now that we're not sharing secrets anymore," Luna smiled. "I heard you out in the hall that day. I enjoyed giving you a little show, hoping you might come in and join me on the bed."

"Oh, Luna," I gushed, feeling the powerful jet spraying against my tingling clit. "I've wanted you from the minute I first saw you–"

"The feeling was mutual," Luna said, looking me squarely in my eyes as her own pleasure beginning to escalate from the jet caressing her covered vulva.

She pulled her hands out of the water and stripped off her swimsuit, throwing it on the deck of the hot tub.

"Fuck it," she said. "No more playing around. I'm going to enjoy this hot tub the way it was intended. I want to come this time watching you orgasm with me."

"Yes, baby," I panted. "Come with me while I watch you. I'm already close."

"I'm coming, Jade," Luna suddenly grunted as her eyes glazed over.

"Uhnnn," I groaned, gazing at her as we both shuddered under the swirling water.

We watched our heads bobbing in spastic union for a few moments, then we both smiled.

"That took a lot longer to happen than I planned," I said.

"Why don't we go upstairs and *finish* this properly?" Luna smiled. "It's about time I felt your soft skin against me instead of these artificial jets or a silicone sex toy."

"Are you sure you want to do this?" I said, hardly believing my own ears. "I mean, we'd be overstepping the bounds of our arrangement..."

"We're both adults," Luna said. "What Ms. Laurent and my parents don't know won't hurt them. I need you so bad. Please make love to me, Jade."

"You're twisting my arm," I said. "But just to be sure the neighbors don't get suspicious, why don't you put your swimsuit back on before you get out of the tub? I'll join you in a few minutes after I make sure the coast is clear."

"Good idea," Luna said, pulling the suit off the deck and squeezing her body back into it under the cover of the water. "I'll be waiting for you in your bed upstairs."

The next two minutes seemed like an eternity as I thought about my sexy angel waiting for me naked and dripping wet. After a short waiting period, I glanced around me at the surrounding yards to make sure nobody was watching, then I scampered out of the hot tub and ran upstairs, not even bothering to dry off. When I saw Luna spread out naked on my bed with the covers pulled down, I jumped on the mattress next to her, wrapping my arms and legs tightly around her.

"Luna," I panted, feeling electrified from the sensation of her warm body next to mine. "I can't believe we're finally going to do this. I've waited so long..."

"Me too," Luna purred, pressing her hips and breasts against mine. "I always wondered what it would be like to make love to a woman. And I can't imagine a more perfect partner. I've grown very close to you these past few months."

"Oh baby," I sighed. "I feel exactly the same way. I haven't felt like this in such a long time."

"Is this your first time with a woman also?" she asked.

"No," I smiled. "But it's the first time with another woman I've felt so close to."

"Make love to me, Jade," she purred. "I want to feel your love as you caress me."

"Yes, baby," I said. "I'm going to love every square inch of your body."

I inserted my thigh between her legs and pulled it up toward her crotch, feeling her slippery lubrication coating the inside of her thighs. When I pressed my leg against her pussy, she moaned, thrusting her tongue into my mouth while we kissed each other passionately.

"Mmm," she hummed. "You feel so soft. I want to feel you *everywhere*."

"Oh you *will* baby," I said, edging myself lower down her body.

When I reached her neck, I nibbled on her skin then sucked her flesh into my mouth.

"I thought we were supposed to be careful about letting people know what we've been up to?" she said. "You're going to leave hickeys all over me!"

"Who's to say they were from *me*?" I smiled. "You're a big girl now. Isn't this what teenagers do to each other behind the portables at school?"

"You're very bad, Jade," Luna panted.

"You have *no* idea," I said.

Feeling her tits caressing the sides of my neck, I moved my face lower, swirling my tongue over her beautiful brown medallions while I sucked her erect nipples into my mouth with a loud popping sound. I'd dreamed of sucking her tits ever since I saw her in her tight sweater. Feeling her finally in my soft, pliant mouth was driving me insane with desire, and I could feel my juices coating her thighs as I rubbed my body against her. I lifted my face and squeezed her tits with my hands, kneading the firm flesh between my fingers.

"You have no idea how much I've wanted to touch you like this," I said, blowing softly on her puckering teats.

"Oh, I have an idea," she groaned. "Between the sexy lingerie set you designed for me and the cutaway swimsuit, you seemed to be overly focused on my girl parts."

"You got that right," I said. "Do you mind if I take a moment to fulfill one particular fantasy I've been harboring ever since I saw these beautiful breasts up close and personal?"

"I can't imagine what you're thinking," Luna smiled. "But I want you to do everything a woman can do to another woman in the remaining time we have together. I don't ever want to forget this time we have left."

I lifted my body up and knelt over her torso with my knees straddling her chest, then I lowered my dripping pussy onto one of her tits. When she felt my warm vulva touching her skin, she reached down and grabbed her breast with two hands, rolling it back and forth over my throbbing slit.

"Oh *God*, Luna," I panted, feeling her erect nipple pressing into my opening. "Fuck me with your beautiful breasts. That feels incredible."

"This is way better than playing with a *sex toy*," she said, smiling up at me.

"Even that special *white* one with the bendy finger and realistic tongue action?"

"There's no comparison," she said. "You're softer, warmer, and wetter. And besides, you can't make *love* to a sex toy, even one that imitates human movement so well."

"Oh, Luna," I said, bending forward to kiss her. "I've fallen in love with you these past few months. I don't ever want you to leave."

"Let's enjoy the little time we have together to the fullest," she smiled. "We have a lot of catching up to do."

"Mmm," I said, rolling my sopping pussy all over her firm mounds. "You feel so good, baby. Keep tribbing me with your tits."

As Luna flapped her breast against my quivering pussy, I moaned louder and louder into her mouth, rapidly approaching my peak. Sensing I was getting close, Luna grabbed the sides of my hips, slowing my movement.

"Can I feel you come in my *mouth* instead this first time?" she asked. "I want to watch your face while I kiss you in your most intimate place. This has been *my* fantasy these past few months."

"As long as you let me return the favor," I said, lifting my head and gazing into her eyes. "Are you sure you're going to know how to do this?"

"How hard can it be?" she smiled. "I'll just imitate the action of the Osé sex toy that I used while you were watching me a few days ago."

"Mmm," I nodded. "I've come many times imagining that was another woman's mouth on my pussy. But something tells me this time it's going to be a hundred times better."

"Only a *hundred*?" Luna smirked.

"Come here," I said, shimmying my hips overtop of her head and lowering my steaming cunt onto her rosebud lips. "Suck my pussy with those pretty lips."

"Mmmm," Luna moaned, feeling my erect nub in her mouth as I coated her face with the juices streaming out of my slit.

She looked up at me and grabbed both of my tits with her two hands, squeezing them firmly. Seeing her pretty face framed by my thighs straddling her head drove me crazy, and when we locked eyes expressing how close we felt to one another at that moment, a tear rolled down my cheek.

"Luna," I groaned. "I love you, baby. It won't take me long now. Can I come on your sweet, beautiful face?"

"*Mm-hmm*," Luna nodded excitedly, squeezing my tits with three quick pulses to show that she returned the sentiment.

"Here's it comes, baby," I gushed. "Oh God, I'm *cumming. Nnngh!*"

As my orgasm washed over me, my entire body began shaking as I gushed all over Luna's flushed cheeks. She blinked her eyes in surprise but never stopped caressing my clit as she sucked it tightly in her mouth. While I sat convulsing over her face, she peered up at me with her aquamarine eyes, cupping my breasts lovingly in her hands. When I finally finished coming, I lifted myself off her and lay down next to her, tasting my juices on her lips as I intertwined my tongue with hers.

"That was *incredible*," I said, pulling back to look into her eyes.

"Was I okay for my first time?"

"*Okay*?" I said, widening my eyes. "You're a natural at this. Now I'm going to miss you all the more when you leave. Nothing's going to make up for you being gone."

"Not even that special rabbit vibrator with the rotating shaft and the flapping ears?"

"Not even *that*," I laughed, leaning in to kiss her again. "But it's your turn now. I've been dreaming about touching *another* part of your body for quite a while. It's time for me to taste *you* and feel you come in my mouth now."

"I'd like that," Luna smiled. "But we've still got a few days to explore each other's bodies. Can you *hold* me when you make love to me this time? I want to feel *every* part of you rubbing up against me when we come together."

"*God* yes," I said. "You've been reading my mind."

I rolled Luna onto her back then lifted myself on top of her, straightening my legs between hers as I pressed my pubis against her mound. She lifted her knees and spread her legs apart as she angled her hips upward, pressing her wet vulva against mine. We both moaned and grabbed each other's heads, pulling our lips together. As our tongues danced in each other's mouths, we began to rock our hips in unison. I could feel Luna's tits pressing against mine, and my entire body tingled from the sensation of her rubbing up against me.

She rocked her hips awkwardly against mine, trying to lock our pussies together, but in our missionary position it was difficult to get traction on both of our clits. I lifted my body and moved up a few inches, straddling her stomach with my thighs, then I pressed my sex down over her bald mound. She spread her legs further apart at the same time, tilting her hips upward until our glands touched. When she felt my hard clit rubbing against hers, she groaned deeply into my mouth, pressing her fingers into my back.

As we began to hump each other, I could hear the sound of our wet pussies smacking together while our juices rolled down the insides of both our thighs. Feeling her warm flesh pressed against mine was everything I'd dreamed of, and it didn't take long for me to feel the familiar pangs of a powerful orgasm rising within me again.

"Luna," I panted. "I've wanted to feel you like this for so long. I'm going to come soon. Let me feel you come *with* me while I hold you in my arms."

"Yes, Jade," Luna grunted. "I feel so close to you. Oh *God!*"

Suddenly she dug her nails hard into my back as she squeezed my hips tightly with her thighs, grunting loudly into my mouth. Feeling her hot pussy against mine when she came soon pushed me also over the edge also, as I sprayed my juices all over her gaping hole while I pressed my cunt hard against her. As we both squealed and groaned into each other's mouths, I held her tightly until we finished coming. When we finally finished quivering in each other's arms, I lay down beside her, softly stroking her cheek as I gazed into her eyes.

"Do you know what we French girls call an orgasm?" she said, smiling at me.

"I have no idea," I said, shaking my head.

"We call it *la petite mort*," she said. "It means little death."

"That's funny," I chuckled. "I guess that's kind of fitting, given all the convulsions we experience at the moment of climax and the way we go limp afterwards. But that reminds me. I haven't spent nearly as much time as I'd hoped learning your language while you've been with me. There's so much more I was hoping you could teach me."

"I'll be happy to," Luna said, suddenly rolling back on top of me. "But something tells me you've still got plenty to teach me too."

As our bodies melded back together again, I couldn't help smiling. This cultural exchange program had been far more beneficial for both of us than I'd ever imagined.

VOLUME THREE

THE FIRST LADY

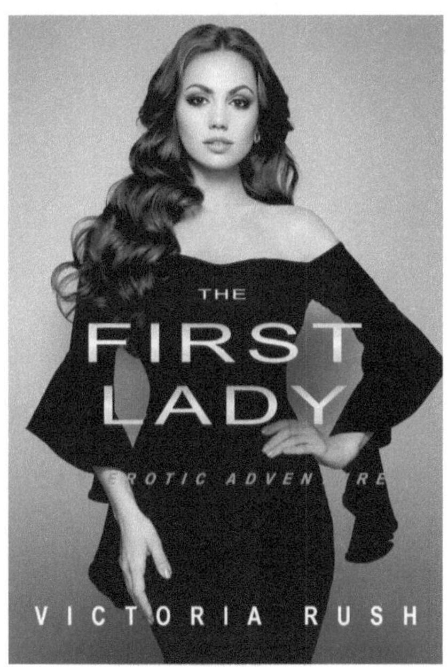

1

———

After a long day of schmoozing at my local political fundraiser, I dragged myself into the nearest Starbucks for a much needed break. I'd been invited to the event by the mayor's wife, and knowing that an election was just around the corner, I was eager to plant some seeds for potential work designing the team's campaign material. A commission helping to design their website and political banners would be a major feather in my cap and be a major stepping stone for networking with other bigwigs in the party apparatus. But after three straight hours of genuflecting and kissing ass, I needed some downtime to rest my brain and reclaim my soul.

After grabbing my almond-milk Americano at the pick-up counter, I ambled over to the one remaining seat in the corner of the shop, where an attractive woman sat alone nursing a warm beverage. It seemed odd to me that she was wearing a headscarf and sunglasses indoors, and although it was obvious that she wanted to be alone, I desperately needed to get off my feet.

"Do you mind if I take this last open chair?" I said, motioning to the chair directly opposite her.

"No, of course," she said distractedly, lost in thought.

"I'm sorry to intrude," I said, kicking off my shoes under the table. "But I've been standing all day and my feet are killing me."

"I know the feeling," the woman said, smiling half-heartedly.

Her face looked vaguely familiar, but it was hard to place her under her heavy camouflage. She looked to be about my age, maybe just a few years older, with wavy brown hair and perfectly coiffed, arching eyebrows. With her soft flushed cheeks and clear lip gloss coating her full sensuous lips, she could have easily passed for a matinee idol.

But it was her unusual *outfit* that attracted my attention the most. Wearing an off-the-shoulder, tight-fitting black chiffon dress with flared sleeves and sparkling diamond hoop earrings dangling from her ears, she definitely didn't look the part of the average Starbucks customer.

"You look like you could use a little respite from the elements too," I said. "What brings you into our community coffee shop on this cold wintry day?"

"Just needed a break from all the hubbub, I guess. A few too many boring meetings."

"*Meetings*?" I said, glancing down at her curvy figure outlined by her clingy dress. "If you don't mind my saying, you don't look dressed for a typical business meeting. I gotta say, you're *rocking* that dress."

"Thanks. They're not your typical business meetings. There's a lot of high-powered people. I guess I'm expected to look the part."

I caught her glancing in the direction of an adjacent table where two stiff young men dressed in gray business suits wearing earpieces watched her intently. I jerked suddenly when I began to put the pieces together. High powered business meetings. An important political convention in town. A classy woman dressed to the nines accompanied by a security detail. I had the crazy fortune to be sitting next to the President's wife!

"Oh my God!" I gasped. "You're the–"

"*Shh!*" she whispered, lowering her head and turning her body toward the corner of the room. "It's hard enough trying to maintain a low profile with these goons following me everywhere I go. Can we try to keep this little secret between the two of us?"

"Of course," I said, pushing back in my seat in shock. "I didn't mean to... It's just–"

"No worries," the First Lady said. "No need to get overly excited. I'm just another commoner in our humble little republic."

"I'd hardly call you that," I chuckled. "Even without all the trappings of political office, you're a long way from *common*."

"Thank you," she said, blushing slightly.

"Are you here for the Democratic fundraiser?" I asked. "I didn't see you at the convention center today."

"I try to leave all that political glad-handing to the big boys," she said. "I put in an appearance every now and then to demonstrate that all is happy and well with the first family and so the president can show off his eye candy, but otherwise I try to stay out of the affairs of the state as much as I can."

I peered at the First Lady through squinted eyes and nodded. It must have been tiring following her husband all around the country to various official functions, having to put on her game-face all the time. But there was something in her slack jaw and sad eyes that suggested there was a little more at work than just the harried life of a high-ranking political wife.

"I can appreciate that," I nodded. "Having spent enough time around all these politicos myself, I understand how exhausting it can be."

"What's *your* connection to the fundraiser, if I can ask?"

"I'm a freelance graphic designer. It's mostly a bunch of networking. There's a lot of money flung around these political campaigns. Just trying to get my small piece of the pie, I guess."

"These things tend to be pretty closed-door affairs," she said. "Do you mind my asking how you scored an invitation?"

"I know the mayor's wife in a roundabout way," I said, reflecting back on our little dalliance in the wine cellar of billionaire Steve Bannon's estate at last year's Halloween costume party.

"Haley's a doll," the First Lady nodded. "How do you know her exactly?"

"We're just casual friends," I fibbed. "I think she was just throwing me a bone as a favor, to be honest."

"Mm–hmm," she nodded, pinching her eyebrows together suspiciously. "What kind of design work do you do? Maybe I can throw you little bone, too."

"Oh, ah–" I stammered, momentarily taken aback by her generous offer. "Mostly website design, banners, logos, that sort of thing. It's kind of boring actually..."

"Are you kidding me?" the First Lady said. "Online fundraising has long since eclipsed the traditional form of fundraising by a large margin. I wouldn't sell yourself short. My husband needs to take advantage of every little edge he can find. Do you have any samples you can show me of your work?"

"Sure," I said, tapping my phone to pull up my photo portfolio and turning it around for the First Lady to see. "These are some of the corporate commissions I've worked on. There's no government applications to speak of, but some of my logo and signage work could be easily adapted for political purposes."

The First Lady took my phone out of my hand and began swiping her finger across the screen, nodding her head as she scrolled through my portfolio.

"These are actually pretty good," she said, pursing her lips in appreciation. "I think my husband's tired old campaign team could use some fresh ideas like these. Do you have a card I can pass along to our national campaign manager?"

"Wow, um–thank you," I stammered. "That's very generous of you."

"From the looks of some of these *other* pictures in your library, it appears that you know Haley a little more than just casually. Are these photos from Steve Bannon's infamous annual Halloween Ball?"

"Yes," I said, wrinkling my forehead at the thought of her viewing my personal pictures. "I got an invitation through a friend of a friend–"

Suddenly the First Lady's eyes flung open as she continued swiping through my photo library.

"Is this *you* wearing that provocative cowboy costume? You were really letting it all hang out at the costume party!"

I reached out and retrieved my phone, blushing a deep shade of crimson when I saw that she'd seen me dressed up in full regalia with my faux cock and balls dangling between my open leather chaps in the Lone Ranger costume.

"Bannon's invitation encouraged the guests to be creative and wear as little or as much as we desired. I guess I wanted to make a statement around all those self-absorbed high-rollers and show them that men aren't the *only* ones who can swing a big dick around."

"Humphh!" the First Lady coughed into her coffee, spilling some of it onto the table as she held out her hand to her security team to signal that she was okay.

"I like your style, young lady," she said, wiping up the table with a small serviette. "I think you're exactly the kind of free-thinking woman my husband needs on his starchy old campaign team. What's your name?"

"Jade," I said handing her my business card. "Jade Jackson. I'm not exactly sure how I should address you. Shall I address you as Madame First Lady?"

"*God*, no. Technically, I'm a private citizen, just like you. The job of First Lady refers a role, not a public office. So there's no need for such silly honorifics. You can call me Liz."

"It's a pleasure to meet you, Madame—I mean, Liz," I said, holding out my hand.

"The pleasure's all mine," Liz said, clasping my hand warmly.

We held onto each other's hand for a long moment, and I felt a buzz of electricity course through me while I watched her pupils dilating in excitement as another part of my body throbbed in arousal.

"How would you like to attend a different kind of fundraiser, at the White House next week?" she asked.

"Who–*me*?" I said incredulously. "You're inviting me to the *White House*?"

"Yes," she said. "The President's hosting his annual Correspondent's Dinner next Saturday and I could introduce you to a few people in his inner circle who might be interested in your services. Of course, you'll have to dress a little more conservatively than you did at Mr. Bannon's party. A ball gown might be more appropriate in this case."

"I think I could manage that," I said, clearing my throat. "But how do I get in? I'm sure there's exceptional security..."

"I'll send you an invitation with a special entry code. Just show your credentials at the guard shack. I'll leave your name for them to usher you in. Do you think you'll be able to make it?"

"I'm think I might be able to clear my schedule," I joked. "Thank you for your kind invitation."

"You can bring a partner with you if you'd like. I'll likely be pretty distracted with official duties at the affair, so I don't know how much attention I'll be able to give you. Just enjoy yourself and try not to ruffle any feathers. If you present yourself well enough, I'm sure we can connect you with the right people to further your career."

"Thank you. I look forward to seeing you again."

"That makes two of us," the First Lady said, motioning for her security team as she stood up to leave. "I'm looking forward to having you join the team. See you next Saturday."

As the First Lady gathered her belongings and swooped out the front door of the coffee shop with her security detail in tow, I sat back down on my chair with wobbly legs. I could scarcely believe what had just happened. Not only had I met one of the most intriguing and powerful women in America, she'd invited me into the White House to meet the President and his inner circle. But there was something *more* than that. I sensed we'd developed a powerful bond in the short time we'd been together, and I sensed she felt it too. I slumped back in my chair breathing a huge sigh, wondering what was in store with this sexy, beautiful woman.

2

On the day of the President's ball, I flew to Washington, D.C. then checked into a hotel to prepare myself for the big event. I didn't want to get all rumpled and sweaty flying in my dress clothes aboard a packed commercial airliner. Besides, it would look pretty strange boarding an aircraft in a ball gown and high heels.

The only gown I still had in my wardrobe was a frumpy old prom dress from twenty years ago, so I definitely felt the need to upgrade for such an important occasion. I wasn't sure how extravagant I should be, but Liz had told me to dress conservatively, so in the end I chose a midnight blue satin gown with a long pleated skirt and a V-neck bodice that revealed just enough of my cleavage to show off my best assets.

Gathered at the waist with a round bump in the rear, it was suitably understated and sexy at the same time. To finish off the look, I bought some black Christian Louboutin four-inch pumps with his trademark red lacquer sole. I didn't know if anyone would be looking down that far at the gala, but if they did, I didn't want them thinking I was so destitute that I'd blown an entire year's clothing budget on this one ensemble (which I very nearly had).

At two p.m., I went to my pre-arranged appointment at the city's premiere hair salon, where I sat for two hours with a stylist who created a flat wave design that looked minimal but still contemporary and chic. When I climbed out of the chair, my hair shone with a radiance that reminded me of my teenage years swimming in the lakes of Northern Wisconsin, where the clear waters and natural sunlight created a soft, natural look. I had just enough time after my appointment to get back to my hotel and put myself together for the scheduled start of the reception at seven o'clock.

When my taxi pulled up beside the White House, I walked up to the guard shack where a uniformed officer checked my credentials. After confirming my name on the guest list, he unlocked a heavy wrought-iron gate leading to a stone pathway adjacent to the curved central driveway. Signs pointed the way to the reception area, where randomly spaced Secret Service agents made sure I didn't stray off the marked path. When I reached the tall colonnaded Front Portico of the White House, I ascended the front steps barely believing I was entering the home of the President.

After stepping into the main entrance hall, ushers directed me down a long hallway lined with pictures of past presidents into a ballroom the size of an olympic swimming pool. Lined with floor-to-ceiling palladian windows and three enormous crystal chandeliers, the room sparkled in the glow of the late autumn sunset. But what really attracted my attention was the guest list. Milling about the packed ballroom I caught glimpses of Beyonce, George Clooney, Leonardo DiCaprio, Scarlett Johansson, and many other celebrities. Scattered among the clustered groups were various members of the President's inner cabinet, including the Secretary of State and the Vice President. But nowhere to be found was the First Lady.

Feeling isolated and exposed among the high-powered group of guests, I headed over to the bar where I ordered a stiff cocktail to calm my nerves. After a few minutes, a handsome local news anchorman sauntered over next to me to make small talk and begin flirting with me. As relieved as I was to have someone to talk to, there was really only one person I was eager to see. Gazing out at the milling movie stars and celebrities while the newsman continued pestering me with his lame pick-up lines, I wished I had the courage to join some of the other important people in the room.

After my third drink, I noticed a flash of red emerging from the middle of the crowd, and Liz caught my eye as she began walking in my direction. Wearing a clingy off-the-shoulder, crimson-colored gown with a long sweeping train, she showed off all the exquisite curves of her voluptuous figure. With her hair pulled back in a pretty French braid, she dominated the scene as the most beautiful woman in the room. Which was saying a lot, given the glittering guest list.

When she approached the bar, she smiled at me, motioning for the bartender to refresh her spritzer.

"Jade!" she said, flashing her pearly-white teeth as she clasped my hand warmly between hers. "I was afraid you didn't make it. I've been looking for you all evening."

"Are you *kidding*? I wouldn't miss this for anything. But I've been kind of hiding out here at the bar. I feel a little self-conscious mingling among all these famous people."

"There's no need to be shy," Liz said, glancing over at the hunky newsman still standing uncomfortably close to me. "Is this your date?"

"No," I grimaced. "I came alone. My preferences lean more in the feminine direction. But I felt self-conscious bringing a girlfriend with all the political implications and everything..."

"Nonsense!" Liz said, as my would-be paramour finally got the message and drifted off into the crowd. "Half the people in this room are gay or bisexual. Come on, let me introduce you to some interesting people."

She took my hand and led me to the other side of the room where I recognized some familiar political faces. She pulled me to the edge of one cluster and the group turned around to acknowledge her.

"Jade, this is Bill Holland, our national campaign manager. I've told him about some of the excellent work that you do and he was eager to meet you."

"Pleasure to meet you, Jade," Bill said, extending his hand. "The

First Lady mentioned you've worked on some high-profile corporate digital campaigns. We could use some fresh ideas to extend our reach into the ever-growing millennial group."

"I think Liz–I mean the First Lady–might be overselling my portfolio a tad, but I'd be happy to talk with you about some of the programs I've managed and how we might be able to adapt them to meet your needs–"

"*There* you are!" a deep voice suddenly interrupted us as a tall distinguished man in a black tux joined the group. I looked up to see the President smiling at Liz, and he stepped next to us, clasping her hand tightly. "I wondered where you'd scurried off to. I feel naked without my beautiful wife by my side."

He looked more handsome close-up than he appeared on TV, and with his broad shoulders and imposing size, he certainly looked the part of Commander-in-Chief.

"You didn't look so lonely chatting up Scarlett Johansson and Jennifer Lawrence on the other side of the room a bit earlier," Liz said with a wry smile.

"Just trying to keep our guests entertained, dear. It never hurts to be seen in the company of some of the key media influencers–am I right, Bill?"

"Being seen with high-profile celebrities definitely adds to your star power, Mr. President," Bill nodded, kowtowing to his boss.

"Speaking of," the President said to Liz. "There's someone I wanted you to meet. Warren Buffet's been one of our biggest campaign contributors, and he's been talking about making a big donation to one of your causes. He's just over there on the other side of the room–"

Liz jerked the President's hand as he began to pull her away.

"I'd like to introduce you to a friend of mine, first," she said, turning toward me. "Jade Jackson will be joining our campaign team and I really think she can help take your online fundraising efforts to the next level."

"Pleased to meet you, Jade," the President said, shaking my hand politely. "I'll look forward to talking with Bill about how you might be able to help us. But right now, I've got some other important matters to attend to." He peered at his wife with a steely expression. "Liz, will you join me?"

As I watched the President and the First Lady walk away from our group, I sensed a certain tension between the two of them, with Liz walking a half-step behind him with her arm outstretched as he pulled her along. She turned around and mouthed the words *see you later* to me, and I smiled and nodded passively toward her. I really didn't expect to see much of her again for the rest evening, except when the gala was over and the first couple bade farewell to their guests.

For the next five minutes or so, the campaign manager and I exchanged ideas on how to spruce up their online website, then he drifted away toward another group of heavy hitters. I was glad when the ushers announced that dinner was ready and began directing everyone into the adjacent State Dining Room. The room was filled with a collection of circular white-linen-covered tables festooned with gleaming crystal dinnerware and tall bouquets of fresh flowers. One of the ushers directed me toward a table half-way back from the Guest of Honor table with a small stage to the left, and he motioned for me to sit down in front of a tent card bearing my name.

I noticed the names of two other women in front of the adjacent chairs, and before long I was joined by the President's press secretary and the First Lady's chief of staff, straddling either side of me. They introduced themselves and made polite small talk while the rest of our table guests were seated, mostly comprising low-level press correspondents and administrative officials. The two women were both single and pretty, and I wondered if Liz had requested a last-minute seating adjustment after she'd heard I came without a date and that I had a sexual preference for women.

After the first course was served, the President stood to make a speech sprinkled with homilies praising the First Amendment while poking fun at some of his counterparts in the press. Then Jimmy Kimmel took the stage and launched into a monologue making good-natured jokes about the President and some of his more controversial political policies. It was all highly entertaining, and I enjoyed peering around the room at all the famous celebrities laughing and clapping along dutifully, but it was the First Lady who my attention was fixated on for most of the evening.

After Jimmy Kimmel finished his piece and the chairman of the correspondent's association took the stage to thank the attending newsmen and women for their journalistic integrity in a thinly veiled attempt to curry favor toward the incumbent President, I excused myself and asked to be pointed in the direction of the ladies' room. I didn't really need to use it, but all the political glad-handing was giving me an uneasy feeling in the pit of my stomach. I'd never been a strong proponent of any one political party, and all this genuflecting was making me rethink the whole idea of helping to push the President's agenda. Especially one who didn't seem to give his wife the proper respect and attention I felt she deserved.

After checking my makeup in the powder room mirror, I went into one of the cubicles and pulled out my phone, tapping on my favorite game of Candy Crush. I couldn't believe that I was attending the most coveted event in the most famous residence in Washington, and here I was sitting in a dingy cubicle playing a solitary video game. After a few minutes, I heard the clack-clack-clack of a woman's shoes entering the marble-floored restroom, and I peered under the door recognizing Liz's long red dress train.

I turned off my phone and held my breath while I listened to her attending to herself in the mirror, but it seemed to take an eternity for her to finish whatever she was doing. Feeling a bit self-conscious waiting for her to leave, I decided to flush the toilet and emerge from my hiding place to say hello. I didn't know when I'd have a chance to be this close to her again, and when she saw me emerge from the cubicle, she gave me a broad smile.

"Jade," she said. "I saw you head toward the washroom and when you didn't return, I grew worried about you. Are you enjoying the evening?"

"Yes," I lied. "It's fascinating watching all these beautiful people mingling, but to be honest I don't have much of a stomach for all this political maneuvering. I just needed to come in here and freshen up."

"I know exactly how you feel," Liz said. "Seeing all these rich and powerful people gushing over one another and self-congratulating themselves can get a bit tiring. You should try doing it twenty-four/seven, three hundred and sixty-five days a year."

"I can only imagine how difficult your job must be," I frowned. "You must feel like a prisoner sometimes locked up in this big fortress, having to play second fiddle to the most powerful man in the world."

Liz coughed, momentarily taken aback by my outspoken opinion.

"You seem to have a special insight on my unique predicament, Jade. Most people think I have one of the most glamorous jobs in America."

"I've been watching you most of the evening," I said. "It's not hard to see the signs of tension between you and the President."

"Is it *that* obvious?" Liz chuckled. "Have you at least been enjoying the company at your table? I hope Julie and Emma have been keeping you properly entertained."

"Yes, they've been lovely. But honestly, it's *you* that I haven't been able to take my eyes off the whole evening. You look absolutely ravishing in that form-fitting dress."

"As do you," Liz said, taking a step closer to me. "That blue satin gown complements your eyes perfectly. You look sexy and elegant at the same time. You chose well. Bill has already complimented me on how smart and creative you are. I hope you won't let all of this political backslapping get in the way of your helping with the campaign."

"I'll be happy to do it as a favor for you," I said, feeling my pussy flutter the closer she got to me. "Anything to keep me working close to you–"

Suddenly, Liz stepped forward and planted her lips against mine, running her fingers through my hair as she plunged her tongue deep into my mouth. I gasped at the unexpected intrusion, but as we pressed our bodies together and ground our pelvises against one another, I flung my arms around her, running my hands down over the curvature of her ass. She pulled me toward one of the cubicles while we continued kissing, then she locked the door behind us and slammed me against the metal partition wall.

While we groped each other's bodies pulling on each other's dresses, I pushed her back against the other side and slowly pulled up the hem of her long red gown. When I finally managed to hike it up over her hips, I snaked my hand between her legs and felt her panties soaked as wet as a dishrag. Pulling them to the side, I thrust two fingers deep into her slit and she threw her head back against the wall, grunting in pleasure.

"Oh Jade," she sighed. "You have no idea how much I've been dreaming of this from the moment I saw you. I haven't felt like this in such a long time..."

"You mean *wet*, or the touch of another woman?" I smiled, thrusting the palm of my hand firmly against her snatch.

"Wet, and *turned on*. James is such a passionless lover. The constant demands of his office have left me cold and dry for the longest time. You're the first woman I've been with this way."

"I'm glad we found each other," I said. "Because I haven't felt this turned on in a long time either."

"But you said you've been with other women–"

"Yes, but I haven't felt this strong a connection with anyone in a long, long time."

"Is it just because–"

"Like you said," I interrupted. "Being First Lady is a *role*, not a job. I like you for a million other reasons."

"We better do this quick then," she said, looking through the crack in the door. "Before my security detail begins to worry about me and checks up on me."

"Even in the White House washroom?!" I said.

"You have no idea how short a leash I have around here."

"Just lie back and enjoy it then," I smiled. "I want to make you feel pleasure you haven't experienced in a long time."

I knelt down slowly until I reached her midsection, then I placed the bottom half of her dress over my head while I pulled her panties down to her ankles. Then I leaned forward, engulfing her inflamed clit in my mouth, running circles over the hard nub while I curled my fingers inside her pussy toward her sensitive G-spot. It didn't take long for Liz to begin moaning more loudly, and as her pleasure began to inexorably rise, she placed her hands over the back of my head, caressing me softly while my tongue danced over her burning gland.

After about sixty seconds of sustained stimulation on her bulb, she lifted her right leg and tilted her pelvis toward my chin, pressing her pussy harder into my face. I could feel the inside of her vagina beginning to tent and I knew she was nearing the precipice, so I sucked her button hard into my mouth while fluttering my fingers against her G-spot. Within seconds, she gasped as her whole body lurched forward in a series of spastic jerks as the walls of her pussy pulsed firmly against my embedded fingers.

I held her gently in my mouth until her contractions stopped and her breathing began to return to normal, then I lifted myself up and kissed her gently on her lips. We heard the sound of another woman's shoes entering the room, and Liz lifted her finger to her lips signaling for me to be quiet while she peered through the crack in the door. Then she quickly pulled her panties back up and leaned in to whisper in my ear.

"It's one of my security guards," she said. "You'll have to wait in here while I pretend like I'm finishing up my business."

"Can I see you again?" I said, looking desperately into her eyes. I didn't want this little tryst to be the last time I saw her.

"I'll call you. Right now, I've got to get back to the function or the President will begin to worry and send his whole squad after me. Thank you Jade–you were even more magnificent than I imagined. Bye for now."

She gave me a little peck on the cheek, then opened the door partway and headed toward the sink to wash up. I peered through the crack and saw a pokerfaced woman with short cropped hair and a business suit nod toward her while she stepped back as Liz fixed her hair and makeup in the mirror. Then the two women exited the room as quickly as they had entered, leaving me alone and breathing heavily in my little cubicle. After they left, I tore off my panties and fingered myself to the quickest orgasm I'd had in ages while reliving the electric moment when I felt the First Lady's warm, pulsing flesh in my hands.

I didn't know when I'd see her again, but at this precise moment I felt like I'd lived a thousand years in the blink of an eye.

3

A fter the dinner finished and the guests began streaming out of the White House, I joined the long line where the President and First Lady thanked everyone for coming and bade them farewell. When it was my turn to face them, the President shook my hand politely and Liz winked at me, saying she was looking forward to working with me on her husband's campaign. When I got back to my hotel, I must have come a hundred times replaying the erotic scene from the White House powder room over and over again.

But the following morning, I woke up uneasily, wondering if the whole thing was just some bizarre fantasy. The President hadn't even remembered talking to me earlier in the evening, and his campaign manager had made no attempt to reconnect with me before leaving the building. Having not heard back from Liz and not knowing when or if she'd contact me again, I began to pack up my belongings to leave the hotel before check-out time. But just as I was about to close the door behind me, I heard the phone ring and I scurried back inside to pick it up.

"Hello?" I said breathlessly, pouncing on the bed.

"Jade?" a familiar voice said. "It's Liz. I wanted to call you before you left town. Did you enjoy the party last night?"

"Yes, of course," I said. "But it was all a bit of a blur, really. I felt a little out of my element around all those celebrities and high-powered political figures. Except when I was with *you* of course. I haven't been able to get you out of my mind ever since our little rendezvous in the restroom."

"Me too," Liz said. "I can't bear the idea of you returning home so soon. I was wondering if you'd like to meet up for lunch so we can continue our discussion about your helping with the campaign team."

"At the White House?" I said, wondering if she was going to invite me back into her inner sanctum.

"It would be better to meet you alone, where we won't be disturbed by the President's minders. Can I meet you at your hotel?"

"Of course," I said, feeling my pussy beginning to flutter at the thought of being alone with her again. "I'm staying at the Marriott Marquis, downtown. Would you like to meet in the lobby?"

"I'd rather see you privately, away from all the prying eyes of the press and the public. What room number are you staying in?"

"1402," I said, feeling my panties beginning to moisten, hoping we'd have a chance to pick up where we left off.

"Will two p.m. work for you?"

"I'd wait until the end of time to see you again," I said, elated to hear that she wanted to meet me again.

"I was hoping you'd say that," Liz said. "See you soon!"

After she hung up, I called downstairs to extend my check-out time, then I went back into the washroom to touch up my makeup. I wasn't sure if Liz had the same thing in mind that I did, but I wanted to make myself as irresistible as possible to maximize my chances.

The next three hours passed by agonizingly slow as I tried to pass the time catching up on my email and browsing through stories of the First Lady's public appearances and personal causes. When I read that her personal passion and primary cause was helping spread the word about the importance of animal rescues, I felt even closer to her. Not only was she drop-dead gorgeous with a body to die for, she also had a heart of gold.

Shortly after the appointed hour, I heard a soft tap on my hotel room door, and I peered out the peephole to see Liz looking back at me, glancing from side to side nervously. I opened the door and invited her in, then closed the door softly behind us. She melted into my arms immediately, and we pressed our bodies together, kissing passionately.

"You're going to smear all your lipstick," I said, pulling away momentarily. "What about lunch–"

"*Screw* lunch," she said. "I'm feeling hungry for something *else* right now. Besides, we won't have much time before my husband begins to wonder where I've gone..."

"Doesn't he have more important things to worry about?" I said, shaking my head.

"You'd think so," Liz frowned. "But he's always been overprotective of me and a bit jealous of other people stealing my attention. I suspect it has something to do with his incessant need to be in control."

"What about your Secret Service detail? Won't they suspect what we're up to if we stay in here too long?"

"They've learned to mind their own business and respect my boundaries. Besides, my lead agent probably already knows we've got something going on after she walked in on us in the White House washroom last night."

"We better get *busy* then," I smiled, pulling Liz closer to my king-size bed.

"You have no idea all the ways I've been dreaming of making love to you since you left last night."

"Oh, I think I might have an idea or two," I said, pulling the bedspread down and throwing her onto the mattress. "I've been replaying this moment in my mind pretty steadily for at least the last twelve hours."

While the two of us groped and kissed each other awkwardly, we pulled on each other's clothes and undergarments until we were both naked on the cool hotel room sheets.

"Oh my God," I gasped, seeing her fully exposed for the first time. "You're even more beautiful than I imagined underneath that sexy ball gown. I've been undressing you with my eyes from the moment I saw you. I had no idea you'd be as exquisite as this."

Liz was tall and slender, with the tight, toned figure of a ballerina, her long legs seeming to go on forever. Her hips curved sexily around her bare mound, tapering to a narrow waistline, before flaring again to reveal perfectly shaped, full breasts that glistened in the bright morning light streaming through the sheer curtains of my hotel room. Devouring her like she was the last person on earth, I took her erect teats into my mouth and sucked on them voraciously while squeezing her firm tits between my hands.

"Jade," she panted, arching her back to lift her bosom toward my mouth. "God, how I've dreamed about feeling your lips on my skin again."

"My *fingers* weren't cutting it last night?" I teased, nibbling on her hard nipples with my teeth.

"Oh, they were *cutting* it, alright," she purred. "I liked the way you parted my folds and made me squeal like a little girl."

"You don't look so much like a little girl right *now*," I said, nibbling my way down her stomach while I caressed her firm mounds with my hands.

"*Hey*," she said, grabbing the sides of my head and pulling me back up toward her face. "It's my turn to return the favor. If *anyone's* going down on anybody in the little time we have together, it's gonna be me."

"Just how much time have we got?" I said, peering into her eyes with a wrinkled brow.

I'd hoped that her meeting me in the privacy of my hotel room would give us more time to explore each other than in the hurried and confined space of the White House restroom.

"I dunno, maybe a couple of hours–"

"That's plenty enough time for us to pleasure one another any *number* of ways. Why don't we try stimulating ourselves *together* before we start worrying about who's looking after whom?"

"I like the sound of that," Liz said, wrapping her legs around my ass while I moved up higher on her body, grinding my pelvis into hers as we kissed each other passionately.

With her hips tilted slightly upward, my bald pubis rubbed against her flaring clit, and she moaned into my mouth. I could feel her wet juices coating my mound as I ground my hard symphysis into her sopping slit while my own juices began pouring down the insides of her thighs.

"Oh God, Jade," Liz moaned. "You feel so good between my legs. Fuck me with that beautiful pussy of yours."

Up to this point, I would have been perfectly happy to bring her to orgasm without paying much attention to my own needs. But when she started talking dirty to me, I reached down and pulled her legs upward, pushing them far to the sides while I lifted myself up and squatted over her, mashing my dripping pussy onto her slippery slit.

"Holy shit!" Liz gasped. "*Fuck*, yes! Fuck my pussy with your hot cunny. You feel amazing–"

I leaned forward, kissing her passionately while we pressed our tits together, dancing our tongues in each other's mouths. While we rolled our hips against one another rubbing our nubs together, I arched my back and pressed my sex harder against her. I could hear the sound of our two voices moaning with increasing urgency as the sound of our wet pussies slapping together filled the room, and I wondered if her Secret Service agent was standing outside the door once again listening to all the noise we were making. But at this moment, that was the last thing I wanted to focus on as I reveled in the sights and sounds of this beautiful woman writhing and moaning underneath me.

As we rolled our slick lips together, I could feel Liz press her hips harder against mine while her grunting and breathing escalated in pitch and velocity. Suddenly, she dug her fingernails hard into my back and jerked her body in a series of spastic heaves as she moaned into my mouth.

"Yes, Jade!" she groaned. "I'm cumming, baby! Oh God–I'm cumming so hard in your hot, sweet pussy. Come with me!"

When she told me she was falling over the precipice, all the tension that had been building up inside me suddenly released like the floodgates of a dam, and I began gushing all over her flapping pussy as one powerful contraction after another began consuming me. I held her close while we pulsed against one another, fucking each other's mouths with our tongues.

It seemed to take forever for us to stop cumming together, but when the waves of pleasure finally subsided, I collapsed beside Liz and kissed her gently on her neck, breathing on her pinched nipples standing pertly atop her mounds like two alert sentries.

"Holy shit!" Liz panted. "I've never been made love to like that in my entire life."

"Because you've never been made love to by another *woman* before?" I said.

"No–because I've never been with anybody who exhibited that kind of passion before. It's like comparing a filet mignon with third-grade hamburger."

"I'm not sure the President would like to hear you referring to him as third-rate hamburger."

"Well, when it comes to lovemaking, I hate to say it, but that's kind of how I feel. Though he may have a number of other admirable qualities, he's never been terribly attentive or giving in the bedroom."

"Maybe he just feels the weight of the world on his shoulders..."

"Maybe," Liz said. "But I think it's a lot more than that. We just never seemed to develop that spark. I think he always viewed our union as more of a political expediency than a match made in heaven."

"So where does that leave us now?" I said, wondering how we'd ever be able to reconcile our rapidly growing attraction to one another with her continuing role as First Lady.

"Well, I don't know about you, but I'm in no hurry to end this. I can't imagine our going our separate ways, regardless of whatever working arrangement you set up with our campaign manager."

I peered at Liz with a pained expression, hoping to separate our professional relationship from our personal one.

"Isn't there some way we could find a way to work more closely together? At least close enough that we can find some more private time to be together like this?"

Liz paused for a moment while she considered the possibilities.

"There might be *one* way," she said as a sly smile formed on the outside corners of her lips. "Normally, the campaign team works out of their own headquarters on the other side of town. But I might be able to find a space for you to work in the East Wing if you'll be doing mostly solo design work on the website. I've already told the President we're friends. I think I can persuade him to carve out a space for you on my side of the executive wing if I beg and plead hard enough."

As excited as I was to hear her proposing to find me a permanent position at the White House, I couldn't help worrying about the implications of our involvement with her continuing relationship with her husband.

"I don't want you to overstep your bounds," I said. "I wouldn't want the President to suspect we've got something more serious going on than just a working relationship..."

"He's far too wrapped up trying to save the world and being the President of Everything to notice. Once I've got you installed in the White House, we'll have plenty more opportunities to carry on our little affair."

"Okay," I said, looking at her like a child who'd just had an ice cream cone pulled away from her. "But is that all you see this as–an *affair*?"

"Of course not. I didn't mean it that way. Right now, I can't imagine being separated from you for more than a millisecond. I haven't felt this way with someone in the longest time–perhaps *ever*. I see your job, as much as I honestly think you can help my husband's campaign, as really just a cover to keep us together. Let's take this one day at a time and see how it plays out. Once my husband is out of public office, we'll have more opportunities to explore taking our relationship to the next level."

I shook my head, realizing the irony of my helping to get him re-elected, knowing full well it would just make the hiding of our relationship all the more difficult.

"Okay, but I wouldn't want to drive a wedge between the two of you–"

"Don't worry about any of that right now," she mewed. "Let's just enjoy what we've created and savor the time we have together. Life's too short to worry about the pitfalls of following your heart."

Liz suddenly rolled on top of me, spreading my legs apart as she pressed her moist pussy against mine once again.

"But speaking of *wedges*," she grinned. "I wouldn't mind getting another piece of this before we have to separate for a little while..."

4

The following morning, Liz invited me back to the White House, where she greeted me at the front portico then walked me down a long corridor, pointing out some of the areas of interest.

"To your right is the Kennedy Garden, which is a lovely place for an outdoor lunch when the weather is good."

I gazed out the tall windows lining the colonnade at the immaculately manicured garden with its pretty holly trees and colorful flower beds.

"And to the left," she said, opening a door to a large room with a giant screen and plush theater chairs, "is the Family Theater Room."

"Did you and the President ever consider having children?" I asked, peering into the cavernous space.

"We just never got around to it, I guess. With his busy schedule, we feared there wouldn't be enough time to give the kids, and he seemed far more interested in his political career than building a family.

"That's too bad," I said, peering down the long hallway with all its nooks and crannies. "This looks like the ultimate playground for young children, and with all the support staff at the White House, you'd have lots of help caring for your children."

"I suppose," Liz said. "But with the current strain on our marriage, I'm not so sure about our prospects for staying together. I'd never want to subject them to a messy public divorce..."

I looked at Liz with sad eyes, realizing how much she felt like a prisoner in her own home. With all the eyes of the world focused on her and her husband, it must have been extraordinarily difficult for her to keep up appearances when she felt so unhappy.

When we reached the end of the corridor, we entered another large building and turned right down another long hallway.

"This is the East Wing," she said. "Which officially houses my office."

"This looks like a pretty big building for *one* person's office," I said, peering up at the tall ceilings and imposing pictures on the wall.

"It also houses a few other functions like the office of the White House social secretary, the Calligraphy Office, and the correspondence staff. But fortunately for you, unlike the West Wing where the President and his staff work, there's a lot of unused space in this building."

Liz stopped near the end of the hall and turned to open an oak door leading into a large, brightly lit office.

"This is my office, with a nice view of the garden and the South Lawn. I keep the door open most of the time, and you're welcome to come visit me anytime you have any questions or you just want some company."

I looked at Liz with a raised eyebrow and smiled.

"Knowing the kind of trouble we seem to get into when we're together, you might want to rethink that open-door policy..."

"You might be right about that," she said. "Fortunately, I'm about as far from the President during working hours as one can possibly be on this big estate, and he rarely comes down this way. So if you're feeling lonely any time, don't hesitate to barge in."

I peered around her office at the pretty paintings and the various artifacts arranged on her shelves. Prominently displayed on her desk and shelves were various photos of her and the President at various stages in his career. I picked up a wedding picture of the two of them on an adjacent shelf and smiled.

"You both look so handsome in this picture," I said.

"And *happy*," she said. "Those were our carefree days, before James started his political career."

"How old were you when you married?"

"Not long after college," she said, taking the picture from my hand and peering at it with sad eyes. "We met at Yale, where he was studying law at the time. I thought he was so dashing and handsome back then."

"He still *is*," I said, beginning to wonder if it was such a good idea for me to be working so close to her when she obviously still had feelings for her husband. "Where were you thinking of putting me up?"

"Oh," she said, putting the picture back on the shelf softly. "I almost forgot. I moved a few things around and put you in the office two rooms down. Come, let me show you."

Liz led me across the hall to a room on the other side of the building and opened the door, inviting me to step in. It was modest in size, but a large window streamed in bright sunshine, and the tall bookcases lining the walls made it look much larger than it was.

"It's not quite as big as my office," she said. "But you've got a nice view facing south and all the equipment you need to get you started on your project. I've left the login information for the computer on your desk. Bill has already sent you an email with some suggestions for updating the website. I've left his number in your Rolodex, so you can reach out with any questions at any time. Is there anything I can do for you before you get started?"

I looked around me at all the official trappings, feeling my heart beating a hundred miles an hour, suddenly feeling conflicted about my new role.

"Liz," I said, turning toward her with a furrowed expression. "I'm not so sure this is a good idea–"

"Shh," she said, placing her finger on my lips. "I'm sure this all seems overwhelming at this point. You'll have the support of my personal staff whenever you need anything–"

"No, it's not that," I said. "I could do this work just as easily from home, or from the campaign office for that matter. Are you sure–"

"Don't get cold feet on me now," Liz said, stepping forward to hug me gently. "I don't want you thinking you're getting in the way of James's and my marriage. It's been a marriage of convenience for a long time now. For all I know, he's carrying on an affair behind *my* back too. I want you here next to me. Give it a few weeks at least. If you don't feel as strongly about us being together as I do, I'll understand and we'll go our separate ways. But don't give up on this yet."

"Okay," I sighed. "I suppose it can't hurt to work on the campaign website for a little while, at least until we've revamped it according to the President's liking..."

"That's my girl," Liz said, raising my chin and kissing me sweetly on the lips. "Take your time easing into this. There's a kitchen at the other end of the hall where you can help yourself to coffee and snacks. Let's plan on having dinner together when you finish up today. I have some special plans for us later this evening."

After Liz returned to her office, I sat down at my computer and logged in, reading the long email from Bill Holland providing instructions on how he wanted the campaign website tweaked. Most of the suggestions made sense, and I tried to keep busy developing new design ideas for the next couple of hours. But I found myself becoming increasing distracted as the day went on, peering out the window at the large White House lawn with all the groundskeepers and Secret Service agents milling about. The more I thought about it, the more convinced I became that I'd gotten myself into a situation that could only end with someone hurt.

How could Liz and I hope to carry on our clandestine affair with all these staff and security people constantly milling about? Was our relationship destined to be another flash-in-the-pan, ignited by the undeniable passion we both felt for one another, but doomed to extinguish under the constant pressure and demands of her role as First Lady? What if our relationship *did* grow to become something deeper and more meaningful? How could she ever hope to extricate herself from the expectations of a watchful nation? America was just starting to acknowledge the idea of gay couples, but accepting a lesbian *ex-First Lady* was a whole other matter.

By the end of the day, I was having serious second thoughts about my continuing role in her life and thinking of heading home. But when Liz poked her head into my office around 4:30, she didn't give me a chance to tell her what I was thinking.

"Are you hungry?" she said. "The White House chef makes a mean stroganoff."

"I don't know Liz," I frowned, not quite ready to tell her I was thinking about leaving. "Maybe it's best I head back to the hotel..."

"At three hundred dollars a night? You'll go broke if you try living out of a hotel in this town. I insist. You simply *must* have a sit-down dinner at the White House at least once. Besides, there was so much more I wanted to show you—"

"Will the President be joining us?"

"He's got a late cabinet meeting that will keep him busy for another couple of hours. It'll just be the two of us. Come," she said, pulling me out of my chair. "Let me show you some more interesting parts of the White House."

For the next hour or so, Liz gave me a grand tour of the three floors of the grand residence, pointing out special points of interest such as the library and bowling alley on the ground floor, the beautifully appointed Red, Green, and Blue rooms on the State Floor, and the personal bedrooms and family dining room on the third floor. After showing me the master bedroom and personal living quarters on the top floor, she led me into the Yellow Oval Room, which led out onto the curved balcony of the South Portico overlooking the enormous South Lawn with its sparkling fountain and the Washington Monument rising majestically in the distance. The sun was setting to the west, and the white obelisk glistened with an orange hue in the fading dusk.

"It's magnificent," I said, looking at the picturesque setting with my mouth agape. "How could you ever grow tired of this view?"

"Well, you know what they say. Home is where the heart is. I'm afraid there hasn't been much warmth in this home these past three years. But enough of the depressing news. Come—let me show you where you'll be staying tonight..."

"*What?*" I said, peering at Liz with a shocked expression. "You want me to spend the *night* here?"

"By the time we finish dinner, it'll be too late for you to find another place to stay. Besides, who hasn't wanted to spend a night in the famous Lincoln Bedroom?"

5

Liz grabbed my hand and led me back inside, where we turned into a large sitting room on the other side of the Yellow Room leading into a huge boudoir dominated by a large four-poster bed and a stone fireplace. Gold velvet curtains framed the two large picture windows, with tasteful Victorian-era chairs and settees placed around the foot of the bed.

"*This* is the Lincoln Bedroom?" I said with wide eyes. "It's even bigger than the *President's* bedroom!"

"Well, technically, they're the same size. Ours just has a bit more closet space. But yeah, it's pretty big, especially for one person."

Liz stepped toward me and kissed me hard on the mouth, thrusting her tongue inside my cavity.

"But we might be able to solve that problem with a little extra company."

Suddenly, I felt dizzy from the bombardment of my senses, and I went limp while she held me. As much as I'd wanted to run away from her only a short while ago, I was suddenly at her mercy, with all the same feelings and cravings circulating inside me.

"Liz," I tried to protest. "This is seriously too much. I don't deserve any of this."

"Nonsense," she said. "You've rekindled a passion and a joy for living that I haven't felt in ages. It's the *least* I can do to repay the favor. Besides, having you stay overnight gives us the perfect excuse to steal away when the mood strikes..."

She pushed me toward the bed and lay me down on the soft mattress, pushing my thighs apart with her knee as she looked at me with a devilish grin.

Suddenly, a loud ding sounded, and Liz turned around, frowning.

"That's the dinner bell. We better not keep our chef waiting. The staff's gone to a lot of trouble to prepare us a special meal, and we'll want to catch it while it's still hot. There'll be plenty of time for more play time later. Come–I'm famished!"

Liz led me to the northwest corner of the top floor to the family dining room, where the kitchen staff had prepared three place settings. The two of us sat down kitty-corner at the end of the table, where the staff proceeded to serve us a delicious three-course meal. By the time we'd finished, the sun had begun to set and I glanced out over the front lawn of the White House with its pretty, illuminated fountain. Just then, the President entered the room and peered at me with a surprised expression.

"I didn't know we were expecting *company* this evening," he said, obviously irritated.

"It's Jade's first day working on the campaign, dear," Liz said. "I set up a special office for her in the East Wing, and we were working a bit late. I thought I'd show her around and invite her to enjoy Pierre's specialty of the house. Since you were tied up in meetings and all..."

"Of course," the President said, pulling up a seat on the opposite side of the table next to Liz. "Is there anything left over for me? I didn't realize how hungry I was until I smelled the beef stroganoff."

"No trouble, Mr. President," the chef said, bringing another serving into the room and placing it in front of him with gloved hands. "And of course, we've saved an extra serving of your favorite dessert, crème brûlée."

"Thank you, Pierre," the President said. "You always know the best way to a man's heart."

"My pleasure, Mr. President," the chef said, backing into the adjacent kitchen.

"So how did you find your first day working in the White House?" the President said, peering at me as he took a mouthful of creamy pasta.

"It was all a bit overwhelming," I said, still hardly believing I was sitting down to have dinner with the President and the First Lady in their private dining room. "Liz has been such a gracious host and has provided me with *more* than I need."

The President looked at me suspiciously, then glanced over at Liz and smiled.

"How long have you known each other?" he said. "Liz said you were friends."

"Not that long actually," I blushed. "We met when you were attending the political convention in Chicago last week."

"You two seem to have formed an unusually strong bond in such a short period of time," he said. "Normally, Liz takes quite a while to warm up to new acquaintances. You must have made an especially powerful first impression."

"When Jade told me about the digital design work she's done," Liz interjected, "I thought it would be a perfect fit for our campaign. We just struck up a conversation and one thing led to another. We have a lot of the same interests and passions–animal rescue, AIDS research, gender equality..."

"It's good to have *passions*," the President said, nodding toward Liz. "I haven't seen the First Lady this animated about anything in a long time. Will you be staying with us long?"

"Actually, I've invited Jade to spend the *night*," Liz said. "She's a long way from home and I thought it would be fun for her to experience staying in the Lincoln Bedroom for one night. You know, something to tell her kids about someday..."

The President peered down at my right hand and cocked his head.

"Oh? Do you have children, Jade? I don't see a wedding ring."

"No, my first husband and I never got around to it. We split up long before the idea crossed our mind."

"So you're *single* then?" he said. "We've got lots of eligible young bachelors working in various administrative capacities in the West Wing. Perhaps you'd like to work on the *other* side of the executive campus where all the action happens–"

"I think Jade is perfectly happy with her *present* arrangements, dear," Liz interrupted. "It's getting late. I think I'll show Jade to her room and get her set up. Will you be coming up to bed soon?"

"I've got a late meeting with my chief of staff," the President said. "I'll join you in another hour or so."

Then he looked at me with a penetrating gaze.

"I hope you have a pleasant sleep, Jade. I'm looking forward to seeing some of your new work in the days ahead."

"Thank you, Mr. President," I smiled. "It will be my pleasure. I hope you like some of the new designs I've been working on."

"I'm sure I *will*," he said, stealing a quick glance down the top of my partially unbuttoned blouse.

After the President left to return to his office, Liz and I went back across the hall to prepare my room.

"That was kind of *scary*," I said to Liz when she closed the door behind us. "Do you think he has any suspicions what we've been up to?

"I think he's far too focused on his own self-important work to dream about any mischief going on behind his back."

Liz suddenly stepped forward, pushing me back down onto the mattress, then she climbed on top of me, spread-eagling her legs around my stomach. "But now that you mention it, there was one other dessert course I was looking forward to having before we turn in."

"Right *here and now*? In the *Lincoln Bedroom*?!"

"You wouldn't be the first guest to enjoy a little late-night tryst while sleeping over at the White House. It's kind of like being a member of the mile-high club. It's on every social climber's bucket list in this city."

"But I'm not a social climb–"

"I know," Liz said, beginning to unbutton my blouse. "That's just another thing I love about you. You don't have a selfish bone in your body. And you're not the least bit political. It's refreshing to have someone like you hanging around this ivory tower."

"Are you sure we've got enough *time*?" I said, peering nervously toward the closed door.

"He said he'd be gone at least an hour," Liz smiled. "That gives us plenty of time to enjoy a turn or two. Besides, there's something I've been dreaming about doing to you..."

Liz unbuttoned the rest of my blouse and removed my bra, then tore off her clothes, straddling one of my breasts while she rubbed her wet pussy over my erect nipple.

"Mmm," she purred. "There's *so* many ways to make love to your beautiful body."

"Oh yeah?" I grinned, suddenly forgetting all of my previous concerns and grabbing my breast between two hands, rubbing it sexily over her slippery vulva. "Do you like that? Do you like fucking my tits?"

"Yes, I do," she moaned, looking at me with a Cheshire Cat grin. "But do you know what I'd enjoy fucking even *more*? Your beautiful face, and those puffy rosebuds lips."

"Mmm," I said, pulling her hips higher up on me until they covered my face. "Sit on my face, Liz. I want to watch you writhe and moan while I eat your pussy."

"*Fuck*, yes," Liz groaned, lowering her dripping pussy onto my lips. "Suck my cunt like you enjoyed that crème brûlée."

"Mmm," I purred. "You're *much* more moist and tasty than the President's favorite dessert."

"Yes, she *is*, isn't she?" a deep baritone voice suddenly said from the other end of the Lincoln Bedroom.

We both jerked our heads to see the President standing in the open doorway with his hands on his hips.

"I *knew* you two had something more going on ever since you both ducked out in the middle of the Correspondent's Dinner."

"James," Liz said, bending over to cover up my exposed body and pulling the sheets overtop the two of us. "I thought you had an important meeting?"

"What could be more important than watching my wife sit atop of a beautiful woman's face, moaning in delight?"

"You mean–you're not *angry*?"

"Are you *kidding* me?" he said. "I'm just thrilled that my wife has found a way to reignite her passion, even if it *is* with another woman. Besides, you know this is every man's fantasy..."

Liz peered at me under the covers, shaking her head in dismay.

"I'm sorry to put you in this predicament, Jade," she whispered. "I'll get dressed and get him out of here so you can have a little privacy."

"It's not a problem, really" I said, smiling at her under the covers. "It's not like I haven't been in this situation before. Why don't we make the most of it and have a little fun now that the opportunity presents itself?"

"Your mean–you don't mind playing it *both ways* sometimes?" she said.

"If the right man presents himself," I grinned, "I never pass up the opportunity to mix it up. And this man is certainly one in a million."

"What did you have in mind, exactly?" Liz asked.

"Why don't we give him a little show to start with? See if we can rev up his engines and rekindle some of that passion you say has been missing from your marriage all these years?"

"You're a *very* naughty girl," Liz said, giving me a huge smile.

"What do you say, dear?" the President said from the other side of the room. "Are you two going to have all the fun under the covers, or were you thinking of sharing in the spoils?"

Liz flew the sheets back toward the end of the bed and turned around to face her husband.

"Why don't you just sit down and *watch* for a little while?" she said. "I'd like to give you a little lesson in self-control for a change."

"Can I–um–at least *enjoy* myself while I watch?" the President said.

"No," Liz smiled. "I'd like to take a turn at being the Commander-in-Chief for a change. You're just going to have to sit there and squirm while the rest of the world revolves around *you* this time."

"If you *insist*," the President said, scrunching down in one of the old armchairs and spreading his legs with a huge bulge in his pants.

"What do you say, Jade?" Liz purred. "Shall we pick up where we left off?"

"By all means," I said, grasping the sides of her ass as she lowered her pussy back down onto my face.

But this time, Liz leaned forward over my head and rested her elbows on the pillows above me, giving her husband a wide-open view of her exposed ass and vulva grinding against my chin.

"Oh my God," the President groaned as he watched his wife roll her hips on my face and moan in delight.

"Does that turn you on, babe?" Liz said. "Do you like watching your wife getting eaten out by a beautiful woman?"

"*God* yes," he said, unzipping his fly.

"No *touching*, remember?" Liz said, grinding her snatch into my face as her juices began streaming down over my chin and my neck.

"I promise," he said. "I'm just freeing the beast. Otherwise, I might rip a hole in my pants from how hard you're making me right now."

"*Good*," Liz said. "Enjoy the show. Maybe you can pick up some pointers."

For the next two or three minutes, Liz proceeded to grind her pussy into my eager mouth while I danced my tongue over her clit and the President hummed and groaned in delicious torture from the other side of the room. For some reason, I didn't mind him seeing my exposed breasts exposed behind Liz's bare bottom–it just added to the eroticism of the moment. Before long, Liz began to shake her hips more vigorously against my face, and I sucked her clit deep into my mouth knowing she was getting close to reaching her climax.

When it finally hit her, she squealed out loud while I watched her tits bouncing and shaking above me in the throes of ecstasy. I cupped her ass tightly in my hands until I felt her buttocks stop shaking, then she lifted her leg and turned around to face the President. When we both looked in his direction, we saw that he'd pulled his pants all the way down to his ankles with his erection flapping up excitedly against his abdomen and a small stream of pre-cum dribbling down the underside toward his tight balls.

His cock was larger than most, perhaps eight inches long with a perfectly straight shaft and a large, glistening circumcised crown. He looked at the two of us with lust in his eyes, gripping the arms of the Victorian chair so tightly his knuckles were blue.

"My oh my, James," Liz teased. "I haven't seen you in such a state of excitement in years. Maybe we should invite an extra paramour into our bedroom more often. You look like you could pop off any second."

"It's taking every ounce of my strength not to pounce on top of the two of you right now," he said. "This is torture watching you."

"Good," Liz scoffed. "Now you have a sense what it's been like being neglected all these years. I want you to see what it's like on the other side of the coin for a change. You just continue sitting there for a little longer while Jade and I have some more fun."

"Liz..." the President protested. "You can't leave me hanging like this–"

"Oh, I can, and I *will*. Just pretend you're sitting in the Situation Room with all your military advisors while you watch helplessly as the North Koreans taunt you with repeated missile launches over the North China sea. *I'm* the one in control, this time, dear."

"You're evil, you witch," he groaned.

"You have *no* idea," Liz smiled. "Jade, do you mind if I *watch* my husband suffer this time while we have some more fun?"

"Whatever you say, boss," I smiled. "I'm just enjoying watching you two build the sexual tension."

"May I remove the rest of your clothes?" she said, winking at me.

"We're in this pretty deep already," I smiled. "Knock yourself out."

Liz leaned over and unbuckled my belt then pulled my dress pants and panties down over my feet and threw them on the adjacent settee. Then she pressed my thighs upward in the same way I'd done with her earlier at the hotel, but this time she turned around and lowered her ass onto my pussy facing toward the President, in the reverse cowgirl position. With both of our legs splayed wide apart mere inches away from the President's ogling eyes, he could clearly see our dripping pussies touching and rubbing against one another.

Liz leaned forward slightly then arched her back as our engorged glands touched, and we both moaned in pleasure. I could hear the President groan also, and I could only imagine what kind of pain he was suffering not being able to join us or touch himself. As Liz began to slide her wet pussy over mine and moan in delight, she continued to taunt and torment her husband.

"Do you *like* seeing our wet pussies rubbing together, James?"

"God, yes," he grunted.

"Do you wish your cock was wedged between these two beautiful cunnies while we soaked you with our juices?"

"*Fuck*, yes," he groaned.

"Would you like to bury your big dick in my snatch while Jade's tribbing my hard clit?"

"Oh God, Liz," he whinnied. "You have no idea."

"I can see you dripping all the way down that big pole and over your beautiful balls," she said.

"*Please*, Liz," he pleaded. "Let me *touch* myself at least. You're killing me."

"I want this to be a lesson to you," she said. "About the power of a passionate, emotional connection. Like the one every husband and wife should share."

"Yes, Liz," the President nodded.

"Like the one every husband and wife should savor together..."

"Yes, baby," he panted.

"Do you want to watch me cum all over Jade's pretty pussy?"

"God, yes. Let it go, baby. Come for me while I watch your beautiful body shaking and quivering in ecstasy."

"Are you ready to cum with me, Jade?" Liz said, turning her head halfway around to peer at me.

"Damn straight, girl," I moaned, feeling my own climax barreling toward me like a freight train.

"Okay, Jade," Liz's voice squeaked, suddenly rising in volume. "I'm going to cum. Let me see you gush all over my twat. I'm cumming, baby!"

I grabbed the sides of Liz's ass and curled my pelvis up toward her hole, feeling the insides of my pussy beginning to throb and contract tightly. As Liz wailed at the top of her lungs in delirious ecstasy, I gushed hard jets of fluid against her pulsing vulva while my anus snapped open and shut mere inches away from her apoplectic husband. While the two of us bucked and screamed in orgasmic union, I could have sworn I heard the sound of slapping skin coming from the President's chair.

When Liz and I finally came down from our highs, Liz lifted herself off me and kissed each of my breasts before giving me a peck on the cheek. Then she lifted up both of our bras lying beside us on the bed and slowly ambled over to the President's chair.

"You've been a *very* bad boy, Mr. President," she said, noticing him holding his purple pecker in both of his hands tightly. "I told you no touching. I'm afraid we're going to have to take more drastic measures now."

As the President looked at her sheepishly, she pulled his hands off his dripping cock and forced them behind the back of his chair, tying them tightly to the backrest with the two bra straps. When he was sufficiently immobilized, she walked around in front of him and slapped her tits across his face, making them redden.

"You don't *look* like the most powerful man in the world now," she teased. "How does it feel to be subjugated and controlled by the whims of a distracted partner?"

"Not so bad, actually," he smiled. "I could kind of get used to this."

"That's not what your *little* head seems to be saying," she said, noticing the streams of precum cascading down both sides of his engorged cock like a waterfall. "Don't you want to feel my warm, slippery pussy taking your big thumper inside me?"

"Yes, please Liz," he pleaded. "I want to feel you inside. I want to make love to you so bad right now."

"What do you think, Jade?" Liz said, smiling over at me. "Should I put him out of his misery, or are you enjoying this show too much?"

"Maybe just a little bit longer," I teased. "We don't want him to forget what it takes to please a woman and who's in charge now."

"You little–" the President started.

"*Uh, Uh!*" Liz shook her head, chiding him. "That's my new best friend you're talking about. From now on, *I'm* the one calling the shots as to what happens to her and what kind of role she's going to play in our campaign. Is that clear?"

"Yes, dear," the President groveled. "I'll do anything to reconnect with you. I just want to feel your beautiful, warm body next to me."

"That can be arranged," Liz said while circling around him, shimmying her ass mere inches away from the tip of his cock.

"Do you promise to love me, and hold me, and cherish me for the rest of our days?" she said.

"Yes, Liz. I've always loved you. I just never gave you the attention you deserved."

"Do you promise to tuck me in every night with a sweet bedtime kiss?"

"Yes, baby."

"And make love to me whenever either one of us feels the urge?"

"Oh *God* yes," the President panted, staring between Liz's legs at her glistening gap while she bent over him, tantalizing inches away from his throbbing crown.

"Even if North Korea or China have just declared war on the U.S.?"

"Um..."

"I'm *kidding*, you big brute," Liz said as she finally placed her dripping slit over his pulsing member and slowly slid herself down his shaft.

"Oh my God, Liz," the President groaned. "You've never felt so good..."

"Is that just because you're all turned on from watching me make love to Jade?"

"No, it's because I've never felt this close to you. Now I finally recognize how important you are to me. I'll never neglect you again."

"Okay, baby," Liz smiled. "I believe you. Now fuck me with that big

President Johnson and let me feel you squirting inside me. I'm going to come again."

"Yes, Liz," the President groaned. "I'm going to come for you. I'm going to come like I've never come before in my whole life. Squeeze my cock while I come inside you."

While the President unleashed a howl of pleasure, Liz grabbed the two sides of the armrests and threw her head back in ecstasy while her pussy clamped down on the President's cock. I watched the two of them rocking and thrashing their hips together while the base of the President's dick pulsed in a series of powerful surges as he emptied his seed inside her.

I wasn't sure what my future would be in their administration, but there was one thing I was certain of at this moment. The President would no longer take his wife for granted again, and their bond would forever be unbreakable from this moment forward.

VOLUME FOUR

THE THERAPIST

1

———

"Every time I see you, I want to tell one of those bad gynecologist jokes," I said to my sex therapist friend Hannah at our weekly luncheon.

Hannah rolled her eyes as she took another bite of her salad. Her practice seemed to be the never-ending butt of jokes among our friends, but she'd learned to take the digs with good humor.

"Well you know I'm a far cry from a gynecologist, but I could use a little laugh today, so if you really need to get it out of your system, lay it on me."

"Ok, so this old lady goes to see her dentist," I started. "When her appointment is called, she sits in the chair, lowers her underpants, and raises her legs..."

"Uh huh," Hannah murmured, lifting a glass of soda water to her lips to signal her disinterest.

"So the dentist says," I continued, 'Excuse me, but I'm not a gyne-cologist.'"

I paused long enough for Hannah to begin swallowing her water. "'I know,' said the old lady. 'I want you to take my husband's teeth out.'"

Hannah lurched forward, spewing her soda water all over her salad as she raised her hand to her mouth, coughing loudly.

"Are you okay?" I said, glancing at the surrounding restaurant patrons alarmed by the sudden commotion at our table.

"Y–yeah," Hannah gagged. "The water just went down the wrong way. I wasn't expecting that punchline."

"Pretty good, right?" I smiled.

"Better than most, I'll grant you," she nodded. "But I don't know why you guys always make fun of my practice. *Someone* has to help all the sexually dysfunctional people out there."

"I know," I said, frowning sheepishly. "It's just hard to imagine what goes on in your office when people talk candidly about their sex lives."

"You'd be surprised," Hannah said, taking another swig of water to clear her throat. "In fact, I was thinking of inviting you to one of my sessions sometime."

I pinched my eyebrows and shook my head, surprised at her offer.

"As a *patient* or as an observer?"

"You don't need any help with your sex life," she said. "You're already miles ahead of me with all your wild escapades and adventures. I'd like to present you as more of a role model for what a healthy, sexually uninhibited person looks like."

"What would you have me *do* exactly? Don't you have to protect patient-doctor privilege? I thought you guys had to keep everything at arms-length, so to speak."

"I've been experimenting with some different strategies lately," Hannah smiled. "Let's just say I've been trying out some more *active* therapeutic techniques."

"No way!" I said, widening my eyes as I rested my cocktail on the table so as not to spill it. "Isn't that against the rules? I thought you had to maintain a certain degree of professional distance or risk losing your license."

"I still do. The only difference is now I encourage them to practice some of the prescribed self-empowerment techniques in my *office* instead of at home, so I can coach and guide them more actively. Besides, everybody signs a waiver before we take it to the next level."

"Holy shit!" I said, shaking my glass incredulously. "While you *watch* them touch themselves intimately?"

"Sometimes," Hannah nodded. "But most patients prefer to be concealed behind a protective screen when they first start the process."

"So you basically guide them through a facilitated *masturbation* session?"

"In a manner of speaking, yes. I find most patients need a little more active engagement to get them over the hump becoming comfortable enjoying sex with another person. You'd be surprised how many sexually dysfunctional women there are out there."

"So most of your patients are women?"

"Yes–I find them much more interesting to work with."

"Oh my God," I panted, beginning to feel my panties moisten under my tight jeans. "I'd love to be a fly on the wall in one of these sessions. How do you manage to stay focused when things start to heat up? Don't you get aroused while these women pleasure themselves?"

Hannah shifted uncomfortably in her chair, signaling for the waiter to bring her another cocktail.

"I do. At first, I just kind of squirmed in my chair and squeezed my legs together in frustration. But I've discovered a more animated way to keep myself stimulated while I watch my patients enjoying themselves."

My eyes flew open as the fluid in my cocktail glass began to tremble.

"You stick a *vibrator* down your pants?!" I said. "Isn't that kind of noisy? How do you hide that from your patients?"

"It's not just *any* vibrator," Hannah said with a crooked grin. "Our friend Cheryl from the local Babeland store introduced me to a new kind of toy. It's designed by a woman to mimic the touch and movement of real fingers and lips. It doesn't buzz so much as *hum* as it undulates both inside and on the outside of your vulva."

"Jesus!" I squealed, furrowing my brow in frustration. "Just when I thought I had the full collection of the latest toys. What does this thing look like?"

Hannah opened up her purse and passed me a large finger-shaped device attached to a hollow cone at the base.

"I just happen to carry one with me wherever I go," she said. "See for yourself."

I peered at the strange-looking object, stroking the soft silicone surface gently.

"It sure doesn't look like anything I've seen before. How does it work if it doesn't vibrate?"

"The long finger-shaped appendage goes inside you and bends in a series of come-hither motions against your G-spot. Give it a try by tapping the control button on the base one time."

I pressed the button and the finger began waving toward me like some kind of animatronic alien finger.

"*What the fuck*?" I said. "That's insane! It moves just like a real finger. And it hardly makes a sound."

"That the best part. You can use it anywhere. Even in a crowded restaurant. You should give it a try. Pretend that you're reclining on a couch in my office."

I glanced around the table to make sure no one else had seen the strange device that I was fondling at the table.

"It's tempting," I said, peering into the orifice at the top of the cone. "But what's with this little hole near the bottom of the device? What goes on there?"

"See for yourself," Hannah smiled. "Tap the button a second time. You might be in for a bit of a surprise."

I tapped the button again and a long, tongue-shaped object pushed up out of the hole and began undulating like a hypnotic snake against my palm.

My eyes grew wide as saucers as Hannah nodded at me with a huge smirk.

"Like I said," she grinned. "It's not a vibrator so much as a *replicator*. Doesn't it remind you of a real finger and tongue?"

"In a weird, perverted, *ET* kind of way–yeah."

Hannah lowered her gaze and nodded toward my midsection.

"You've got to feel it down there to really appreciate it. Go ahead–give it a try. No one needs to know besides us girls."

"Seriously?" I said. "Right here?!"

"Why not? There's a long skirt surrounding the table. You can loosen your pants and insert it inside you without anyone knowing. Let me have a little bit of fun watching you pleasure yourself for a change. We haven't been together that way in quite a while."

"I have to admit," I huffed. "I *am* insanely horny right now. I'm dying to try this thing out. But what are you going to do while I amuse myself?"

"I'm going to eat my salad like we're having a normal luncheon. This is all about *you* girl, don't worry about me. Knock yourself out."

"I can't believe I'm thinking about doing this," I said, watching the tongue slither back into its hole as I turned the toy off temporarily.

"It should be pretty easy to insert it if you're already properly worked up," Hannah said, lifting her glass to her lips.

I glanced to both sides of our table to make sure nobody else was watching, then reached under the tablecloth and unzipped my jeans, pulling them down to the floor. I could feel my juices already pooling on the wooden chair between my legs as I lowered the device under the table.

"Just be sure to position it so the hole is over your clit," Hannah whispered.

"I'm all over that," I nodded, slowly inserting the bulbous tip into my opening.

It slipped inside my slit smoothly, and I gasped as I pushed it all the way up inside me.

"It's not like just *any* old finger, is it?" Hannah grinned.

"No," I panted. "It's longer and fatter than most."

"It's designed with the ideal shape and form to stimulate your G-spot. If you've got it pressed all the way inside, turn it on to see what it feels like when it's animated."

I glanced around me nervously, watching the other restaurant patrons lost in conversation with their partners.

"Are you sure I'm going to be able to control myself in full view of all these customers? What if I break out into a Meg Ryan in front of all these people?"

"That'll be up to you to keep things under control as much as you can. But if not, what's the worst that can happen? Just like in the movie, everybody will want to know what you ordered that made you so happy."

"Very funny," I said, fumbling to find the control button on the base of the unit resting over my mound.

I pressed the button and began squirming in my chair as the long pointed finger began caressing me like no lover I ever had.

"Uhnn," I groaned, feeling the unusual stimulation inside my pussy.

"Not too bad, is it?" Hannah smiled. "Imagine all that going on while you're watching one of my patients pleasuring themselves."

"Is that really *possible*?" I said, getting even more turned on at the thought of watching one of her clients playing with herself in Hannah's private office.

"I've been thinking about it for a while," Hannah nodded. "It's the logical next step in the process of learning to become fully functional in a paired relationship. I've already had a few of my patients suggest they'd like me to guide them through their first encounter with another partner."

"You know how I like to *watch*," I groaned, as my eyes began to glaze over from the delicate sensation of the long finger rubbing up against my G-spot.

Hannah crossed her legs under the table and began to bob up and down as she flexed her buttocks and thighs together watching me get off.

"I do," she said, lifting her cocktail glass off the table and sliding her tongue around the rim suggestively. "Try the tongue action now."

"You're such a tease," I hissed, reaching under the tablecloth and tapping the control button one more time.

When I felt the flexible appendage push out of the hole and begin rolling over my hard clit, I bent over my place setting, grasping the handles of my chair tightly.

"That's it, babe," Hannah purred. "Feel the rhythm. Close your eyes and imagine it's your fantasy partner licking your pussy. Surrender to the feeling..."

"Is this how you do it with your clients?" I panted. "Talking to them all sexy while they play with themselves?"

"Sometimes," Hannah smiled. "Or sometimes I just let them do most of the vocalization while they tell me what they're doing behind the screen."

I spread my knees further apart imagining myself in one of her sessions.

"Do they ever get to the point where they're comfortable letting you watch them?"

"That's the ultimate goal. I've had a number of clients reach that level already. But I'd like to try taking it one step further. That's where you come in–"

"Tell me, Han," I moaned, beginning to lose myself in the fantasy. "Tell me what you want me to do with your sexy patients."

"We'll start out slowly at first," she instructed. "We'll just have you listen to them moan and purr as they begin the process of self-discovery behind the safety of their protective screen. But you'll have to be quiet at first to not distract their self-focus."

"At *this* point," I said, beginning to feel the pleasure spreading over my entire body. "That might be enough. With this amazing device doing its thing, I could probably get off listening to the sound of running water."

"That's the intent," Hannah laughed. "At least for my clients. But in order for them to become truly uninhibited and be able to function competently, the next step would be for the two of you to emerge from your hiding places and become comfortable watching each other in a face-to-face setting."

"*Fuck, yes,*" I panted. "If I can help another soul learn to enjoy the full pleasures of lesbian sex, count me in!"

"I know *you* won't have any trouble participating in this next phase of the process," Hannah smiled. "Just try to keep some of your more extreme methods in check for a while so you don't scare away my customers."

"I promise to keep my big dildos at home if you insist," I smirked.

"Once we get them feeling comfortable touching themselves and achieving climax in this voyeur scenario, the last step will be for the two of you to join together on the same couch and explore each other with more direct contact."

"Can I break out some of my favorite moves then?"

"If you find your partner is responding appropriately. Just be careful to always be gentle and focused on her needs. If you get to the point where she feels comfortable getting more inventive, by all means–"

"Oh, I've got the *means* alright," I moaned, imaging myself straddling one of her patients with her legs splayed wide apart as we ground our pussies together and I watched her come all over me. "How soon can we set this up?"

"I've got a certain patient in mind. She's young and never been with another woman before. She's had some unfulfilling experiences with men and confided that she's always fantasized about being with a woman. We'll just have to ease her into it carefully. Are you up for the opportunity, assuming she's game?"

"You know I am," I grunted, pressing harder down against the artificial tongue. "But first, tell me more about this girl..."

"She's nineteen, a sophomore in college, with a cheerleader's body–"

"She's athletic then?"

"Oh yes," Hannah smiled. "Tight ass, firm tits, and legs that could wrap all the way around you while you tribbed her virgin pussy–"

"Oh God, Han," I moaned. "I can't take it any longer. Sign me up– I want to taste her sweet pussy in my mouth..."

"Yes, Jade," Hannah purred. "Let it go, hun. Surrender to the feeling–"

As I imagined the co-ed writhing in ecstasy sitting on my face, the pleasure generated by the lifelike sex toy suddenly peaked, and I bit my lip as I began convulsing in my chair. I'd never fought so hard to remain quiet during a powerful orgasm in my entire life. There was something about the experience of cumming surrounded by scores of oblivious restaurant patrons that made the experience all the more erotic. While I twisted and squirmed in my chair, Hannah smiled as she raised her glass in toast to me.

"Congratulations, Jade," she said. "You've just passed the first test with flying colors."

2

———

With every passing day after our luncheon, I grew increasingly excited about the idea of participating in one of Hannah's guided therapy sessions. When she finally called me back, I almost dropped my phone fumbling to answer it.

"Han?" I answered the phone expectantly.

"Are you sure you're up for this?" Hannah asked.

"Are you kidding me?" I said. "It's all I've been thinking about since I last saw you."

"I've got another session scheduled with my target client for this Thursday at eleven a.m. Are you available?"

"With the young co-ed?"

"Yes."

"Absolutely!" I gushed.

"Ok," Hannah said. "We're going to have to set this up carefully. I don't want to put too much pressure on either one of you during this initial encounter. I think it's better if she doesn't even know you're there at first. I'll talk to her while she begins to explore her body behind the safety of the protective screen, then broach the subject of introducing a potential partner at the next session."

"Okay," I said. "But where will you hide me?"

"As strange as it may sound, I think the only safe place to be sure you're not discovered is in my closet. You can open the door a crack and listen if you promise to be absolutely quiet the entire time. That way, I can protect her identity in the event she doesn't wish to escalate things to the next level."

I shook my head at the idea of spying on her like a peeping Tom, but the dampness in my panties betrayed my true feelings.

"I'll feel like a bit of a lech hiding in the closet, but if that's what it'll take to make sure she's comfortable, I can work with that."

"Okay then," Hannah said. "Meet me at my office at 10:45 and I'll get you situated. And remember–not even a peep."

"I promise to be on my best behavior," I smiled. "If I can stay silent surrounded by a hundred restaurant customers, I think I can handle one uptight schoolgirl."

"And don't bring any toys either. I don't want to take the chance she'll hear anything other than my soothing voice."

"Not even your special vibrator that doesn't make any noise?"

"I'm not sure I can trust you with that thing. Besides, it's already going to be put to good use while you're in the closet."

"No fair!" I protested. "*You'll* be the one having all the fun!"

"I'm sure you can find other ways to amuse yourself," Hannah said. "You'll have plenty of chances to get more actively engaged during the next session. Just don't trip over anything in there when things start to heat up."

As soon as Hannah hung up, I rushed into my bedroom and positioned my dressing room mirror in front of my clothes closet. Then I opened the door a crack and imagined it was the schoolgirl I was watching while I jilled myself to a quick orgasm.

This should be interesting, I thought, quivering in the darkness. *I just hope her patient will find it as erotic as I do, knowing someone else is on the other side of the curtain.*

On the day of the scheduled session, I arrived fifteen minutes early as requested, while Hannah reiterated the ground rules and gave me final instructions. She made me promise that I wouldn't open the door until her client was safely behind the protective screen. She knew she was already pushing the boundary of professional ethics, and she wanted to make sure that her patient's identity would be protected until the girl felt comfortable introducing another person into the mix.

When I got into the closet, I pushed the coats to one side to produce an open space for me, then I peered through the louvers as I heard a soft tap on Hannah's office door. The slats were angled downward, so I could only see the floor a few feet ahead of me, but that was enough to get my heart racing in excitement already.

"Good morning, Haley," I heard Hannah say as two shadows crossed the floor in front of me. "Can I get you a coffee or tea? It's a bit chilly out there today, and you probably need to warm up."

"I'm fine, thank you," a young woman's voice spoke softly. "I'm pretty nervous about today's session and I don't think I should be holding any hot beverages in my trembling hands."

"There's no need to worry," Hannah assured the girl. "We're going to take things slowly, at your own pace. May I take your coat?"

"Yes, thank you," the girl said.

I heard the rustling of clothes then the sound of footfalls moving toward the closet. The door on the opposite side of the closet opened and Hannah reached in to fetch an open hanger, then she hung the girl's coat over the crossbar. I could smell her perfume on the garment, and my pussy twitched when I realized how close she was to me on the other side of the door. But neither Hannah nor I so much as made eye contact, to protect the secrecy of our little ruse.

"Have a seat, please," Hannah said, and I heard the sound of the girl reclining on the office divan.

"If you remember from our last session," Hannah continued, "we talked about trying something a little different today. You shared your discomfort about touching yourself intimately based on your prior family history, and that you thought it might be helpful to have me coach you through a private session. Are you still feeling comfortable taking it to this next level?"

"I think so," Haley said. "But you mentioned the possibility of my having a bit more privacy. I'm not sure I'm ready to have you watch me just yet."

"Of course," Hannah said. "It'll be easier for you to concentrate on exploring your body and focus on what you're feeling without any outside distractions. I can move the linen screen between the two of us to protect your privacy, but I'd also like to place this long dressing mirror in front of your couch so you can watch yourself and begin to get more comfortable with your body. Will that work for you?"

"I suppose so," Haley said, hesitating. "Do you have any expectations for today's session? I mean, in terms of achieving climax or anything like that?"

"None whatsoever," Hannah said. "This is all about you becoming comfortable in your own skin and beginning the process of self-exploration. The only desire I have is that you learn to relax and accept the beauty of your own body. This is a journey, not a destination. You need to learn how to love *yourself* before you can begin to think about loving someone else."

Oh, she's good, I thought. If only every girl could have this kind of advice when they're first experiencing the strange feelings of puberty and early adulthood. Far too many parents make their kids think sex is dirty and that enjoying any kind of carnal pleasure before marriage is sinful. For a moment, I reflected back on my own awkward attempts at sex with my first husband, realizing how much time and pleasure I'd forsaken until I learned to explore my sexuality on my own and with other like-minded women.

I listened to the sound of furniture moving across the floor as Hannah positioned the mirror in front of Haley's settee then placed the curtain between their two chairs.

"Does that make you feel more comfortable?" Hannah asked the girl.

"Yes, thank you," Haley said.

"Good. Now first, I just want you to look at yourself fully clothed in the mirror. Look at your pretty face and the curves of your figure and recognize that you're a beautiful woman who was designed to enjoy the natural pleasures of your body. And that this is also part of the natural process of pairing with a partner and enjoying the shared union that is part of the human experience."

"Okay..." Haley said with a hesitating lilt.

As I listened to her soft voice, my mind raced imagining what she looked like lying on the divan, watching herself in the mirror.

"But first you need to get fully comfortable in your own skin," Hannah said. "And begin to experience the pleasures that you've been naturally endowed with as a healthy young woman. Unfortunately, our society has learned to cover up our bodies as if they're a shameful thing we should hide. I want you to see your body as a beautiful thing and recognize the pleasures it can deliver to you, both when you're alone and with a partner."

Damn straight, I thought, feeling the blood rushing to my pussy as I reflected back on my own first tentative explorations of my young body that led to my first climax.

"Now I want you to take off your blouse and your bra,'"Hannah continued. "And lie back against the chair as you examine your body and begin to explore some of your erogenous areas."

I heard the sound of soft rustling behind the screen, followed by awkward silence.

"Can you see your naked torso in the mirror in front of you?" Hannah asked.

"Yes..." Haley said softly.

"Look at your breasts and examine their shape. Did you know that every woman has her own unique shape? Some have large breasts, some have small breasts, some have pointy breasts, and some have floppy breasts. It's all part of the female expression and what makes you unique."

More awkward silence.

"Do you like the shape of your breasts, Haley?" Hannah said.

"I suppose so…"

"I want you to cup them in your hands and feel how soft and pleasant they feel to be held and coddled. A woman's breasts are a beautiful thing, and they serve many purposes. Besides feeding a newborn child, their shape is meant to attract other partners whose bodies you can likewise enjoy and appreciate. And of course, your breasts can be a source of intense internal pleasure for yourself. Did you know that some women can climax just from the feeling of their babies suckling on their teats?"

"I had no idea," Haley said.

While Hannah talked the girl through the process of self-examination, I mimicked her movements and gestures, trying to imagine how she felt and how her body was responding. I unbuttoned my blouse and opened my bra, feeling an electric charge race through my body as I felt the fullness of my breasts in my hands.

"Now I want you to pinch your nipples gently between your thumbs and forefingers as you cup your breasts and roll them between your fingers, telling me what you feel."

"It tingles a little bit," Haley confessed.

"In a good way?"

"Yes–I think so."

"Do you notice any changes to the size and shape of your nipples?"

"Yes," Haley said. "They're growing larger and firmer."

"That's another one of the amazing reactions our bodies experience when our erogenous zones are properly stimulated. Do you like the feeling when you touch your breasts in this way, Haley?"

"Yes," she panted softly.

The girl's visceral reaction to touching herself sent a chill down my spine as I felt myself getting wetter and wetter by the moment.

"Look at your body in the mirror as you touch yourself. Do you see your chest flushing and your breasts subtly changing shape?"

"Yes."

"That's from your blood rushing to the area to provide more oxygen and nutrients to feed the increased stimulation. Isn't it wonderful how our bodies naturally respond when we stimulate it in a pleasant way?"

"Mmm," Haley purred.

"Now I want you to bend your head down and lift one of your breasts toward your mouth. You've been blessed with larger breasts than most, and if you can suck and lick your nipples, I want you to tell me how it feels."

Soon after, I heard the sound of liquid sloshing and the smacking of lips. I knew that Haley was sucking her plump nipples, and the thought of it sent rivers of fluid running down the inside of my legs. I was glad that I'd chosen to wear a dress instead of jeans so I'd have freer access to my pussy in the tight confines of Hannah's closet.

"How does that feel?" Hannah asked.

"Heavenly," Haley sighed. "I've never really explored my body in this way before."

"You'll be amazed at all the ways you and your partner can create exciting sensations like these using different techniques and body parts to explore the different areas of your body. Look up at your nipples in the mirror every now and then, but don't let me stop you from continuing your exploration."

I could hear the sloshing and smacking sounds increasing in frequency and pitch, along with Haley's moans and sighs. I had to bite my lip to keep from moaning myself, as I imagined what she must have been feeling at this moment.

"What do you see and feel?" Hannah asked.

"The dark ring around my nipples is getting smaller and my nipples are getting harder the more I lick and suck them."

"Mmm, that's good," Hannah said.

I could tell Hannah was getting just as turned on as I was from the exchange, and I wondered if she'd turned on her vibrator yet.

"Mix up the way you stimulate your nipples," she said. "Try circling your tongue around the perimeter and flicking it over the ends of your nipples every now and then. Most of the pleasure in exploring our bodies is discovered from the many different ways we can stimulate ourselves and others. Squeeze your breasts with your hands, pinch your nipples, suck and play with them as you lose yourself in the moment."

"It feels good," Haley panted. "I think I'm ready to try some of those other new techniques you mentioned now."

I smiled when I realized Haley was losing herself in the process and beginning to surrender to the pleasurable feelings flooding her body.

"Let's get comfortable seeing your *entire* body in the nude then," Hannah continued. "I want you to take off the rest of your clothes and throw them to the side. There are so many other ways to give yourself pleasure."

I heard some more rustling of clothes, this time more urgent-sounding, and the telltale sound of clothes dropping to the floor. It was obvious to me that Haley was getting more and more worked up and that she no longer cared if her clothes got a little wrinkled or dirty.

After the rustling sound stopped, Hannah paused for a moment to let the silence in the room escalate the sexual tension. Her professional technique was working for more than just her client, as I froze with my hand still as a statue against my dripping pussy while I imagined the pretty schoolgirl looking at her naked body on the chaise lounge chair.

"Are you fully naked now, Haley?" Hannah asked.

"Yes," the girl said.

"Examine the curve of your profile for a moment. See the way your waist tapers and the swelling of your hips above your long, shapely legs. Do you think you're beautiful, Haley?"

"Yes," she said. "I feel good all over."

"Good," Hannah said. "Now I want you to spread your legs and knees apart a little bit so you can examine your private area. Can you see your skin glistening on your vulva and on the inside of your thighs?"

"Yes," Haley panted.

"That means your body is enjoying the stimulation you've provided so far and that you're feeling aroused viewing your own body. Can you see the slit between your legs?"

"Yes–"

"I want you to run your hands gently down the front of your torso, feeling the softness of the skin on your abdomen..."

"My tummy is trembling," Haley said.

"That's a natural reaction to the excitement you feel as you caress yourself and move closer to your magical place."

"Magical place?"

"You'll see what I mean soon enough. Can you see the natural hairs covering your private area?"

"Yes," Haley said.

Both Hannah and I guessed that a girl this young and innocent wouldn't have learned yet to trim her pubic hair in the manner of the modern custom.

"I want you to run your fingers through your bush and tell me what you feel."

For a moment I envied the virgin schoolgirl with her natural muff. It had been a long time since I'd felt the wonderful feeling of my pubic hairs being caressed and stroked in this way. By way of consolation, I raised my slippery fingers up from my crotch and spread my juices over my bare mound.

"It feels kind of ticklish," Haley said from behind the screen. "But in a good way. I feel all warm and tingly inside."

"That's your body's way of saying it's enjoying the sensation of being touched this way. Now the blood is rushing to an entirely different area of your body. Can you feel yourself becoming wetter and wetter around your opening?"

"Yes," Haley said. "It's a good thing you put a blanket down over your chair. Otherwise, I'd be making a mess of your pretty office."

"That's perfect," Hannah said. "I'd like nothing more than for you to make a mess of my office. That just means that you're enjoying the experience and that your body is reacting the way it was meant to."

"I can feel things beginning to heat up down there," Haley grunted. "And there's other changes too–"

"Spread your legs further apart now and tell me what changes you see. And what you *feel*."

"I can see my lips are getting wetter and darker. And my little bean is getting plumper and harder. I feel like I'm tingling all over now..."

"Move your hands between your thighs and feel the slippery wetness as you caress the sides of your labia. How does that feel?"

"It feels *good*," Haley panted. "It's so warm and wet. I'm feeling some other sensations now..."

"Isn't it wonderful how good you can make yourself feel just by gently exploring your body and appreciating your natural beauty?"

"Yes, Dr. Marshall."

"Please, call me Hannah. At this point, we don't need to stay so informal, plus it will make it easier for you to vocalize what you're feeling. Now, I want you to explore a very special place on your body. Trace your fingers up along the edges of your labia until they meet at the top, then touch your little nub and tell me what you feel."

"*Huh!*" Haley gasped. "Oh, that feels–different. It's a much more intense type of tingling now."

By now I was rubbing my button furiously as I imagined Haley playing with her clit for the first time. As I peered through the slats trying desperately to catch any sight of her shadow or movement on the reflective floor, I could hear the soft sound of my own juices as I became more and more excited by the sensory deprivation of being locked in the closet.

"Yes," Hannah said, encouraging Haley on. "We women are lucky to be endowed with the most sensitive organ on the human body. Our clitorises are bestowed with more than eight thousand nerve endings–more per square inch than even on the end of a man's penis. Rub your fingers softly over your jewel and close your eyes as you savor the feeling."

"Oh God," Haley moaned. "That feels so good. I had no idea I could make myself feel this way."

"We're just getting started exploring all the possibilities," Hannah said, her own voice starting to become ragged. "Run your fingers over your clit, trying different movements. Sometimes it's nice to pinch it gently between your fingers, and sometimes it feels good to rub your fingers in circles over your button. Can you see anything *else* changing in your vulva as you rub yourself this way?"

"Yes," Haley groaned. "My lips are getting puffier, and they're beginning to separate a bit."

"*Fuck me*," I groaned under my breath, wishing I could be looking into the same mirror that Haley was viewing at this precise moment. *How I'd love to fuck her sweet little pussy right now.*

"That's perfectly normal and healthy," Hannah purred. "That's just your body's way of saying that it's ready to accept another partner into the equation. Do you think you'd like to try that someday soon?"

"Maybe," Haley said. "But right now I'm having too much fun all by myself. I'm beginning to feel some different feelings now. The tingling is getting much more intense. It almost feels like I have to pee or something..."

"That means you're getting closer to reaching the apex of your pleasure," Hannah said, shifting in her chair. "Close your eyes now and focus on your body as you surrender to the pleasure. Don't worry if things start to get pretty intense. Just lose yourself in the process..."

"Yes, doc–I mean Hannah," Haley squeaked. "I feel it now. It feels like a wave is falling over me. A big, beautiful wall of pleasure engulfing me..."

"Yes, Haley," Hannah mewed. "Let it consume you. Surrender to the passion inside your body."

"Oh God! Oh God!" Haley whimpered. "It feels so good. Something is happening. I feel it coming over me–. Uhnnn! Uhnnn! Uhnnn!"

As I listened to Haley having her first powerful orgasm, I lost all control and began squirting over the floor of Hannah's closet as my pussy clamped together in multiple contractions while I leaned against the wall to steady myself. I'd never heard anything so erotic in my entire life, and my whole body was trembling at the thought of meeting her face-to-face at our next session.

When Haley finally stopped moaning and silence filled the room, I could hear Hannah shifting again in her chair. I wondered if she'd been unable to control herself and had had a powerful orgasm of her own listening to Haley. With that lifelike sex toy embedded in her pussy, I couldn't imagine how she'd able to hold back.

"How does it feel to experience the natural pleasures of being a woman, Haley?" she said.

"Oh my God," Haley panted. "I had no idea I had this inside of me. I want more–"

"There's so much more for you to experience, young lady. I encourage you to experiment with more self-exploration before our next session. Of course, the ultimate pleasure of being a woman happens when you get to *share* this pleasure with another partner. Do you think you might be ready to try this at our next meeting?"

"Um–maybe. But how will that work? I don't think I'm quite ready to jump right into an intimate relationship with a complete stranger."

"With your permission," Hannah said, "I'd like to invite another patient to the session who's expressed similar feelings about being with another woman. We can start slowly at first with the two of you just watching and talking to one another before we consider taking it to the next stage. You should always feel completely comfortable with your partner before agreeing to share this kind of intimacy."

"That does sound interesting," Haley said. "Would we be separated by protective screens again?"

"Only if you both want it that way. But something tells me you're ready to discover for yourself how much higher it can elevate the experience watching another woman pleasuring herself with you at the same time."

"Yes," Haley said. "I think I might like that."

"Let me know before your next session if you'd like to meet this new girl. Because she's definitely ready to meet you."

No shit, I muttered under my breath as my pussy continued spasming over my fingers firmly embedded inside my hole.

I had no idea know how I'd be able to keep it together for a whole week before I met this girl again. I smiled as my juices streamed down the insides of my thighs.

I'll just have to practice as much as I can in the meantime to get ready.

3

The intervening week before Haley's next scheduled session felt like the longest week of my life. I couldn't stop thinking about what she looked like and how she'd react to watching me respond to Hannah's instruction the way she had. I spent long hours lying on my couch with my dressing mirror propped up in front of me, fantasizing that it was Haley watching me instead of myself.

I must have cum a hundred times contorting myself into different positions trying to make myself look as sexy and alluring as possible. I didn't want to take any chance that she wouldn't respond positively to me in this shared therapy session. Beyond my desire for her to enjoy the experience to the fullest extent possible, I didn't want anything getting in the way of her moving on to the final step in her journey of sexual awakening. Every time I thought about actually touching her, my pussy throbbed and I had to tear my clothes off once again to quell the yearning desire within me.

When the appointment day finally arrived, I spent most of the morning trying on different outfits I thought might strike the right balance between sexually enticing and emotionally guarded. After all, Hannah was presenting me as another repressed patient who'd reached out for help overcoming her fear of intimacy with other women. I finally decided on a pleated mid-length skirt with inch-high pumps and a creamy silk blouse that hugged my breasts just enough to highlight the fullness of my bosom.

Hannah had asked me to arrive at her office five minutes after the hour so she could prep Haley first and confirm that she still wished to proceed as intended. The plan was for her to send me a quick text with either a smiling or frowning emoji to signal her readiness. When I still hadn't heard anything by 11:15, I shifted uncomfortably in her waiting room, wondering if Haley had gotten cold feet.

I couldn't blame her if she had. This whole idea was highly irregular and must have been kind of frightening for her. It was a far cry from meeting someone the natural way, getting to know them over a period of time before deciding to initiate intimate relations. But if she was too afraid to approach another woman the traditional way, I had every intention of making this experience as comfortable and uplifting as possible.

When my phone pinged and I saw the smiley-face symbol in my message thread, I stood up and nervously smoothed out the wrinkles in my blouse. I chuckled at the realization that I was just as anxious as the young schoolgirl at the prospect of our chaperoned playdate. Hannah stuck her head out her office door motioning me inside, and I straightened myself out and walked confidently into her office.

The girl was standing a few feet to Hannah's side, smiling nervously at me when our eyes met. I was surprised how young she looked in her skinny jeans, tight t-shirt, and Keds sneakers. She had long blonde hair, big bright eyes, and the plump skin of an adolescent who hadn't lost any of her youthful collagen. I must have looked ancient almost fifteen years older than her, as I pulled my shoulders back trying to lift my chest and press my breasts against my tight blouse.

Hannah turned toward the girl, arcing her arm toward me.

"Haley," she said. "This is Jade. In spite of your difference in age, I think you'll find you actually have a lot in common. I've brought the two of you together today to share some of your mutual experiences and learn to become more comfortable expressing your intimacy in the presence of another woman."

Hannah peered at the two of us and smiled.

"Would you like a drink before we get started?"

"Have you got some *tequila* behind your bar?" I joked.

"That might not be such a bad idea to help you both loosen up," Hannah chuckled. "But unfortunately, all I have to offer is coffee or tea."

"I'll have a coffee with a bit of cream and sugar then," I said.

"Tea is fine," Haley nodded.

"Cream and sugar also?" Hannah asked.

"Yes, thank you."

As Hannah turned to prepare our drinks, I moved closer toward Haley and extended my hand. She looked even prettier up close, with thick natural eyebrows and long dark lashes.

"Pleased to meet you, Haley," I said. "Hannah's told me so much about you. You're even more beautiful than she described."

Haley reached out and clasped my hand softly, and I could feel the nervous dampness in her palm as we touched for the first time.

"Thank you," she said. "You're very pretty also."

Her eyes blinked as she stole a glance down my body, peering at the cleavage formed by my push-up bra peeking out of my loosely unbuttoned blouse. My breasts were at least full size larger than hers, and I stood three or four inches taller in my elevated pumps.

"You remind me a little of Marilyn Monroe in that white blouse and skirt," she said.

"That's very kind," I smiled. "I could never hold a candle to her, though I feel a certain affinity given my own little seven-year-itch. It took me at least that long to break free of the oppressive bonds of my first marriage."

"Have you married again?"

"No–I guess I'm still discovering myself. I've kind of been looking for a change of pace lately. I never felt fully satisfied in my relationships with men."

"I've never felt comfortable approaching *either* gender, actually. My parents were pretty strict about the whole dating thing when I was growing up–"

Hannah returned from her kitchen and handed each of us a steaming mug.

"I see you two are beginning to get more comfortable," she said. "I'm glad to see you hitting it off so quickly. Would you like to get more comfortable?"

Haley and I turned to see two long chaise lounge chairs facing one another about ten feet apart, angled slightly toward Hannah's armchair positioned at the apex of the triangle. I smiled when I realized she'd done this intentionally to facilitate her own enhanced viewing of the two of us once we got loosened up.

We walked toward the settees and I paused, motioning for Haley to take the one on the left side. Both chairs were covered in a long throw blanket, and I kicked off my shoes before sitting back against the curved backrest, crossing my ankles on the end nearest Haley. It felt awkward holding my coffee in this semi-reclined position, and when I leaned over to rest it on the floor beside me, Haley did the same.

"How are you both feeling today?" Hannah said as she sat in her chair in front of us, crossing her legs sexily with her pointed pumps bouncing gently in our direction.

I had little doubt she was wearing her special sex toy under her prim business suit, and I envied her for a moment, knowing she'd have a leg up on the two of us for the rest of the session.

"Good," Haley said, with a gentle lilt.

"Better *now*," I said, smiling toward Haley.

"You've both expressed interest in exploring a same-sex relationship, but also about your reservations initiating the process given your previous experiences."

I nodded, realizing there was more than a hint of truth in her statement, even though I'd long since resolved my reticence about being with other women.

"The purpose of this session is to give you both an opportunity to become more comfortable in the presence of another woman, and to the extent you feel ready, to begin to explore the boundaries of your sexuality in the safe confines of my office. Is this still something you both feel comfortable proceeding with?"

I looked at Haley and she peered back at me, as we both nodded gently.

"Okay," Hannah said. "At first, I'd just like the two of you to gaze into each other's eyes for a moment and pause as you take a moment to acknowledge each other as willing partners and make a silent connection..."

I smiled at Haley and saw a soft flush spread over her cheeks as her pupils began to widen while she peered back at me. Even though neither of us said a thing, the longer I looked at her the more excited I got as my chest began rising and falling from my elevated respiration rate.

"Now, I want each of you to take a minute to look over each other's bodies without making any judgements or feeling self-conscious that you're checking each other out. Take a moment to appreciate the different shapes of your respective figures, and listen to how your body is reacting as you soak each other up."

I was happy to be given free license to leer at Haley's youthful figure, and as my eyes drifted down her body, I could feel my panties begin to moisten in excitement seeing the girl of my dreams reclining directly in front of me. Her breasts looked like they were painted on her body, sitting high and firm under her tight t-shirt. She had a narrow waist and slim but shapely hips, tapering to slender hourglass-shaped legs, looking all the more toned resting gently on the firm surface of her settee.

She in turn ran her gaze all over my body, pausing to stare at my full breasts pushing up against the flimsy silk fabric of my blouse. For a moment, I wished I'd decided to go braless, so she could see how she was turning me on as my nipples pressed against the soft fabric of my lace bra. After a few seconds of lingering, her eyes traced a line further down my body, pausing at the bottom of my skirt's hemline, as if hoping to catch a glimpse into the shadow between my closed legs. When her gaze reached the bottom of my feet, I wiggled my toes playfully, and she did the same with her cute sneakers. Even though we hadn't said a thing to each other for several minutes, I felt like we were already beginning to bond over our strange circumstances.

"Take a moment to revel in the beauty and diversity of the female form," Hannah whispered. "Recognize that everyone is built differently, and that these differences contribute to making each of us all the more interesting and alluring. Can you see the natural beauty within each of your own bodies and in those of your partner?"

"Yes," Haley nodded, tracing her gaze once again up to my pointed breasts.

"Absolutely," I enthused.

"Let's take this to the next level then," Hannah said. "If you feel comfortable, I'd like each of you to remove your tops and lie back in your chair while you admire one another in your undergarments."

As I slowly began unbuttoning my blouse, Haley leaned forward, pulling her t-shirt over her shoulders. When she lifted it over her head, her blonde locks fell down over the front of her cream-colored sports bra. I was a little disappointed to see her covered up so tightly, but her bra only seemed to accentuate the firmness of her perky tits.

When I unfastened the last button on my blouse, I pulled my arms out one side at a time then leaned back against the soft back-rest. It felt electrifying to rest there in my lacy bra as Haley ran her eyes lustily over my exposed chest and abdomen. My brassiere was low-cut enough that she could see the tops of my dark areolas, and they puckered slightly as my hard nipples began to lift the fabric away from my skin.

"Now look at each other's bodies more closely," Hannah intoned. "Examine the shape of each other's breasts, the curvature of your waists, and the smoothness of your stomachs. What do you see that appeals to your feminine senses?"

"I like the fullness of Jade's breasts," Haley purred. "And the way the top edge of her bra angles sexily down toward her cleavage."

"Yes," Hannah said, stretching the S out the end of the word. "Being a sensual woman means we can dress up in different ways to tease and excite our partners as a precursor to more intimate relations. What do you see in Haley's body that you find most attractive, Jade?"

I paused for a moment, examining her tight belly and the subtle striations in her stomach.

"I like the line running down the middle of her abdomen from the bottom of her bra to her belly button. I wish I could be that lean and sexy once again."

"That's the beauty we share as women of different generations. Some women are more lean and chiseled, while others are more full-bodied and curvy. It's all part of the magnificent palette of the human form and what makes it so interesting for each of us to experience. Are you beginning to imagine what lies further underneath?"

"Yes..." Haley said, her cheeks flushing a crimson red.

"Oh, very definitely yes," I sighed, wishing I could jump out of my seat and tear Haley's sports bra off with my own hands.

"If you're ready then, you may remove your brassieres and begin to get more comfortable being naked in the presence of one another."

Haley hesitated for a moment, looking at me to make the first move. Fortunately, the bra I'd chosen to wear had the closure at the front, and as I pressed my fingers together unhinging the clasp and spreading the cups apart to reveal my naked breasts, I heard Haley gasp a few feet away. Her reaction only excited me more as I peered down at my tits, seeing that my nipples had already hardened and extended to their full extent. I pulled my bra off my back and threw it on the floor, and my whole body started buzzing as Haley stared at my torso with wide eyes.

Within a few seconds, she felt emboldened enough to remove her own sports bra as she pinched her thumbs under the lower band and pulled it over her head in one swift movement. Her breasts jiggled softly on her chest and I marveled at how perfectly round and symmetrical they were. They looked bigger than I imagined when I saw her fully clothed, and I began to salivate as I leered at her creamy skin and her light-colored areolas. They'd already begun to bunch up in excitement, protruding like two erasers on the end of a pencil.

Hannah paused just long moment to give each of us a chance to soak up each other's bodies. I could see Haley's eyes darting excitedly between my points as a light dew formed at the top of her chest between her breasts. This just accentuated the youthful look of her glistening skin, glowing like a sexy goddess. As my mouth watered at the thought of taking her moist nipples into my mouth, another part of me began to grow rapidly wetter.

"What are you feeling as you look each other's naked bodies?" Hannah said, interrupting our thoughts.

"I'm thinking how much I want to touch Haley right now," I confessed.

"There'll be plenty of time for that soon enough," Hannah said, admonishing me gently. "What are you feeling at this moment, Haley?"

"I'm just..." Haley panted, her moist lips parting slightly. "I'm just amazed at how gorgeous Jade's tits–I mean *breasts* are. She's looks like a supermodel to me."

"It's okay to use informal terms to describe each other's bodies," Hannah nodded. "It helps to desensitize the experience and lose yourself more readily in the feelings of arousal that you're experiencing. Are you beginning to recognize how each of you are responding to the sight of watching one another in this manner?"

"Yes," Haley said as she locked her eyes on my tingling teats.

"You have *no* idea," I smiled, peering at Haley's quivering tummy.

"I'm happy you're both responding so positively. That means you're attracted to one another and that you're becoming more comfortable with the idea of exploring a different kind of union. Are you ready to take it to the next level?"

"I think so..." Haley hesitated.

"*God* yes," I panted, feeling the wetness in my panties beginning to run down the crack of my ass.

"Why don't you both take off your lower garments now, but keep your panties on for the moment? Part of the attraction with foreplay is taking our time to build the desire and teasing our partners by withholding those things we most crave. Take a moment to look at your naked bodies, but not completely undressed yet."

I leaned forward and unclasped the latch at the back of my skirt, then lowered the zipper and pulled my skirt down the front of my legs, throwing it playfully on the floor. Haley locked eyes on me as she unfastened the front of her jeans, wiggling sexily on her divan while she pulled her pants down, then flipping off her sneakers and throwing everything on the floor beside her.

She was wearing plain white low-cut panties that stretched at least four inches below her navel. I could see the dark outline of her bush under the thin fabric, and my pussy twitched knowing I'd soon get to see her completely naked. She leaned back and fixed her gaze on my crotch while I teasingly separated my feet a few inches. I was wearing matching lace panties and the light color must have shown the giant wet spot that had formed in the fabric. But I couldn't yet see any sign of wetness in Haley's underwear, since she still had her legs closed in a protective posture.

"How does it feel to view another woman like this, nearly naked?" Hannah asked. "Are you noticing any new reactions in your body as you watch your partner disrobe?"

"Yes," Haley panted. "I'm beginning to feel that same tingling sensation I experienced at our last session. It feels like my whole body is on fire..."

"How about you, Jade?" Hannah said, smiling at me. "How do you feel sitting in front of Haley almost naked?"

"Very sexy," I said. "I'm feeling things I haven't felt in a long time."

"So it would appear," she said, glancing at the wet spot between my legs. "Now I want each of you to spread your legs a little further apart to witness the effect you're having on one another. Take a moment to recognize the reaction each of you are experiencing as you become more and more aroused looking at one another's bodies."

As I spread my legs further apart, Haley pulled her feet up a few inches, then angled her knees down onto the divan to reveal the white swath of fabric running between her legs. I could see the indentation of her slit in the tight cotton and the telltale darkness of a small wet spot in the middle of her panties. Seeing her reveal this little slice of her private anatomy raised my excitement level even higher as the wet spot in my own panties slowly spread all the way from one side to the other.

While Haley stared at the widening dark spot between my legs, I noticed her chest begin to rise and fall as she started breathing more heavily. It took every ounce of my willpower to stay seated in my settee and not sprint over to her side and take her for myself. Hannah was right about one thing. All this slow buildup was driving me more crazy with desire and just increasing my longing to touch her.

"Can you see how each of you are responding to one another the more you reveal of yourselves?" Hannah said. "Are you beginning to become more comfortable with the idea of watching another woman being intimate and moving closer to a more formal connection?"

"Yes," Haley sighed.

"*Fuck*, yes," I gushed.

"Let's remove our remaining entrapments then and revel in the naked glory of the female body. You may both remove your last vestiges of clothing if you feel comfortable. Take a moment to soak up one another's bodies and connect with your feelings. A healthy sexual relationship starts with feeling comfortable in both your and your partner's nakedness."

I raised my hips, practically tearing my panties off as I pulled them down my legs and tossing them on the floor. While I kept my legs slightly parted, Haley wriggled out of her little white panties and dropped them sexily on the floor beside her. This time, she parted her legs the same distance as mine as we both stared at each other's wet slits shining in the bright overhead lights of Hannah's office. Haley's light pubic patch formed a perfect triangle over her mound and I clenched the fabric on the divan beside me trying to keep my hands from straying any further.

"There now," Hannah purred. "That wasn't so bad, was it?"

"No," Haley said. "It was actually easier than I imagined."

"How about you, Jade? How do you feel seeing your partner fully naked in front of you?"

"I'd hardly call it *easy*," I groaned. "The hardest part is remaining still on my sofa. My hands want to wander all over the place right now."

"If that's what you feel like doing, don't let me stop you from enjoying the process. I encourage each of you to begin touching yourselves while you verbalize how you're feeling. Communication and openness are the first two essential ingredients in any healthy relationship."

As I watched Haley separate her legs further apart, I lifted my hand to my breast and squeezed it tightly while I lowered my other hand to my crotch and began to circle my button. Normally I'd take more time to tease myself, but at this point I was so horny I needed to get right down to business.

Watching me touch myself and begin to moan softly seemed to encourage Haley, as she moved her hand to the inside of her thighs and began to flutter her fingers over her button. While we both began to moan and roll our hips over our divans, Hannah began to bob her foot more forcefully over her knee and cleared her throat.

"Yes," she mewed. "It's a beautiful thing watching another woman pleasuring herself. Focus on one another as you listen to the reaction of your own body and that of your partner. The biggest turn-on is seeing your partner respond excitedly to your touch."

I wasn't sure if she was talking more about what *she* was feeling at this precise moment, or referring to what we were experiencing. It must have been even more exciting for her watching two sexy women touching their naked bodies only a few feet in front of her. With her special sex toy working its wonders underneath her business suit, I imagined she'd have experienced multiple climaxes facilitating these sessions.

"Don't forget to communicate how you feel," she said. "Tell your partner what she's doing to you right now."

"I'm so excited watching Jade touch herself," Haley said. "I never thought a woman could look this sexy and beautiful before. The feelings inside are even more intense than last time–"

"And *you*, Jade?" Hannah said. "How is your body responding seeing Haley get excited watching you?"

"Oh my God," I groaned. "I want her so bad. I want to touch her and taste her and feel her trembling in my arms."

"Soon enough," Hannah smiled. "For now, I just want you both to learn how to satisfy one another at a distance without the added pressure of direct engagement. Focus on what you're feeling, and surrender to the pleasure engulfing your bodies. As before, feel free to experiment with different forms of stimulation. You can begin learning from one another even before you come together."

I spread my legs further apart and inserted two fingers from my other hand into my hole as I began to rub my clit more quickly.

"Mmm, yes," I panted. "You're so beautiful, Haley. I'm imagining you touching me..."

"Yes, Jade," Haley said. "I want to touch you and feel your wetness. You're making me so hot right now."

Haley mimicked my technique, awkwardly inserting the middle finger of her left hand into her slit while she pumped it in and out as she began jilling herself more rapidly. Our hips began to slowly lift off our divans and our mouths opened in pleasure as we moved inexorably closer to orgasm.

"Yes, baby," I purred. "I want to watch you let it go. Imagine me sucking your jewel as you come in my mouth–"

"Oh God," Haley squealed as she arched her hips higher in the air. "It's *coming*! Suck my pussy, Jade!"

Suddenly, Haley fell back onto the surface of the divan and she hunched over, jerking her body back and forth while she pressed her fingers deeper inside her pussy. Seeing her come just inches away from me was more than I could take. I suddenly flipped over on all fours and pounded my cunt as my tits wobbled excitedly over my chest. Within seconds, my orgasm washed over me like a tidal wave as I began squirting long streams in Haley's direction. While I peered at her between my legs, I saw her mouth gape wider apart as she watched me writhing uncontrollably on the chair in front of her.

I glanced over at Hannah for a moment and saw her slumping rhythmically in her own chair as she watched the two of us cumming with our fingers deeply embedded in our pussies. I smiled, knowing she had her *own* special finger stimulating her G-spot as she surrendered to an entirely different kind of lover.

4

———————

fter we all came down from our highs at Hannah's therapy session, she asked Haley and me if we were ready to proceed to the next stage in our intimacy journey. Knowing this meant we'd be allowed to touch each other, we both quickly agreed, but since we'd used up all the allotted time in the day's session, Hannah scheduled our next meeting for the following week. When we parted, Haley and I kissed each other on the cheek, but that was enough to keep me going until we met next time.

In the intervening week, I ran through all kinds of scenarios imagining how I'd like to touch and caress her. It was kind of fun not using any toys for a change, since I knew those would be off base during our next encounter. Hannah didn't want any artificial stimulation getting in the way of Haley learning to enjoy sex in the natural manner. That was easy for *her* to say, I thought, remembering how she'd responded watching Haley and me writhing on our divans while she let her special sex toy do all the work for her. But I knew she was right, and as I lay on my sofa dreaming of all the ways I could stimulate Haley, I came many times remembering what she'd said to me when she experienced her first orgasm in the presence of another woman.

This time, I thought, *she won't need to pretend that I'm touching her when she comes next to me.*

On the day of our next scheduled session, we arrived at Hannah's office a few minutes early, which gave her a chance to prep us and set the ground rules. The most important thing, she said, was to go slow and make sure our partner felt comfortable before pushing any further.

I looked around her office and noticed that the two settees had been pushed to the side, and I looked at her inquisitively.

"Where did you want us to relax?" I asked.

Hannah smiled as she led us into another room with a four-poster bed. The drapes had been pulled and a series of candles were lit around the room to set the mood. I could smell a hint of lemon-grass from some burning incense on the night table, and I nodded at Hannah's preparation.

"I thought you might like something a little more comfortable to relax on this time," she said. "Plus, I suspect you'll need a little more room to maneuver as you begin to explore each other's bodies. I wanted to make sure you felt as cozy as possible before proceeding to the next step. Why don't you give it a try and see what you think?"

I strolled up to the bed and ran my fingers over the linens. The high thread count made the bedding feel like silk, and I got goose-bumps imagining what it would feel like to lie next to Haley on the sumptuous surface.

"What do you think, Haley?" I said. "Do you think this will be suitable for our purposes?"

Haley stepped forward and ran her hands over the sheets, then turned toward Hannah and smiled.

"It feels like I'm in a five-star hotel," she said. "I've never experi-enced anything so luxurious in my entire life."

"I wanted you to feel completely relaxed in preparation for the next step in your journey of sexual awakening."

"What about *you*?" Haley asked. "Where will you be while Jade and I are resting on the bed?"

Hannah turned to a reclining chair resting in the corner of the room.

"I'll be sitting in the shadows not too far away. I want there to be minimum distraction while you and Jade explore each other's bodies."

"So you'll be with us for the remainder of the session then?"

"If that's what you prefer."

"You were very helpful last time," Haley nodded. "Plus, it somehow seems more erotic knowing you'll be watching us."

Hannah paused as she peered at the two of us with a sly smile.

"I'll try to be less involved this time while I give each of you a chance to experiment with what turns you on. But I assure you that I'll be enjoying the process almost as much as you will."

She walked to the other side of the room and lay down in her chair, crossing her legs.

"To get you in the mood, sometimes it can be more exciting to let your partner take your clothes off before you lie down. Who'd like to begin?"

Haley and I peered at one another, and a blush fell over her cheeks. It was obvious that she wanted me to make the first move, which was fine with me since I'd been undressing her with my eyes from the moment we came in the door. She'd chosen to wear a more formal outfit today, with a collared blouse, wool pants, and suede loafers. Whether she was trying to mimic me or she was trying to project the image of more sophisticated woman, was unclear. Either way, I liked the look, and I felt my heart beating faster as I imagined unbuttoning her blouse.

I stepped forward and reached out my hand to her, and she met mine with her opposite hand, squeezing my fingers gently. I tilted my head down, and she closed her eyes, anticipating my kiss. Pausing an inch from her mouth, I felt her cool breath on my skin, and my pussy twitched when I realized I was about to touch her intimately for the first time.

When our lips touched, she puckered them like they used to in old-time movies. I smiled, realizing that this might have been the first romantic contact she'd ever experienced and that she still hadn't learned the art of erotic kissing. I lifted my hand and cupped her face as I moved closer, pressing my body against hers. She unconsciously tilted her pelvis, pressing her hips against mine. I parted my mouth and nibbled her flesh, feeling the fullness of her lips.

She sighed as we pressed our breasts together, and I circled my arm around her, caressing the indentation of her lower back. I was dying to plunge my tongue into her, but I remembered Hannah's admonition about going slowly, and instead I turned around and sat down on the bed with my knees straddling her hips. While Haley peered down at me, I began to loosen the buttons of her blouse from the top. As I began to spread the panels apart, I smiled when I noticed that she was wearing a lacy bra like the one I'd worn at our last session.

I leaned in and kissed her exposed belly with my moist lips, reaching up to cup her breasts as I squeezed them gently. She began to moan and reached behind my head to run her fingers through my hair. I'd almost forgotten how to properly make love a woman with all my recent escapades, and suddenly I was happy that I'd agree to participate in Hannah's guided session.

Maybe I'd needed this as much as Haley did.

As she pulled my head tighter against her belly, I reached behind her and unfastened the clasp at the back of her bra, pulling it gently over her shoulders. Her brassiere fell below her breasts, and I lifted myself up, licking her pointy tips. Her nipples were hard and warm, and as I sucked them into my mouth one at a time, she gasped, pulling my head harder against her body. As I began to roll my tongue over her tips, I moved my hands to the front of her chest and squeezed her breasts more tightly. They felt full and firm in my palms, and for the first time since I'd entered the office, I became conscious of the warm feeling in my pussy. My juices had been flowing for some time now, and the feeling of wetness between my legs made my nipples harden.

Haley was running her fingers through my hair more wildly now, and I took this to mean that she was ready for me to take it to the next step. I traced my hands down the front of her belly, unclasping the button at the top of her pants, then I slowly pulled the zipper down to reveal a pair of black lace panties. Seeing her wearing sexy lingerie got me even more turned on, and I slipped my fingers over the waist of her pants and began to pull them down over her hips.

My heart pounded as I felt them tighten up when they reached the widest part of her hips, realizing just how curvy and tight her ass must have been. As I pulled them further down her thighs, Haley lifted her feet and kicked off her loafers, stepping out of her jeans. I pulled her blouse off her back, and her brassiere fell softly onto the floor. Now she stood inches away from me, almost naked and quivering in excitement.

Hannah must have sensed Haley's trepidation, as I heard her shift in her chair for the first time and clear her throat.

"Sometimes it's even more erotic to have your partner remove her clothes while you *watch*," she said. "Would you like to undress Jade yourself Haley, or watch her do so herself?"

"I've been dreaming of seeing her naked again this whole week," Haley said. "But I'm not as experienced as Jade in the art of undressing another woman..."

Taking Haley's cue, I stood up off the bed and stepped back a few paces to give her a chance to take in my full figure. I smiled at her as I began to slowly unbutton my blouse. I'd decided to go braless for today's session, and as it became apparent to Haley that I was naked under my shirt, I saw her eyes widening in excitement. After I unclasped the fourth button, I let the silky fabric fall on top of my breasts while I breathed in and out deeply. As my nipples began to harden, pressing against the soft fabric, Haley's lips begin to separate.

I teased her for a moment longer, bringing my hands together and pushing my tits closer together. She panted looking at my cleavage, and I felt my pussy getting wetter seeing her rising excitement. When I undid the last button and threw my blouse on the bed beside me, I watched the flickering light casting sexy shadows over Haley's mounds. I wanted to step forward and trib her pointed nipples with my own, but I reminded myself that this session was all about her.

The more slowly I could build her desire, the more I knew she'd enjoy the moment when we finally came together.

Damn, I thought. It had been a long time since I'd been this patient in seducing another woman. Apparently I needed Hannah's guided lessons just as much as Haley.

As we stood facing each other in the hypnotic shadows, Haley glanced down my midsection and a small curl formed on the side of her lips. For the same reason she'd chosen to dress more maturely, I'd chosen to wear jeans so she'd feel more comfortable seeing me as a peer. But the problem with the tight jeans was that they revealed the widening wet spot between my legs far more easily than when I wore my skirt.

"It looks like you're getting just as excited as me," Haley smiled, locking her eyes on my dark stain.

"Sorry," I shrugged. "I guess I lubricate a little more easily than most women."

"Mmm, I like that," Haley purred. "I can't wait to feel you. I'm beginning to get wet too."

I glanced down at Haley's legs and saw the shimmering slickness on the inside of her thighs.

"Perhaps it's time for the two of you to get more comfortable on the bed," Hannah interrupted from the darkness.

I'd almost forgotten she was there, but far from finding her intrusions irritating, I was glad she knew when we needed a little prompt. I slipped off my jeans, then lay down on the bed with my arm cocked sexily against the side of my head in a come-hither look to Haley. She didn't hesitate to join me on the other side of the bed, and we quickly melted into each other's arms. As I felt her press her body against mine, I kissed her with an open mouth, and this time she parted her lips and allowed my tongue to probe her cavity. Our breasts mashed together, and as we intertwined our legs, we both began to moan passionately. I pulled my leg up, pressing it against her pussy, and she responded by grinding her hips against my thigh.

By now, she'd joined me in thrusting her tongue into my mouth, and as we writhed together on the bed, I grabbed her ass and pulled her closer. The passion with which she was tongue-fucking me made me think she was ready for different kind of tongue lashing, and after a few minutes I disengaged and began nibbling my way down the front of her body. The only sound I could hear from the other sound of the room now was the soft rusting of Hannah shifting in her chair and the occasional soft sigh. I wondered if Haley sensed how much she was enjoying herself watching us, but at this point my only concern was satisfying the pretty girl lying beside me.

As I nibbled on Haley's teats and swirled my tongue over her areolas, she arched her back and pressed herself more firmly against me. It was apparent to me that she'd lost all of her inhibitions about being with another woman, and I hummed my approval as her body responded to my touch. I traced the little indentation running down the center of her tummy with my tongue, and her stomach quivered the closer I got to her private area as she began to roll her hips in anticipation of my touch.

When I reached her panties, I pulled them over her hips while she lifted her ass off the bed. Her bush felt as soft as fur and I rolled my cheeks over it, reveling in it's sexy scent and plush thickness. Beads of lubrication rested on her muff like morning dew on a spider web, and I paused to suck them into my mouth, tasting her sweet honey.

The further down I lowered myself, the further she spread her legs apart, until my shoulders were comfortably nestled between her legs. For a moment, I paused with my head cocked above her clit as I closed my eyes and inhaled her sweet, perfumy scent. After a few moments, she began to shimmy her hips impatiently, eager to feel my touch in her special place. Instead, I dribbled some saliva out of my mouth and let it fall on top of her inflamed jewel. When she felt the unexpected moisture on her button, she groaned and lifted her hips closer to my face.

"Oh God, Jade," she whined. "You're driving me crazy. I want to feel your touch so bad. Take me into your mouth like you said you would last time. Suck my pussy with your pretty mouth."

Her dirty talk just turned me on all the more, and I lowered my head to encircle her burning clit.

"Oh God–Oh God," Haley panted. "That feels so good. Lick my little man with your lips and make me feel like you did when I watched you last time."

Little man, I chuckled to myself. I hadn't heard that expression used by a woman before to describe her clit, and I wondered if this was a euphemism her parents had used when she was younger. But it didn't matter to me–I was just thrilled that she was expressing her desire for me and telling me how much I was turning her on.

As I hummed in delight, I began circling her button with the tip of my tongue, and she began groaning more loudly. While I mixed up my technique between sucking and licking her pearl, she placed her hands behind my head once again and pulled me harder into her crotch. As her breathing began to get more ragged and accelerated, I knew that she was getting close to the point of no return. I was tempted to pull back for a few seconds to prolong her torment, but then I realized there'd be plenty more time to tease and play with her after she released her pent-up sexual tension. She began to lift her hips off the bed as her body became rigid in a tight lock, and I slipped my fingers inside her and began to stroke her tenting G-spot.

"Oh God, Jade," she hissed. "Don't stop. I'm going to cum. *Yes!*" she grunted. "I'm cumming in your mouth!"

Suddenly, I felt the walls of her pussy clamping down on my fingers in rhythmic contractions as she humped her hips against my face while holding me tightly against her. I paused for a moment to feel her body spasming as I peered up and watched her pretty face contorting into paroxysms of pleasure. After what seemed like a full minute of tensing her body in a prolonged and powerful orgasm, she finally dropped her hips down onto the bed, panting loudly to catch her breath.

With the room suddenly quiet, I heard gentle squeaks coming from the other side of the room as Hannah shifted rhythmically in her chair. It was obvious to both of us what was going on in the dark, and we smiled at one another as I pulled myself back up to look into Haley's steamy eyes.

"That was beautiful, Jade," she sighed. "Thank you for making me feel like a woman for the first time in my life. I can't believe how skilled a lover you are. I'm afraid that I'll never be able to meet your expectations–"

"Remember that there are no expectations or targets in this first direct encounter between the two of you," Hannah breathed deeply, collecting herself. "Jade–why don't you show Haley how she can satisfy you. Sometimes it's more fun for the *receiver* to take the lead."

I knew immediately what Hannah meant, and as I lifted myself up off the bed, I looked into Haley's eyes and nodded.

"Why don't you lie there for a little longer and let me do most of the work?" I said.

I raised myself up on all fours and straddled her face with my knees on either side of her head, and she looked up at me with wide eyes and smiled. As I ran my fingers gently through her silky hair, I began to lower myself until my dripping pussy hovered inches over her pouty lips. She flicked her tongue out awkwardly trying to bat my clit, and I cupped her cheeks, lowering myself a little further until my nub pressed against her lips.

"Just open your mouth a little bit and nibble on me for a moment," I said. "Sometimes when you're making love to a woman, less is more. Let me ease into it while I watch your pretty face."

Haley did as she was told, and as she sucked my hard nub into her mouth, I closed my eyes and groaned.

"Yes, baby," I purred. "Just like that. Suck my button and roll it around in your mouth. I like the feeling of your mouth on my body."

As Haley began to roll her tongue over my bulb in a similar manner to the way I'd kissed her earlier, I smiled. She was a quick study, and I felt myself growing closer to her with every passing moment.

"Yes, Haley," I encouraged her. "Just like that. Feel my hard clit in your mouth. I'm making love to your mouth while I watch you. I'm going to cum for you soon."

Haley's head nodded excitedly, and her eyes began to widen as I pressed my pussy harder down onto her face. I could feel the passion rising within me but I didn't want to drown her in another torrent if I came too hard, so as my orgasm began to take hold of me, I lifted my hips and pointed my pussy over her tits while I squirted my juices all over her heaving chest. As she peered down at me between my legs, I saw her face twist into another silent orgasm. Apparently, I'd excited her so much with my waterworks that she hadn't needed any direct stimulation to come once again.

As we both groaned and shook our bodies together on the bed, I heard the sound of gentle sloshing coming from the direction of Hannah's chair. I peered over at her and noticed that her pants were unbuttoned while she rubbed her hands sensuously over her naked mound.

"That was very good, ladies," she sighed. "You're making excellent progress. It's time for the last step in your pair bonding. Now I want you to touch each other at the same time and experience the joy of coming together. Jade, I'm guessing you have a bit more experience in this area."

"Perhaps just a little," I smiled, as I shimmied my hips over Haley's slippery torso toward her quivering pussy. I paused for a moment when I reached her bush once again and tilted my pelvis back and forth over top of her bush, feeling the soft hairs tickling my clit and wet opening.

"Would you like me to make love to you now, Haley?" I purred.

"Isn't that what we've been doing all this time?" she said.

"Not quite *this* way," I smiled. "I think you might find this brings us even closer together and feels even more amazing. Lift your knees up higher and spread your legs for me."

Haley looked at me confused for a moment, and I nodded reassuringly. When she pulled her knees almost up to her chest, I pushed her thighs apart and peered at her inflamed gland, poking its head out of its hood. I kneeled over top of her and slowly lowered my body until the bottom of our thighs rested on one another. Her eyes widened when she realized what I intended to do, and a sly smile formed on my mouth as our clits touched for the first time. As I began to grind our hips together providing direct stimulation to our most sensitive areas, she threw her head back and groaned . I didn't know if she'd even conceived of two women touching themselves this way, but the look of pleasure on her face indicated that she was quickly losing herself in the process.

As I shifted my weight forward and back, stroking her hard clit and rubbing our sopping pussies together, she began to whimper and toss her head from side to side. Seeing her enjoying the tribbing action so much just made me want to fuck her harder. I transferred more of my weight onto her thighs, and she began to rock her hips in concert with mine. The feeling of our nubs rolling over one another as our slits smacked against one another was the most exciting feeling either one of us had experienced. Before long, she began moaning more urgently, and I saw a flush begin to spread over her chest as her nipples contracted even more firmly.

"Yes, Haley," I groaned, seeing the look of ecstasy roll over her face. "Let it go baby. Let me feel you cum with me while I make love to you."

"Yes, Jade," Haley grunted. "I feel it coming. I'm going to cum so hard against your pussy. Fuck me harder."

That was all I needed to hear as I pressed my hips harder down onto her vulva and began humping her more forcefully. When I heard her pussy begin to make sexy gassy sounds, I knew she was cumming again, but this time I stayed connected to her while my own orgasm took hold of me. The sound of my juices spraying onto her gaping hole as she moaned in euphoria was the sexiest thing I'd ever heard. As we came together listening to the sound of our pussies spasming in the height of ecstasy, I leaned forward and kissed her passionately. Haley had come a long way since her first awkward guided session with Hannah, and as our pussies continued twitching against one another, we both sighed in contentment.

Soon after, we heard Hannah moaning softly in her chair, and we turned our heads to see that she'd pulled her pants down all the way and was ramming her long dildo in and out of her pussy.

"I'd have to say you've both graduated with flying colors," she panted as her body jerked softly in her chair.

Haley and I looked at each for a moment with the same thought, nodding our heads in Hannah's direction.

"I think maybe Hannah needs a little therapy session of her *own* now," I smiled.

VOLUME FIVE

TOO CLOSE FOR COMFORT

1

———

As I watched our 787 Dreamliner arc over Biscayne Bay on approach to Miami International Airport, I couldn't help thinking back on fond memories from my youth. My brother Stephen and I had grown up on the northern shores of Chicago, where we made frequent trips to the beaches of Lake Michigan with our parents, frolicking in the surf and playing with our water toys until the sun went down.

But it had been almost five years since I'd seen Stephen after he took an executive position with American Airlines and married his college sweetheart, Gabriella. We'd tried to stay in touch as best we could from afar, but our communications seemed to be more and more focused on his struggling career with the airline. His job as Vice-President of Marketing had become increasingly strained in the midst of continual downsizing and consolidation in the industry following the last big recession.

In addition to the never-ending pressure to boost revenues in the super-competitive business, he'd grown fearful of the constant layoffs, worried when his own job might be on the cutting block. I'd hoped by visiting him that I could take his mind off work for a little while and reflect on happier times. Plus, I hadn't seen Gabby since their wedding ceremony on the North Shore, and I was looking forward to getting caught up with both of them.

As the jet's altitude lowered approaching the city, I could see the trails of motorboats and jet-skis plying the turquoise waters off Miami Beach. Little parasols dotted the beach as people lounged on the sand, periodically wading into the frothy waves. It had been far too long since I'd experienced the sublime sensation of warm salt-water rolling over my bare feet, and I could feel my skin tingling at the thought of finding some quality downtime with Gabby and Steve.

When the plane skidded down onto the runway, I turned on my phone and sent a message to Steve to let him know I'd arrived. He'd promised to pick me up at the airport and drive me back to his home in Coral Gables. After I picked up my luggage at the baggage claim carousel and headed toward the ground transportation area of the terminal, I saw him waiting near the exit door, and he waved at me. He looked weary and pale, but he still had that thick shock of curly blond hair I remembered as a kid and the handsome smile that had convinced his pretty bride to move halfway across the country in pursuit of his new job.

When we greeted, he gave me a big hug and kissed me on the cheek.

"How was the flight?" he said. "Did you enjoy the first-class seats I arranged for you through the Friends and Family Program?"

"Yes," I said. "But it was hardly necessary for such a short flight. Though I did enjoy the view from my window seat on the right-hand side of the plane. The beaches look spectacular along the east side. I'm looking forward to getting out in the sun again after a long winter."

I took a moment to appraise his pallid complexion and two-day-old growth of beard.

"It looks like you could use a bit of sunshine and fresh air your-self. You're looking far too pale for someone who lives right next to one of the most popular tourist destinations in America."

"Humpf," Stephen grunted. "If only I could find the time away from work. With all the pressures and downsizing in the airline industry over the past few years, it's been all-hands-on-deck just trying to stay afloat. If I don't put in the extra hours, I'm afraid my job will be the next one to be made redundant."

"Let's not worry about any of that right now," I smiled. "Let's just pretend like we're eight years old again and lap up this little slice of paradise for the next week or so."

I looked around the terminal for any sign of his wife.

"Where's Gabby? I've been looking forward to seeing her almost as much as you. We never really got a chance to become properly acquainted after you moved to Florida."

"She wanted to prepare a nice homecoming meal for the three of us. Plus, traffic at this time of day is pretty crazy. It's not much fun navigating the smog-choked streets of Miami during rush hour."

"Okay, Mr. Sourpants," I chuckled. "I feel really sorry for you, with your glamorous job and cushy lifestyle in this little patch of Eden.

"Come on," I said, threading my arm between his, and pulling my roller bag toward the exit. "Let's get out of this busy terminal and go see your pretty wife."

***

On the drive back to his place, I tried to take Stephen's mind off his troubles by talking about the old days and laughing about all the shenanigans we got into as kids, but I could tell that his mind was elsewhere as he asked me half-heartedly about what was going on in my life. When we turned into the gated neighborhood of Gables Estates and drove up his long brick-lined driveway toward his pink stucco house, I gasped.

"Holy crap, Steve!" I gushed. "You're really moving up in the world!"

"Hardly," he huffed. "This is just a middle-class property in this part of Miami. The *real* money is out on the islands and in Palm Beach. You should *see* some of the estates along the shoreline."

"I wouldn't sell yourself short," I said, admiring the manicured gardens surrounding his house with tall hibiscus trees and brightly colored flowers. "It looks to me like you're doing pretty well for yourself."

"Come," he said, parking his Audi in the driveway. "You must be hungry after traveling half the day. Gabby's eager to see you again."

He led me into the house, where I admired his marble floors and upscale Miami decor. With tall ceilings and huge picture windows overlooking a large garden, his home looked like the epitome of laid-back southern lifestyle. But when I saw Gabby working in the large open kitchen, my attention was suddenly diverted to the more natural features of the home. Wearing a tight-fitting apron around her curvy figure with her hair tied up in a bun atop her head, she looked even more beautiful than I remembered her at their wedding.

"Jade!" she exclaimed when she caught sight of me entering the room. "It's seems like forever since I last saw you!"

She dropped her cooking utensils and rushed toward me, throwing her arms around my back. I could feel her firm breasts pressing against me, and I blushed self-consciously at the visceral reaction to her touch.

"I know," I sighed. "Five years is way too long for close family not to see one another. I've been looking forward to this trip for ages."

I glanced at Gabby's pretty cooking uniform and nodded approvingly.

"I see the passage of time has been good to you. You look even more gorgeous than ever, as if that were even possible."

"I was just about to say the same thing about you," she said. "I love that new bob hairstyle."

She glanced down my body, running her eyes up and down my figure.

"And what have you been doing to stay in shape? You look as buff as always. It can't just be *yoga* that's giving you all those beautiful curves?"

"I've been getting my exercise in *lots* of novel ways," I smiled, not quite ready to tell her and Stephen about my recent forays into the arms of lesbian lovers.

"Well whatever you're doing, you'll have to share your secret with me. This southern lifestyle can be a little too laid-back sometimes to keep up my girly figure."

"Um, I think you're managing just fine in spite of the unfortunate surroundings you find yourself in," I said, peering sarcastically around their luxurious house.

"Okay, enough self-congratulations, you two lovebirds," Stephen interjected. "I'm starved. What's that exquisite concoction I'm smelling on the stove?"

"I made one of your favorite meals in honor of your sister's arrival," Gabby said. "Ventresca tuna with whole wheat pasta and kalamata olives in homemade tomato sauce. It's just about ready." Gabby handed me a bottle of wine and pointed toward the preset table. "Do you want to pour the wine, Jade? This Malbec goes perfect with tuna."

"My pleasure," I smiled. "I could do with a couple of glasses of wine to decompress after a day of traveling."

***

The three of us got caught up over dinner, and I was happy to see Stephen relaxing a bit while we all laughed about our childhoods and talked about current developments. Steve and Gabby made occasional intimations about developments in my love life after my marriage had quickly dissolved, but I told them I was taking my time exploring the dating field once again.

But I couldn't help noticing a certain emotional distance between the two of them. They hardly looked at each other the entire time during the meal and their chairs at the table seemed unnaturally far apart for a married couple. At first, I chocked it up to the size of their large dining room table, but when Stephen excused himself after an hour or so to get caught up on some overdue work in his study, I couldn't help probing a little further with Gabby while we cleaned up in the kitchen.

"How's everything been going down here in la-la land?" I said, drying off the pots and pans as she placed them in the opposite side of the sink after washing them. "Stephen seems a little more distracted than usual."

Gabby paused for a moment while she nodded toward the suds in the basin.

"He hasn't been quite the same since he took that executive position at the airline. At first, I attributed it up to his desire to get ahead and consolidate his position at the firm. But with all the layoffs and competitive pressures the past few years in the industry, I think he's grown increasingly worried about keeping his job. We're carrying a pretty big mortgage, and he's always been mindful of his role as the primary breadwinner in the family."

"Hmm," I nodded sympathetically. "I can see how that might weigh on his mind. And what about the two of you? Have you been thinking about expanding the family with the pitter-patter of little feet in this marble palace of yours?"

"*God*, no," she frowned. "Now is definitely not the right time. We'd need two fully participating parents to make that work. Besides, it takes a certain degree of physical intimacy to make babies these days. Stephen's been so self-absorbed in his work the past few months, he barely touches me anymore. I can't even remember the last time we had sex."

"Wow," I said. "I'm sorry to hear that. A healthy sex life is an important part of a successful marriage. Maybe we can take his mind off work for a few days while I'm down here visiting. Go down to the beach and frolic in the surf, and all that. Maybe if he sees you in skimpy bikini again, it'll change his mind about attending to your female needs."

"I'd like that," Gabby said, putting the clean pots back into the kitchen cupboard. "But I might need to update my swimsuit if I hope to arouse his passions again. All I've got left in my wardrobe is a frumpy old one-piece suit from back in the day."

I took a quick look at her generous bosom bulging out from the top of her apron and shook my head.

"Well we can't have that Goddess figure of yours all covered up in nylon while we're strutting along South Beach. What do you say the two of us go shopping tomorrow to pick out the perfect temptation? I could use a bit of a refresh to my summer wardrobe too!"

2

———

G abby and I stayed up late after washing the dishes and finished a couple more bottles of wine while chatting about what each of us had been up to in the intervening years. She seemed to be particularly interested in my love life, and after my third glass of wine, I finally confessed about my recent excursions into the realm of lesbian and bisexual sex.

She wanted to know all the dirt on my lovers, with explicit details about the different ways we made love. I could tell she was intrigued, having never experimented outside her monogamous relationship with Stephen, and I found myself becoming increasingly turned on sharing the sordid details of my adventurous new sex life. I noticed her squirming on the sofa while I explained how sex with other women had been so much more fulfilling than the boring, straight sex I'd had with my previous husband.

By the time we retired to our separate bedrooms at three in the morning, I was wet as a leaky faucet and had to relieve my sexual tension by masturbating quietly under the covers. I wondered if she was doing the same thing, and even though I felt guilty about telling my sister-in-law about the pleasures of lesbian love, I figured rekindling her interest in sex in any way could only be good for their moribund marriage.

With the next day falling on a Saturday, after much cajoling and prodding, we finally convinced Stephen to join the two of us for a relaxing day at the beach. Hoping to surprise him with Gabby's sexy new swimsuit, we agreed to meet on the surf side of the Royal Palm Hotel at two in the afternoon. That would give Gabby and me enough time to do a little shopping and develop a plan of attack for enticing him back under the covers with his wife.

Gabby took me to Miami's premiere shopping mall at Bal Harbour, and we flitted from one designer boutique to another before deciding that the Saks Fifth Avenue store had the best selection of swimsuits. We shared a small dressing room where we both tried on different outfits, giggling and baring our bodies while changing clothes. Gabby had a magnificent figure with tall, prominent, scooped-shaped breasts and slender hips that reminded me of a young Gina Lollobrigida. It was hard for me to concentrate while she asked my opinion about the different outfits she tried on while swaying her hips and mouth-watering tits mere inches away from my body in the small enclosed space.

As we changed from one outfit to another, she grew increasingly brazen and forward with her the comments about my revealing bikinis. After forty-five minutes or so of increasing sexual tension in the room, we accidentally bumped our hips together while bending over to remove another outfit, then swung around and straightened up, slapping our bare breasts against one another. We both paused momentarily, surprised at the unexpected touching of our private parts, then we suddenly melded together, embracing each other in a passionate kiss and intertwining of arms and legs.

Within seconds, our hands were running wildly over each other's bodies, dipping into every crevasse and squeezing each other's flesh with reckless abandon. Gabby seemed a little unsure how to engage with me as she groped me awkwardly while rubbing her crotch against mine, trying to increase the friction between our pussies. I lifted her left leg and bent her knee to the side, then raised my opposite knee, pinning her against the wall. When she felt my hot sex press against her own, she gasped, throwing her head back.

Not wanting to make too much commotion in the public dressing room, I pressed my mouth harder against her lips to stifle her moans while I ran my fingers through her hair and ground my wet pussy against hers. I could feel rivers of lubrication running down the insides of my legs, not sure if it was her or me that was getting more turned on by our clandestine public tryst. Deep down, I knew that it was wrong of me to take advantage of her vulnerability, especially in view of her fragile relationship with my brother, but there was something about her innocent inexperience and radiant beauty that I found simply irresistible.

As we rolled our sweaty bodies together and humped our hips together against the flimsy dividing wall of our small room, I could hear the creaking of the framework giving way to our impassioned fucking. Gabby's squeals and whimpering were growing louder and more prominent in spite of my best attempts to keep her vocalizations in check with my tongue in her mouth, but by this time I no longer cared who or how many people could hear us.

I could feel my own orgasm beginning to well up inside me, and from the increasingly tight grip of Gabby's hands on my butt cheeks, I knew it wouldn't be long before her passion crested along with mine. As my climax washed over me, I lifted Gabby's body up in the air, pounding my wet cunt against hers and burying my face in her cleavage as I began to gush like a geyser all over her ass and the dressing room wall. When Gabby felt me squirting on her pussy, her eyes flung open in surprise and she threw her head back against the wall, grunting loudly in the throes of a powerful orgasm.

We held each other tightly while we moaned together in mutual climax, jerking our hips loudly against the thin partition in tandem with our powerful internal contractions. When we finally came down from our intense orgasm, I gently lowered her back down onto the floor as we panted heavily, leaning exhausted against the dressing room wall. After a few moments, we pulled back a few inches and peered into each other's faces.

"Holy shit!" Gabby panted. "*Now* I see why you were so interested in switching sides. That might have been the best sex I've had in my entire life!"

"You were probably just overly excited from all the pent-up frustration of not having had sex with your husband for such a long time. I don't want you to get any crazy ideas. You're still a married woman, you know. To my *brother*, no less."

"We can't ever *tell* him about this," she said, shaking her head as the reality of what we'd just done took hold of her.

"Of course not," I said. "This will be our little secret. What happens in Saks, stays in Saks."

"Ha," Gabby chuckled nervously. "What now? Do you think anybody heard us?"

"I don't see how they couldn't have *not* heard us. You were pretty vocal, and this flimsy wall was shaking the whole time like a snare drum in a seventies pop band."

"Not to mention all the *mess* we've made of this place," she said, noticing the wet stain I'd left on the wall behind her. "I had no idea girls could squirt like that when they had sex."

"You've got a lot to learn, little lady," I grinned. "It's kind of an acquired skill. But I've always been a little wetter than most girls when I have good sex. And that was pretty fucking spectacular."

"Maybe you can teach me how to do that some day," Gabby said, smiling back at me mischievously. "I'm pretty sure if I pulled that little trick out of the hat while I was in bed with Stephen, that would bring some life back into his limp noodle."

I nodded as my pussy twitched watching her still-erect nipples jutting out from her plump breasts.

"We'll see what we can do to find some more private time while I'm in town. But we'll have to be careful that Stephen doesn't find out. I'm sure he wouldn't look kindly upon his long-lost sister taking advantage of his neglected wife while he's hosting me at your house."

I peered at the wet mark left from my spray on the wall as it dribbled down the sideboard.

"Let's clean up and get out of here before they send security to cart us away. Have you decided on a favorite outfit?"

"I was thinking of the cross-hatch-top and high-cut-bottom design in the hot pink color. I like how it supports my boobs and exposes just enough of my butt to highlight my best assets."

"I totally agree," I nodded.

I pulled some wet-wipes out of my purse that I kept on hand for these types of contingencies, then I wiped down the wall and we both got dressed and exited the dressing room area under the watchful gaze of many shellshocked surrounding shoppers. As we paraded down the hall hand-in-hand with everybody's eyes following us, the Saks dressing room attendant smiled and winked at us as we headed to the nearest cash register to pay for our purchases.

A few hours later, we met Stephen at the edge of the shoreline a few hundred feet opposite the hotel, just as Gabby was emerging from the surf with her wet bikini clinging to her luscious figure like a second skin. Stephen peered at her with wide eyes, appraising her from head to foot as he slowly lowered his sunglasses over his nose.

"Glad you could make it," I said, leading him up to our little stand on the beach a few feet way. "I was afraid you might get caught up in your work again and miss this opportunity to catch some fresh air and sunshine."

"How could I turn down an opportunity to mingle with my two favorite girls on such a pretty day?" he said, his eyes still darting over Gabby's sexy figure.

"Hi honey," Gabby said, giving him a peck on the cheek with wet lips as she traipsed up the sand toward us. "Do you like my new outfit?"

"Um–yes," Stephen stammered. "It's quite...*revealing*."

"Oh?" Gabby said, tilting her backside up teasingly to peer at her half-covered ass. "Do you think too much?"

"No..." Stephen said, noticing a parade of buff young men in Speedos checking out his wife as they passed by. "I'm just worried about you attracting the attention of all the *other* men on this beach in that hot outfit."

"I wouldn't worry about any of them," she smiled. "You know I've only got eyes for you. Besides, what about Jade? Don't you think she looks just as sexy in her new outfit?"

"Well–yes," Stephen said, taking a cursory glance at my bikini. "But she's my *sister*, so I wouldn't say she's sexy so much as beautiful. You both look gorgeous as a matter of fact. You guys can definitely hold your own with all these preening teenagers and trophy wives strutting their wares on this beach."

"Well come on, then," I said, grabbing his hand. He looked slim and fit in his tight-fitting boxer-brief swim trunks, but definitely like he hadn't seen any sunshine for a long time. "Let's get that chiseled body of yours all tanned up so you don't stick out like a tourist among all these beautiful people."

Gabby and I grabbed each of his hands and pulled him toward the surf, where he crashed into an incoming wave with the water spraying all over the three of us.

That won't be the only thing spraying over him pretty soon with any luck, I smiled, watching the salty froth running down over Gabby's exposed belly and low-cut bikini.

3

Gabby, Stephen, and I stayed on the beach for a couple of hours before returning later in the day to the hotel for a long dinner and nightcap. I tried to convince Steve to join Gabby and me nightclub hopping along the strip, but he said his sunburn was bothering him, and he insisted on going home to catch up on work email. Not wanting to miss a chance to have more quality time with Gabby, the two of us danced well into the night, bumping and grinding our bodies together on the dance floor, getting more than a little tipsy in the process.

By the end of the evening, we were belting out our favorite pop songs on the taxi ride home while making out in the back seat. I was disappointed when we had to retire to our separate chambers, but neither one of us wanted to raise any suspicion on Stephen's part by having her join me in my bedroom. I had hoped that after seeing her in her sexy new swimsuit and enjoying some downtime away from the distractions of work that it might renew his sexual interest in Gabby. But not long after she closed the door, I was surprised to hear an argument emanating from their quarters instead of the sounds of lovemaking.

After a half hour or so of raised voices, it became quiet again in the house, and I lay awake tossing and turning while reliving the exciting encounter with Gabby in the dressing room at Saks. As much as I'd enjoyed our risky public tryst, I longed to lie down with her in the comfort of my own bed and make love to her slowly and properly. As I began to thread my fingers between my legs to relieve the growing ache in my pussy, I heard my door squeak open and I saw Gabby tiptoeing toward my bed.

"Do you mind if I join you for a little while?" she whispered in the dark.

"Of course not," I said, flipping back the covers. "I was just thinking about you too."

"I couldn't sleep," Gabby said, sliding her naked body in next to me. "I can't stop thinking about what we did in the dressing room earlier today."

"Me too," I said, snuggling closer to her. "But what was all that fighting I heard coming from your bedroom? After seeing Stephen eyeing you up at the beach, I was sure he'd be all over you as soon as you got home."

"It was something he said while we were out earlier in the day that bothered me," she said, looking at me with a pained expression. "That comment about all the pretty teenage girls and trophy wives showing off their wares on the beach. It made me feel old and cheap. I told him that he shouldn't be comparing me to anyone else, and that he should be damn happy to have snared a catch like me. Not many wives would put up with his constant bellyaching and long hours at work."

"I'm sorry to hear that," I said, wrapping my arms around her shoulders. "You're damn right that he should consider himself lucky to have landed you as his bride. You're a million times sexier than any of those silicone-enhanced bimbos, and you're an absolute *angel* to have put up with his neglect these past few years."

I ran my index finger slowly down the hollow of her spine toward the curvature of her tight ass.

"But I'm kind of glad that you came to me for consolation. I haven't been able to sleep either thinking about our encounter in the dressing room, and I was just about to relieve myself when you came in."

"Maybe I can help you with that," Gabby said, nibbling me softly on my neck.

"I was hoping you'd feel that way," I smiled, curving my hand around her back to caress the side of her breast. "But we're going to have to be quiet as mice this time. We can't make the same kind of commotion we did at Saks. Stephen would never forgive either one of us if he found us in bed together."

"I promise to be quiet this time," she said, wrapping her legs around my hips and pulling our crotches closer together. "Can you teach me how to squirt like you do? I want to come all over you like you did with me."

"Maybe we should take it slow, to start," I said. "As eager as I am to feel you squirting all over me, I'm not sure I can trust you to keep quiet under the circumstances. We've got all week to get to know each other a little better. I just want to be close to you right now. I feel like making love to you this time, instead of just *fucking* each other."

"I like the sound of that," Gabby said. "I've been having the same kinds of feelings about you. In fact, I haven't felt this way in a long time."

"You mean sexually?"

"No, I mean emotionally. It's been nice to feel a two-way connection again. And I have to confess, I've always had a bit of a crush on you. I was disappointed when Stephen moved us away from Chicago–"

"Oh Gab," I sighed, pulling her closer. "Maybe this isn't such a good idea after all. I don't want to drive a wedge between the two of you..."

"There's not much more distance you could possibly put between us right now," she said. "He's so self-absorbed in his work, even that sexy bikini I wore today couldn't do anything to perk up his interest in me."

"But what about *us*?" I said, peering into her pretty brown eyes.

"I'm going to have to leave in a few days. This will just make it harder for us to separate–"

"Let's not worry about any of that right now," she said, rolling on her side to squeeze our bodies together. "We could never stay together permanently, anyhow. The rest of your family would never forgive us, and it would forever ruin your relationship with your brother. Let's just live in the moment and enjoy the brief time we have together while we can."

"You're twisting my arm, girl," I smiled, nibbling on one of her ears.

"Mmm," Gabby purred. "I like the feel of your tongue on my skin. I've been dreaming about you licking me all over. You have no idea how much I've fantasized about making love to you ever since we met at Stephen's dorm party all those years ago."

"Well just lie back and enjoy it then," I said, shifting my body lower on her body.

As Gabby lay trembling on the bedsheets with her arms lying expectantly by her side, I nibbled my way down the side of her neck and over the curvature of her shoulder, swiping my cheeks softly against the upper surface of her breasts.

"God, Jade," she moaned. "You really know how to drive a girl crazy. Stephen only seems interested in one part of me, and he's always in a hurry to get there to finish his business."

"We'll have to work on that," I said. "Perhaps you can teach him some of these new techniques. Sometimes I think only a *woman* knows how to properly please another woman."

"Yes," Gabby sighed. "Teach me all the ways of making love to a woman. I want to feel every part of you touching my body. Your skin feels so soft against mine."

"Mmm," I purred as I buried my face in her cleavage, then lifted my head to let the ends of my curls dance over her erect nipples.

"*Huh!*" Gabby suddenly gasped at the pleasant sensation on her sensitive skin. "Damn–I could make love to you every night this way."

"I don't know about *every* night," I said, lowering my lips to kiss her protruding tips. "How sound a sleeper is Stephen?"

"Can't you hear him snoring in the other room?"

I stopped shifting under the covers for a moment and smiled when I heard the familiar wheezing of a man's voice deep in slumber coming from the room down the hall.

"Good," I said. "Maybe that'll help cover up all the noise you make when you make love. Should I get you something to clamp your teeth onto to keep you from waking up the whole house?"

"In due time," Gabby purred. "I'm pretty sure I can find something tasty to chomp on when you're finished down there."

"I'll be happy to oblige," I smiled. "Just pull the covers over your head in the meantime if you need to muffle your moans. Because by the time I'm finished with you, I intend to have you squealing like a pig."

Gabby scrunched further down under the covers and pulled the sheets over her head, then she spread her legs apart, inviting me to go lower. I could feel her nipples tickling my breasts, and unable to resist the temptation any further, I devoured them like a newborn calf sucking on its mother's teat for the first time. She arched her back when she felt my mouth encircle her medallions, groaning softly under the covers. Her tits were soft but firm, and I squeezed them gently while I suckled on her peaks.

I was surprised how big they felt in my mouth, almost the size of a young boy's penis. I circled my tongue around the phallic projection, slipping it in and out of my mouth, making a rude popping sound each time. She groaned each time I did so, and the harder I sucked on it, the bigger it seemed to grow. Not wanting to neglect her other breast, I switched back and forth between each of her tips, teasing and bending them in my mouth.

I could feel her hips gyrating more vigorously against my tummy while I was sucking her, and after five minutes or so of playing with her tits, I drew my tongue down the crease in the center of her stomach toward her quivering pussy. When I reached her pubis, I was surprised at how soft and bare it was, and I peered up at her for a moment.

"You're awfully well-groomed for someone who hasn't had sex in such a long time," I smiled. "Have you been expecting some new attention down here lately?"

"I wanted to make sure I was properly landscaped to show off my low-cut bikini," she said. "But I decided to shave it all off knowing there was a good chance you'd see me naked in the change room."

"Well I *like* it," I purred, sucking her bare flesh hard into my mouth.

"Yes, Jade," Gabby panted. "Suck my pussy. I want you to taste me *everywhere*."

"Mmm, my pleasure," I said, lowering my chin down into her dripping crease.

I could feel the heat from her pussy radiating against my face and neck, and I spread her knees further apart, kissing the insides of her thighs as I slowly worked my way up to her steamy opening. Gabby whimpered as she tilted her hips toward me, begging me to approach her prize, but I wanted to build the tension to make her first experience with lesbian oral sex as memorable as possible. But when I felt her juices beginning to pour down over her thighs and I tasted her aroma on my tongue, I positioned my head over her puffy lips and sucked them into my mouth with a loud sopping sound.

"*Uhnn!*" Gabby grunted, reaching down under the covers to grab the back of my head and pull me harder into her pussy.

She was gyrating her hips harder and faster now that I'd made contact with her most sensitive parts, and the bed started to creak and shake in tandem with her escalating moans.

"You're going to have to be quieter if we're going to do this without waking your husband up," I said, pausing momentarily to chide her. "Stop rocking the bed so much!"

"Sorry," she said, lifting the covers to peer down at me. "But you're making it nearly impossible for me to remain still when you do that to me. I've never had anybody turn me on this much!"

"Do you want me to *stop*?" I teased.

"Don't you dare!" she hissed. "I promise to be quieter. Just suck my pussy a little longer. It won't take long for me to come soon."

"Okay," I said. "But I'll to have to stop if you can't control yourself any better. The last thing we need is for Stephen to barge in here and find his sister eating out his wife's pussy."

"Yes—eat my pussy, Jade," Gabby groaned. "Make me come in your mouth. I'm so wet right now, I feel like I'm about to spray all over you like a *car wash!*"

"Okay, just let your *pussy* do the talking the rest of the way. I'll know we're finished when I feel you cumming all over my face."

"Suck my clit now," she said. "I'm ready to come for you."

As much as I wanted to tease her a little longer, I was mindful of Stephen sleeping only a few feet down the hall, and we needed to get this over with before he suspected any foul play. I shifted my body a few inches higher between her legs, then slowly lowered my face over her folds, taking her engorged button into my mouth.

"Mmmft!" Gabby grunted, gritting her teeth trying to stifle her moans.

I could feel her gripping the sheets beside me with her two fists as she pressed her pussy harder against my face. I slid both of my hands under her ass and grabbed her butt cheeks, squeezing them hard as my tongue circled her nub, sucking it harder into my mouth as she slowly lifted her hips off the mattress. Her breathing began escalating rapidly in both pitch and frequency, and with her hips now raised almost two feet over the mattress and her buttock muscles tensing tightly in my hands, she suddenly let out loud squeal, and I felt her gushing into my mouth.

I threw one of my hands up toward her face, clamping it tightly over her mouth trying to muffle the sounds of her powerful climax, and I could hear Stephen's snoring temporarily interrupted while Gabby whimpered and moaned in tortured silence as her hips buckled against my face and her juices poured down over my chin. For almost a full minute, she stayed in this arched position, jerking her hips spastically against my face as jet after jet of her sweet cum filled my mouth.

When I felt her begin to climax, I stopped moving my tongue over her clit and just held her tightly, feeling her pussy clamping in rhythmic contractions against my face until she lowered her hips back down onto the bed and exhaled in one long, heavy sigh.

"Oh my *God!*" she whispered to me under the covers. "That was *insane!* I've never had an orgasm like that. Did you feel me come?"

"I felt you, I tasted you, and heard you," I said, nestling up beside her and holding her gently in my arms. "I just hope we haven't woken up your husband with all the noise you were making."

We both paused for a long moment to listen for any sound coming from the other room, and after a minute or so, the sound of Stephen's snoring began to fill the hallway again between our two rooms.

"Thank God," Gabby sighed when she realized he'd fallen back into a deep sleep. "Now I can return the favor and give you the same kind of pleasure you just gave me."

"As much as I like that idea," I said, caressing her soft hair. "I thinking we're pushing our luck as it is. Let me just hold you in my arms and enjoy your afterglow while he's still asleep. Maybe we can steal some more time together another night. That orgasm of yours was strong enough to satisfy *both* of us."

"Did I do good?" Gabby whispered, raising her eyebrows expectantly at me. "Did I squirt when I came?"

"Yes," I smiled. "Can't you see the wetness all over my face and breasts?"

"Mmm, yes," Gabby mewed, leaning over to kiss me passionately on my lips. "Tomorrow night I'm going to taste *your* pussy in my mouth and enjoy a little car wash of my *own*."

4

Gabby and I fell asleep together not long after and were awoken a few hours later by a gentle tap on my bedroom door.

"Hello?" Stephen's voice called. "Has anyone seen any sign of my wife?"

Gabby woke up with a start and looked at me with wide eyes, unsure how to handle the awkward situation.

"It's okay," I whispered. "Get up quietly and put on a pair of pj's from my suitcase lying on the chair."

She scampered out of bed and found my pajamas in the case, hopping from one foot to the other while hastily pulling them over her naked body.

"I dunno," I called back to Stephen teasingly. "Have you checked the kitchen?"

"Yes," he said, sounding annoyed. "There's no sign of her anywhere in the house."

"What about the *laundry* room?" I said, getting up to put on some panties and a long button-up blouse.

"Nooo," Stephen groaned, beginning to catch on to my joke.

"Have you tried the garden?" I said, motioning for Gabby to get back into the bed and sit up against the headboard. "She must be *somewhere* around the place doing her wifely duties."

"Ha, ha–very funny," he said as I hopped back into the bed, sitting up beside Gabby with my legs crossed casually in front of me.

"Why don't you come in here and check under the bed? Are you sure you didn't scare her away last night with all your yelling?"

The door creaked open a bit and Stephen poked his head in, noticing us both sitting up nonchalantly in my bed like we'd been up chatting all night.

"*There* you are," he said, noticing Gabby peering back at him icily. "I was worried when I saw the car in the driveway and couldn't find you anywhere."

"I'm surprised you even noticed my absence, with your preoccupation with so many *other* things these days," she said, crossing her arms over her chest. "Maybe if you had a proper *trophy* wife, she'd be a little more doting of your every little whim and need–"

"Gabby," Stephen said, putting on his best puppy dog face. "I'm so sorry I said that. I didn't mean to compare you to anybody. You're the best trophy–I mean *wife*–any man could hope to have. I'm the luckiest man alive to have you put up with all my bullshit."

"Damn right," Gabby said, crossing her legs in front of her in solidarity with me.

"You guys look like two little bees in a bonnet," Stephen said, appraising our unusual sleepwear. "Have you been here all night?"

"Pretty much," I nodded. "You know how us girls like to sleep together and talk all night long. Plus, we got a little tipsy at the nightclub and crashed not long after we got home."

"Hmm," Stephen nodded, glancing at my bare legs suspiciously.

"Are you guys hungry? I was going to scare up an omelette if you're interested."

"I could practically eat a horse after dancing all night long. What about you, Gab?"

"I need to eat *something*, that's for sure," she said. "Are you sure you can manage it all by yourself, dear? Do you need me to crack the eggs for you or show you how to turn on the stove?"

"Very funny," Stephen smiled with a lopsided grin. "I'll give you a shout when it's ready if you need some time to put yourselves together."

"Okay," I said. "See you in a few minutes."

After Stephen shut the door behind him, I peered over at Gabby, pinching my eyebrows.

"That was bit *harsh*, don't you think?"

"You don't think he deserved it, after what he said at the beach?"

"Well maybe, but he *did* apologize and sounded like he was genuinely trying to mend bridges..."

"Possibly," she said. "But this has been going on for a long time and I wanted him to realize that I'm not just going to lay over that easily. He's going to have to *earn* my respect to get me back into his good graces."

"And the matrimonial *bed*?"

"That could take a little longer," she said, rubbing her knee softly against my bare thigh. "After last night's experience, I'm in no hurry to rush back into his arms."

"You can't sleep with me *every* night. This girls' sleepover thing will only take us so far."

"True, but he's a pretty sound sleeper, remember? All we have to do is wait until he nods off then I can sneak back into your room. Besides, I'm not finished with you, yet. There's so many more things I want to try before you have to leave..."

"What's the plan for today?" I said, getting up to put on some pants. "It's Sunday. Surely there's *something* we can think of to entice Stephen out of the house for an entire day to take his mind off work."

"I was thinking we could make a trip out to Key West. It's a beautiful drive over the causeway, and there's so much to do there. Quaint shops, great restaurants, and tons of bars to kick up our heels again if you're up for it."

"Oh I'm up for it, alright," I smiled. "But I think it would be better for you and your *husband* to do a little bumping and grinding instead to begin repairing your frosty marriage."

"Maybe," she said. "But first we need to entice him out of the house and away from his computer. We might need to drag him kicking and screaming."

"If that's what it takes," I chuckled. "I'm determined to get you two reconnected if it's the last thing I do."

"Oh?" she teased, stroking the inside of my thigh softly. "You're ready to ditch me this fast? Have your way with me, then dispose of me like so much flotsam?"

"Don't be silly," I said, leaning in toward her and giving her a long, wet kiss. "You know how I feel about you. It's just like you said last night, we can't stay together this way when this week is over. But I'm always going to have a soft spot for you in my heart, no matter where we find ourselves."

"I hope that's not the *only* soft spot you keep reserved for me," she purred, rolling her hand over the front of my panties and stroking my vulva.

"You know it, girl," I smiled. "Whenever we have a chance to reconnect, I'm ready for more fireworks."

"And *car washes*?" she said, raising a playful eyebrow.

"Absolutely, you can hose down my chassis any time you like."

I reached down behind her back and slapped her butt playfully.

"Now get out there and spend some time with your handsome husband before he burns himself on the stove or cuts himself slicing the onions. The last thing we need is for him to have another excuse not to go out with us today."

After we got dressed, the three of us had a long relaxing breakfast on the back terrace. The smell of the tropical flowers was intoxicating, and I could feel the fresh sea breeze wafting over from the bay a few miles away. After much begging and pleading, we convinced Stephen to join us on our trip to Key West, where we had a relaxing day exploring the shops and enjoying outdoor dining watching the seabirds trying to steal our scraps. Key West had a large and vibrant LGBT community, and we all had a fun time watching some drag shows and cabaret acts, then dancing at some of the town's hotspots until well after midnight. Stephen and Gabby appeared to be reconnecting as they bumped their bodies together on the dance floor and I even noticed them holding hands while watching some of the shows.

By the long drive home, I was convinced the two of them were ready to climb into bed together to begin rekindling their intimate relationship. But when we stopped to refuel the car at a pitstop along the way, Stephen's mood suddenly became more somber when he got back in the car.

"What is it, hon?" Gabby said, noticing the familiar tightening of his face.

"I just noticed a text message from my boss earlier in the day. He wants me to prepare a presentation for an important meeting first thing tomorrow morning–"

"You've *got* to be kidding me," Gabby groaned, leaning sullenly against the side of her door. "Can't those guys *ever* leave you alone and let you enjoy a full relaxing weekend once in a while?'

"I'm so sorry, Gab," he sighed. "Believe me, this is the last thing I want to be working on tonight. I was really looking forward to having you back in my arms and getting back to the way we were. I promise, after this is done, I'm going to find a way to pull back from this ridiculous work schedule. Jade's visit has really helped me realize the important things I've been neglecting these past few years."

Gabby uttered a heavy sigh and crossed her arms, staring out the side of the window at the wide expanse of the Atlantic Ocean on the side of the Overseas Highway. I could feel the tension in the car, but decided it was best for me to stay out of their domestic troubles for the time being. If Stephen was genuine about his intentions, at least they'd have a fighting chance to repair their fragile marriage at another time.

When we got home, Stephen went to his study to begin work on his presentation, and Gabby insisted on joining me again in my bedroom even though her husband would be awake for another couple of hours. She told him that she was going to spend the night with me again and not to disturb us since we were exhausted after spending two nights in a row without much sleep. He nodded grudgingly, and Gabby shut the door of the den behind her when she left him to his work.

"Are you sure you should be sleeping here again tonight?" I said when she joined me in my bedroom, closing the door softly behind her.

"His study's on the other side of the house," she said, walking directly up to me and beginning to unbutton my blouse. "There's two closed doors between us, and he'll be so absorbed in getting ready for his executive meeting tomorrow morning that he'll pay no mind to whatever we're doing in here."

"I don't know, Gab," I said, pulling away a few inches. "You guys looked to be reconnecting tonight, and I don't want to put another roadblock between the two of you getting back together intimately. Maybe you should wait for him to return to bed. It sounded like he was eager to make love to you again..."

"There'll be plenty of time for that after you leave," she said, stepping forward to kiss me hard on my lips. "We've only got a few days together to share some quality time together. Besides, we've got unfinished business from last night–"

"Mmm," I said, beginning to succumb to her gentle caresses and probing of my nether regions. "Maybe just for a few minutes..."

Gabby tore off my clothes and the two of us pounced on the bed together, temporarily leaving our troubles behind. After rolling back and forth, kissing and rubbing our bodies together, Gabby pinned my arms to the mattress and looked me squarely in the eyes.

"It's *my* turn to taste you tonight," she grinned. "I've been dreaming about licking your pussy from the moment you walked into my house three days ago."

"Are you sure you know *how*?" I kidded. "It's not quite the same as going down on a man. Our body parts are configured a little differently you know..."

"Really?" she said. "I had no idea. Maybe I'll just take your lead from last night and copy what you do. You seem to know your way around a girl's body pretty well."

"I've had a bit more practice," I smiled. "But you seem to be picking up the technique pretty fast–"

"Mmm, especially that whole squirting thing. I can't wait to feel you gushing all over my face while I'm planted between your legs."

"Damn, girl," I sighed. "You're not making this any easier for me to resist your temptations."

"Just lie back and enjoy it then," she said, using my line from the previous night. "Because by the time I'm finished with you, I intend to have you squealing like a little girl."

"Yes," I purred. "Suck my cunny, Gab. I want to feel your pretty lips on my pussy and feel me coming in your mouth."

"Your wish is my command," Gabby said, beginning to kiss her way down my body as she nibbled and lapped up my tingling skin.

It didn't take long for her to bring me to the brink of orgasm as she expertly sucked and rubbed every sensitive area of my private parts, culminating with a long and sustained focus on my flaring clit. But when she thrust three fingers into my hole as I was nearing my peak and began to fuck me hard with her hand while she simultaneously sucked on my nub, she quickly put me over the top, and I grabbed her head hard between my legs, shaking and quivering while trying to stifle my moans of pleasure so Stephen wouldn't hear us.

After I came down from my highs, Gabby scurried up next to me and kissed me softly on the lips, smiling at me.

"Are you sure you haven't done that before?" I said, still breathing heavily. "Because that was some pretty first-rate pussy-licking you were doing right there."

"I might have watched a few lesbian porn videos awaiting your arrival," she smirked. "I wanted to be ready just in case I had the chance to divert your attention away from your brother."

"It looks like you've accomplished your goal," I said, tasing my juices on her tongue as I kissed her passionately.

"Maybe not *entirely*," she said, wrinkling her brow at me. "I didn't feel you squirt when you came, like last time. Did I do something wrong?"

"No, of course not," I said, drawing her closer. "It's not something you can just turn on and off. It depends on a lot of things. How wet I am, how long of a buildup I've had, the position I'm in, and other things. But it felt wonderful, believe me. I had a lovely long orgasm and it felt incredible feeling your face between my legs when I came."

"I'll guess I'll have to take your word for it," Gabby frowned. "But I was kind of looking forward to another 'car-wash' experience, like the one we had in the dressing room at Saks. That was incredibly hot!"

"Oh?" I said, looking at her mischievously. "You like grinding our pussies together and feeling me spraying all over you when I come?"

"Fuck yes," Gabby said, rubbing her mound against mine under the covers.

"I've kind of been wanting to do that again *too* since the last time," I said. "But with both of us moving around together on the bed, we're going to have to be extra careful not to distract Stephen from his work. Are you sure you're going to be able to keep relatively quiet if we do this?"

"I promise," Gabby said, holding up three fingers with the Girl Scout's pledge. "I just want to feel your wet pussy against mine again. Maybe we can experience a little waterworks show together this time."

"I like the sound of that," I said. "But let *me* do most of the work so you don't have to move around too much."

"Whatever you say, boss," Gabby smiled. "Have your way with me. I'll be the sub and you can be the domme. Isn't that kind of how it works with lesbians most of the time?"

"Sometimes, I said. "It depends on who's playing the bottom and who's on top, so to speak. But I'll be happy to take charge this time."

I grabbed Gabby's legs and pushed them apart into a scissors position then turned my body around and wedged my hips between hers.

"Now come here little girl while I give you a proper lesbian fucking."

"Mmm," Gabby purred. "Rub your cunt against mine and make me squeal like a little girl. I want to *watch* you this time while you spray all over my bare pussy."

I grabbed Gabby's knees and pulled her hard toward me, and she groaned when our wet pussies touched. As I began to rock my hips in rhythm with hers, I could hear the sloshing sound of our snatches grinding against one another, and she reached out her arms to join hands with me while we looked into each other's eyes as our passion slowly escalated. The closer we came to approaching our climax, the more tightly we pulled on each other's arms while curling our bodies together, until her back was arched over the mattress and I was kneeling over top of her, grinding my cunt into her upturned pussy.

I could see Gabby's mouth progressively widening as she approached her orgasm, trying desperately not to cry out in pleasure with her body consumed in passion. The sight of her prostrated beneath me at the height of ecstasy, with her pretty tits swaying in tandem with our hips and her big nipples pointing up at me, was simply too much for me to hold back any longer. With one last hard grunt, I mashed my pussy hard against hers and began spraying my juices in every direction as the tight connection between us acted like a spigot, drenching her upper torso and face with my pent-up lubrication.

"Oh my God!" Gabby groaned. "I'm going to come, Jade. I'm going to cum so hard against your pussy. *Uhnnnn!*"

Suddenly, we had *two* powerful jets of lubrication spraying out the sides of both of our pussies, soaking our bodies and the bedsheets thoroughly. I barely noticed how much noise the two of us had been making while lost in the throes of one of the longest and most powerful orgasms I'd experienced in a long time. But just as we began to slow the jerking our hips together in the final stages of our mutual orgasm, we heard another loud tap on our door, and we quickly scrambled under the covers.

"Is everything okay in there?" Stephen called out. "I heard some strange sounds and wondered if something happened."

"Everything's fine," I called back. "We were just laughing about that drag show we were watching earlier in the day."

"I'm finally finished preparing my presentation," Stephen said. "Are you coming to bed, Gabby? I really was hoping we could spend the rest of the night together."

Gabby peered over at me, and I nodded.

"You should go now," I whispered. "Go spend some quality time with your husband while you have the chance. Just clean up quickly in the washroom so he doesn't suspect what you've been up to. Go get your groove on, girl."

"I *am* still kind of horny," she said, smiling at me. "Are you sure you're going to be alright spending the rest of the night alone?"

"Absolutely," I said. "Nothing would give me more pleasure than to hear the sound of you two renewing your intimate relationship." I nudged her in the side and playfully pushed her out of the bed. "Now go scoot and get reacquainted what it feels like to make love to a *man* for a change!"

"I'm coming babe," Gabby called out. "Just give me a minute and I'll be right there. Maybe you could light some candles and put on some sexy music to get me in the mood..."

"I'm way ahead of you girl," he called back. "And Jade, maybe you should put in some earplugs or wear your headphones for the next hour or so. I wouldn't want to interrupt your sleep any more than I've already done."

"Don't you worry about me," I said. "I'll be fine here all by myself. It's about time you two got back together. Just don't break a gasket or something trying to make up for lost time!"

5

——————

After Gabby left my room and joined Stephen in their bedroom, I could hear some muffled voices under the soft music. But after a few minutes, the bed began to squeak and I heard some gentle moans. As the thumping sound began to grow louder and faster, Gabby became more vocal, and I could hear them quite distinctly.

"Yes, Steve," she panted. "Fuck me, baby."

"Uhnn," I heard Stephen groaning, as the bed squeaked more forcefully.

Even with the sound of soft music playing in the background, I could make out almost everything they were saying, and I wondered if Stephen had also heard Gabby and me making love earlier in the night. *Had hearing her enjoying herself while having sex with me been the cause of his renewed interest in his wife?* I knew most guys were obsessed with the idea of two girls getting it on, or even better, a three-way *menage*, but getting turned on with his sister in the mix seemed kind of creepy.

Nevertheless, the more noise they made from the other room, the more excited I became listening to them. I could still feel Gabby's juices dripping down over my tits and stomach, and while I listened to them making love in the adjacent bedroom, I threaded my hand down between my legs and began to play with my clit.

"*God*, Gabby," Stephen panted. "You feel so good. We have *got* to do this more often."

"I hope so," Gabby said. "You don't want me looking for *other* outlets for my sexual needs, do you?"

"It depends what those outlets are," Stephen said. "You know how much I used to love watching you play with your vibrators."

"Yeah, well, sometimes a girl needs to feel some real flesh and juices once in a while."

"I'll be giving you some of *my* juice pretty soon," Stephen grunted, renewing his pace.

"Hold up for a sec," Gabby said, and suddenly everything stopped in the other room. "I want to feel you come in me from *behind*."

I heard the sound of the bed squeaking and the rustling of sheets, then Stephen groaned when he slid his cock back into Gabby's pussy in the doggy-style position.

"*That's* the way I like it," Gabby hissed. "Pound my ass with your big meat, Steve."

"Jesus, Gab," he panted. "We haven't done it this way since our college days. What's come over you?"

"Quite a bit, actually," she teased. "Let's just say I've gotten a new appreciation for adding a little variety to my sex life."

"Whatever the reason, I *like* it," Stephen said, beginning to breathe more heavily as the headboard pounded harder against the wall.

"Yes, Steve," Gabby panted. "Pound my ass harder. Slap your balls against my wet pussy."

"Yeah, baby," he said. "Talk dirty to me. We haven't had sex like this in ages."

"There's a lot more of this waiting for you if you can drag yourself away from work more often. Lean over and squeeze my tits. I want to feel your hot breath on my neck when you come inside me."

"Fuck, yeah," Steve grunted, shifting his weight forward. "You know I love your tits. Your nipples feel so firm."

"Pinch them, baby," Gabby growled. "Squeeze me harder. I'm going to come all over your big dick soon."

"Here it comes, baby," he said. "Oh God–I'm coming!!"

"*Ngah!*" Gabby suddenly groaned with a loud sloshing sound.

"What the–" Stephen said. "Holy fuck! *Unghhhh!!*"

I heard both of them moaning for many long seconds as it became apparent that Gabby was showing off her newfound squirting skills with her husband, and Stephen was undeniably enjoying the sensation of her spraying all over his balls while he rammed her from behind. The image in my head of my two favorite people in the world climaxing together in a mutual shower of cum made me overjoyed, and I rammed my fingers into my pussy, soon after reaching my own climax.

Seconds later, I rolled over and flitted my eyes shut, feeling the effects of the late nights catching up with me as I began to nod off.

It looks like my work is done here, I smiled contentedly.

Ready for more erotic chills and thrills? *Choose your next toe-curling fantasy from over thirty-five spicy stories in Jade's Erotic Adventures. Browse the full collection here:*

Click to scan your favorites...

FOLLOW VICTORIA RUSH:

Want to keep informed of my latest erotic book releases? Sign up for my newsletter and receive a FREE bonus book:

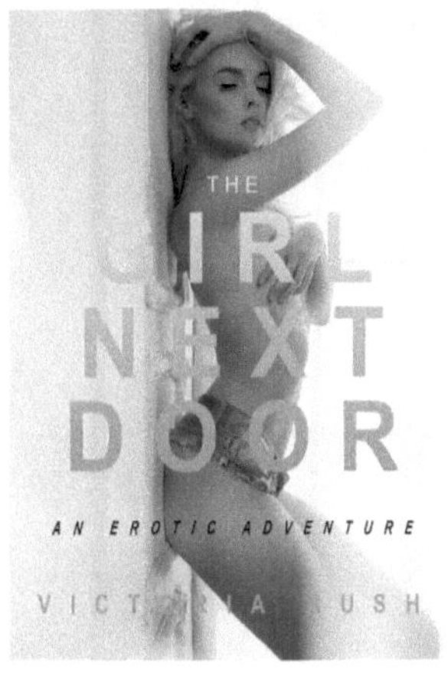

Spying on the neighbors just got a lot more interesting...